THE BREAKING SEASON

THE BREAKING SEASON?

K.A. LINDE

PARANORMAL ROMANCE

BLOOD TYPE SERIES

Blood Type ✦ *Blood Match* ✦ *Blood Cure*

YOUNG ADULT FANTASY

ASCENSION SERIES

The Affiliate ✦ *The Bound*

The Consort ✦ *The Society*

The Domina

PROLOGUE

Today I was marrying a man I didn't love.

And only my best friend, Lark, was waiting in the wings with me. Trying to talk me over the cliff. Not off it.

"Okay, this is what we'll do." Lark immediately went into planning mode. I was another project she had to fix. A fire she had to put out. I barely heard what else she said. Just the end. "Poof, runaway bride."

I ran my hands down the front of my one-of-a-kind designer wedding dress. The bodice was strapless with a sweetheart neck. Made out of the softest, most delicate white lace with dozens of tiny white buttons running up the back. It swept down to my feet with an impressive train that flowed out behind me. A twenty-foot empire veil would be affixed to the intricate braided design at the top of my head. White. Perfect, virginal white.

"No wedding. No Camden," Lark continued.

My eyes found hers in the mirror. "I can't."

"Physically, you are able."

"I can't," I repeated.

"But you don't love him!" Lark gasped. "How can you do

this when you don't even *like* him? It can't just be the money. We all have money. The crew has money. You can have mine. I don't need it."

"Lark," I said, shaking my head.

"Is it the bet?"

I frowned. My dark red lips turning down at the corners. I'd lost the bet to Penn. I'd wagered a wedding date. I was here to deliver. But still, that wasn't it.

"No. I just have to do this."

"I don't want to see you unhappy," Lark told me.

I almost laughed. But I couldn't even manage it.

Unhappy? I'd been unhappy for years. Happiness didn't belong to a girl whose father had lied, cheated, and stolen everything from her. Who ended up in prison for securities fraud, destroying my mother, who hadn't even been able to look at me for years. It certainly didn't belong to a girl whose brother had abandoned them all at the first sign of trouble.

I wanted my old life back. The one before my father had been arrested for his enormous Ponzi scheme. The one when I'd had everything. When I had been on top of the world, and I hadn't had to pretend to love or even like Camden Percy to build that future for myself.

It wasn't as if Penn was going to suddenly change his mind, to go back to the boy I'd known who worshipped at my feet. I'd been so naive then, thinking he'd always come when I called. And now, he wasn't here to save me. But to feed me to the wolves.

"I'll manage," I finally got out.

"You're miserable. Camden makes you miserable. Katherine, please listen to me. We've all been saying it from the beginning. We *know* the kind of person that Camden is. You do, too. You shouldn't subject yourself to his whims."

She was right. Camden twisted me around his little finger. He fucked with my head. At least the sex was good. That was about all he had going for him other than the string of Percy hotels he owned.

"Why are you so set on this?" Lark asked.

I didn't even know how to explain it to myself. It wasn't just about security. I had the penthouse overlooking Central Park. I still had a dwindling trust fund that I could probably stretch if I had to. It was more than that. It was an arrangement. Something Camden and I had crafted together for our mutual benefit. As far as I was concerned, I was getting the better end of the deal, as he now knew exactly how little money I owned. We'd had to fork over tax and bank account information before signing prenups. It worked. We worked somehow... even when we hated each other.

"Maybe I don't want to fail at one more thing."

Lark sighed. "It wouldn't be a failure. You deserve better."

A knock sounded on the door, and the wedding planner, Virginia, burst in. "Time to go, Katherine. Are you ready?"

Lark shot big, round eyes at me, silently begging me to change my mind. But I couldn't.

"Yes," I told Virginia.

"Great. I have the veil. Let's get you both in position."

Lark and Virginia helped me from my pedestal and picked up the long train of my dress. We marched down the hallway and to the back of the church. Virginia tucked my veil into my hair and then moved to cover my face.

I held my hand up. "Leave it."

She shrugged and left my face uncovered. I wanted to face this down with clear eyes. Alone. As always.

The music started. Virginia hurried the bridesmaids out on cue. Lark shot me one last look of despair before stepping into the church in her dark red dress with a bouquet of white flowers.

"Okay, let them get all the way down, and then it's your turn." Virginia beamed at me. "Don't forget to breathe."

"It's just another runway," I muttered.

Canon in D filtered through the church as it moved from the strings of the quartet I had chosen. The sound bloomed and magnified. The doors opened before me. I stood, silhouetted in the atrium of St. Patrick's Cathedral, as hundreds of guests rose to their feet to watch my entrance.

For a split second, I faltered. Debated. Wondered if Lark was right. If I should turn around and run. But it was a moment, and then it was gone.

I stepped forward. Virginia straightened out my train and then the never-ending veil as I walked past row after row of guests. Their faces were a blur. I kept my eyes forward as the altar came into focus. The priest in his cere-monial attire. A line of bridesmaids and groomsmen. Everyone identical.

Then Camden.

He stood in a tuxedo that had been handcrafted by a designer in London. I wasn't close enough yet to discern his expression. That was probably for the better.

I began to recognize more people. My crew taking up the front rows. My mother seated so regally beside my brother, David, and his little Texas bride. Camden's father, Carlyle, seated next to Elizabeth Cunningham. To my surprise, they'd recently eloped. Next to Carlyle was Camden's heinous sister, Candice, and then Elizabeth's daughter, Harmony, who hated me. My new "family."

And then I landed on Penn. My Penn. I just wanted him to look at me. To object. To *do* something.

But he just made eye contact with me. Looked sad for me. Pity.

Penn Kensington pitied me.

I'd told Lark that I wouldn't run. But I hadn't known until that moment that I'd been hoping Penn would object. Not just stand there with his new girlfriend as I went through with it. He really wasn't going to stop it.

I swallowed and turned back to the man I was marrying. I was finally close enough to see the smirk on Camden's strong features. A beautiful exterior hiding a dark interior.

His look said only one thing—*mine*. After tonight, I would belong to him. He'd own me.

And no one was even going to object.

Not even me.

I stepped up to the dais. No one was there to give me away. I had made this deal with the devil. And I would be the one to give myself to him.

Despite all of Camden's faults, he was handsome. N, he was gorgeous. It honestly wasn't fair that someone with that face and body also had the keys to an empire. His dark hair shone in the low lighting. His expression was stern and purposefully blank. As if, even here, even now, he didn't want me to discern what he was thinking. No emotions from him. Not even on his wedding day. I'd expected it from his lips, but I never could understand how he hid behind his eyes. They were dark, so very, very dark. As if I were sinking into the Dead Sea. Drowning. They should have been windows. Instead, he'd closed the shutters, and he was once again a mystery.

"Katherine," he said evenly as he held out his hand.

This was the moment.

I could turn here. I didn't have to go through with this arranged marriage. I didn't have to marry him for his money.

I didn't have to live by this new contract. I could be a runaway bride.

Something hardened in his face as he waited a heartbeat and then another. Then I placed my hand in his.

I wasn't running from him, but... to him. The only person willing to save me.

He helped me up the steps and before the priest. His eyes never wavered from mine. They were unreadable, but still, there was something else in them at that moment as the priest began the service. I hardly heard what was said. The words so familiar that they didn't register. All that really existed in that moment was Camden Percy. There was no reassurance.

I knew what he wanted from me, what I had signed in that contract. My body in exchange for his money and name.

I had no interest in his heart, and he had no interest in mine. It was better this way. Easier.

The priest gestured to me. "Do you, Katherine, take Camden for your lawful husband, to have and to hold from this day forward, for better, for worse, for richer, for poorer, in sickness and in health, until death do you part?"

The room went perfectly silent. As if everyone was waiting on bated breath for my answer.

Camden nodded his head once, decisive and clear. And I knew there was no turning back.

I squeezed Camden's hand and nodded. "I do."

PART I

I DON'T

1

KATHERINE

My patent leather high heels clicked against the hardwood floor. I reached the wall, pivoted, and walked back the length of the room, wearing a path in my penthouse.

My phone buzzed. Again.

I knew precisely who was messaging me and why. I had time to get in a cab and make it to dinner. If I left now, I wouldn't even be late. And still, I paced back the other direction.

A muscle fluttered in my jaw as I heard my phone go off one more time. I froze, forcing my body to stop its incessant movement. Then the phone started ringing. I grumbled and wrenched it off of the counter.

"What?" I snapped.

"Happy anniversary to you, too, darling," Camden said silkily on the other line.

A facade. He didn't care about our anniversary.

"Why do you keep messaging me?" I asked him irritably.

"There's time for me to pick you up in the limo."

"I already said that I'd take a cab."

He said nothing, didn't even sigh, gave not the slightest bit of notice that he was frustrated with my attitude.

Today was the one-year anniversary of our arranged marriage. I couldn't act like it was anything else even if he could.

"I don't see the need," he finally said.

"I will meet you at the restaurant."

"You *will* be there, correct?" His voice was low and guttural as if it irked him that he even had to ask.

"I just said that I would."

Though I had thought of every available excuse to get out of it, including sneaking onto Lark's private jet and heading down to the Caribbean a few days early. But I knew none of them would pass muster. Camden would just meet me at the resort and be *furious* with me. And I knew what would happen from there. What always happened when his temper flared.

Heat ran up my throat, and I touched my fingers to it.

"I'll be there," I said a little breathlessly.

"Good. *Don't* be late," he growled before hanging up.

"Fucker," I snapped back at him.

I wouldn't be late, but fuck, did I want to. No, I didn't want to go at all. I knew what this whole fucking pretense was about. Why he'd scheduled this dinner and forced me to stay behind while my friends darted off to sun and sand and frozen drinks with little umbrellas.

One year ago, I'd agreed to be his wife.

This year, he wanted everything else I'd signed away.

Time for me to live up to my end of the bargain.

I released a breath and forced my face back to neutral. This wasn't who I was. I showed no fear. I was Katherine Van Pelt. Sexy, fierce, and formidable. Not even the likes of Camden Percy could make me waver.

It was just dinner.

A stupid fucking dinner.

It didn't mean that I had to give in to his demands. I *never* gave in. Well... not anymore. There had been a moment—barely even a moment, if I was honest—when I thought that this marriage could work. I'd gone to the Maldives for our honeymoon, thinking it would be the worst month of my life. We'd come back, changed.

I shook my head. I didn't want to think about the past. A few months where we hadn't wanted to kill each other didn't mean that this was going to work as a marriage. Not how I'd thought in those days. No, this had been arranged. We had the contract and prenup to prove it. No point in thinking about what could have been. Not with the present circumstances.

Which meant that I was going to this dinner as a formality. A courtesy really.

Camden Percy didn't care about me. Not more than anything else he'd purchased with his billion-dollar fortune. I wouldn't forget it again.

I stuffed my phone into my black patent leather Hermès bag, double-checked my ruby-red lipstick, and headed for the door. With my armor in place, I left my apartment, ready to handle myself in this shitshow. Just like everything always was with Camden.

Traffic was a nightmare. Thank god I wasn't stuck in Camden's limo. Though I didn't much prefer the taxi either. My foot tapped impatiently on the floor of the cab as I texted with Lark.

Miss you already!

Below that message was a picture of Lark, English, and Whitley in bikinis, doing shots poolside. *Bitches.*

Stop having fun without me!

Enjoy your anniversary dinner. We'll see you soon.

Soon. But not soon enough. Not only did I have to endure this dinner, but I'd also already agreed to do Christmas Eve dinner with Camden's family. I couldn't think of something that I liked less, but Camden had insisted. So, I was going.

Finally, the cab pulled up in front of the building. Prime was located on the thirty-fifth floor with impeccable views of Manhattan and the most expensive steak in the city. Camden had taken me here on our first "date." The rich interior and three-hundred-dollar bottle of wine hadn't convinced me that this wasn't a business deal any more than it would today. I was just a new sort of client for him. A new challenge.

I headed inside, bypassing the man at the front who greeted me. I already knew which table Camden had claimed. The one where we were most visible.

And there he was.

He was seated at the center table against the floor-to-ceiling glass. The panoramic view was stunning. Nearly as stunning as my husband.

He was pure control. It was outlined in every inch of his Savile Row suit. The broad sweeps of his shoulders, the tight lines of his muscular thighs, the sharp cut of the suit to his narrow waist. His hand cradled a glass of red wine with all the delicacy of a newborn baby, but I knew that his proclivities leaned toward destruction rather than comfort.

I forced myself to keep moving as his keen eyes landed on me in my skintight black Elizabeth Cunningham dress. They crawled over my long, lean legs; my slim hips and waist; and my perfectly perky, fake breasts—the best money could buy. Then finally—*finally*—to my face.

He was blank. I wondered what he saw when he looked at me. What went on in that head of his. He was calculated and strategic in every aspect of his life. But I never actually knew what he was thinking. He never yielded an inch.

When I reached him, he stood and wrapped a possessive arm around my waist. "You made it," he said as he pressed a kiss to my cheek.

I swallowed. "I said I'd be here."

"Nice dress."

I narrowed my eyes at him. "It's new."

"I like it."

I stepped out of his grasp. What was he playing at? I couldn't read him. I had no idea if he was just making fun of me. He'd made fun of my shopping habit enough over the last year. I didn't need it on the night of our anniversary, too.

"Sit," he commanded, gesturing to the table. "I ordered your favorite wine."

The sommelier poured me a glass, and it *was* my favorite. I was surprised. He didn't normally bother. Just let me order for myself. Usually vodka because being in his presence after the shit from the last year was excruciating in so many ways. I wondered what the catch was.

"You're late," he said after the sommelier left.

"Traffic." I raised one shoulder and glanced down at my menu. A hundred-dollar steak sounded appetizing with mashed potatoes and macaroni and cheese. My stomach grumbled, but I ignored it. Too many carbs. I'd be sick as a dog if I ate any of that.

"I could have picked you up."

"We've already been through this," I said, scanning the menu for the salads.

The waiter appeared then with a warm smile to take our order.

"I'll take the twenty-two ounce forty-five-day dry-aged rib eye, medium rare, with béarnaise sauce," Camden ordered without even looking at the menu. "Scalloped potatoes and green beans."

"Yes, sir. Excellent," the waiter said, taking his menu. "And you, miss?"

"Greek salad. Dressing on the side."

I offered up the menu. Camden's eyes smoldered.

"A salad?" he asked.

I shrugged. "I'm not that hungry."

He looked up at the waiter. "Bring her a steak, too."

"Yes, sir," he said before departing.

"I don't *need* you to order for me," I growled.

"You *need* to eat. You look like you've lost more weight."

I rolled my eyes and flung my hair over a shoulder, taking a long sip of my wine. "Most people think that's a good thing, Camden. I've been working out with this trainer, who coaches dancers from New York City ballet. It's clearly paying off."

"Well, I'm sure your *trainer* will tell you that you need to eat more calories to make up for the deficit."

"I do protein shakes," I said dismissively.

"Katherine..."

"You know I didn't come here for you to be an ass about my eating habits," I said evenly.

"Fine," he snarled.

The conversation lapsed as we waited for our food. But I helped myself to more wine. I was into my third glass, feeling the first hints of a buzz when our food showed up. I accepted the salad first and let them put the steak down next to it. It did look good, but fuck, it was so much food. No way was I going to finish that.

"Are you excited about the resort?" Camden asked.

"Yes," I said flatly. "I'd already be there if I wasn't here."

Camden's face hardened into stone. "Poor thing."

"I'm *almost* used to it."

"Could you cut the attitude for one night, Katherine?"

"*Me?*" I asked with a half-laugh, stabbing my fork into my salad.

"Yes, you. Do we have to fight each other through this entire dinner? Can we not just enjoy ourselves?"

I shrugged. "I don't know, Camden. Can we? Have we ever?"

"We did in the Maldives."

I pointed my fork at him. "That was different, and *you* know it."

"Why does it have to be?"

"You know why," I ground out.

"Because you ran back to Penn?" he spat.

I stopped breathing. "And you ran back to Fiona," I challenged. "I haven't forgotten Halloween."

"Katherine..."

"Why don't we just *eat* before the food gets cold? Save our cheery disposition for later."

Camden ground his teeth and dug into his steak. The bloody thing looked like something he'd massacred in his rage rather than something that he should be eating. But the turn of the conversation just made me feel sicker. I didn't touch the steak, just picked around at my salad. I'd lost my appetite.

Silence lingered as our plates were cleared.

"Dessert?" the waiter asked eagerly.

"I'll pass," I said.

Camden's jaw clenched. "Just the check."

"As you wish, sir."

"I thought you liked their bread pudding," Camden said.

"I can't stomach the carbs." I shrugged. "Next time."

Camden paid the check while I polished off our third bottle of wine. I was feeling good now. This dinner hadn't been half as bad as I'd thought. Not that I thought the night was going to get better from here.

I set down my empty glass and began to rise, but Camden halted me. "Wait."

I sank back down and arched my eyebrows.

Camden reached into his suit coat and pulled out a small navy-blue box with the letters *HW* on the front. Harry Winston. Shit.

I froze in place, going as still as a statue.

"Happy anniversary," he said, sliding it across the table to me.

"What's that?"

"Open it and find out."

I didn't reach for it. "Why did you get me something?"

"Because we've been married a year," he said evenly. "Now, *open it*."

His command sent a shiver through me, and I tentatively reached out for the box. I had no idea why he was giving me this. We'd never exchanged gifts before. Not on birthdays. Not for our wedding. Not for anything. I hadn't expected a gift. Did it come with strings?

I popped the lid. Inside was a pair of obscenely large diamond earrings. They each featured a central diamond with smaller diamonds haloing around it, and then five teardrop-shaped diamonds winged out across the bottom, like feathers. They were gorgeous and must have cost a small fortune. I should have swooned over them. Instead, my stomach constricted, and the chains of our binding cinched tighter.

"Why?" was the only word I got out.

"I saw them and thought of you."

I shook my head. "You do nothing that isn't out of your own self-interest. I know who I married... and why."

His eyes hardened. "You don't accept them?"

"I want to know what strings are attached."

"Why must you be difficult?"

"You knew who you married, too," I shot back.

He said nothing for a moment, as if considering and then deciding to continue. A deliberate, calculated move like everything he did. "I thought we could... discuss what comes next in our relationship."

I swallowed. "What comes next..."

"We've been married a year, Katherine."

"I know how long we've been married," I said, clenching the box.

I knew what he was going to say. The one thing that he truly wanted from me out of this arrangement. More than the linking of our two powerful names. More than submission in the bedroom. More than his desire to break me completely.

"I want us to have a baby."

2

KATHERINE

"No." The word tumbled out of my mouth before I could think. Before I could even process what I was saying.

Camden coiled like a viper. He was dangerous, deadly even, when he looked at anyone like that. I should have feared that reaction, but I couldn't respond any other way.

I knew that I'd agreed to this. That I'd said I'd have his child, his *heir* to the great Percy fortune. His family couldn't hope for one from his sister, Candice. God only knew which continent she was on at this moment.

But even though I'd known, I'd agreed, I wasn't *ready*. It wasn't that I never wanted a baby. I just didn't particularly care one way or another. I always thought that when I fell deeply, hopelessly in love, it would happen naturally from there. I'd want it. He'd want it. And together, we'd be happy. Not... this.

And now, blind panic.

I wasn't ready to have a child. To be responsible twenty-four hours a day, seven days a week for another human being. Of course, there were nannies and governesses and au pairs. All the wonderful things *I'd* grown up with so that my parents could fuck up my childhood past the point of repair. It was irresponsible to bring another child into this fucked up world. Especially one where the kid's parents didn't even like each other. I knew what that did to a kid.

"We should talk about this," Camden growled, low and predatory.

I stood from my seat. "Table it."

He opened his mouth to argue with me, but there must have been something in my expression to stop him dead, and halt whatever planned speech he'd likely concocted for this precise moment.

"Fine. We'll take the limo," he said.

Then his hand was on my elbow as he steered me out of the restaurant.

"Katherine," he said as I exited the building.

I glanced back at him in question right when a camera flashed.

Oh. Of course. He'd wanted to warn me about the press. Had he tipped them off to let them know where we'd be? At least I'd turned to look at him. I probably looked like I adored him rather than like I wanted to bite his head off. That picture would be spread all over *Page Six* tomorrow.

"Anniversary quota fulfilled," I said, beelining for the limo.

The driver was there, helping us into the back and angling the media out of our faces. Once we were safely inside, the door closed on the media circus. I sat back with a frown. This was my life. Anniversary dinner meant a newspaper appearance. Typical socialite bullshit.

I leaned over into Camden and held my phone out in front of me. "Smile."

He didn't, of course. But he shot the camera a devilish look. Good enough.

I filtered the image and blasted it all over my social network. *Fuck you, paparazzi.* I didn't have to abide by their rules. I would much rather post all of my own photographs than have them sell my image to the highest bidder.

I watched the numbers tick up on the post. The comment section was out of control with anniversary congratulations. It'd be a solid post. Too bad it relayed none of my actual anniversary sentiments.

"I don't know why you bother with that," he said.

"Part of my job."

"Your job," he said derisively.

"I'm not the first socialite you've met, Camden. You don't have to be a little bitch about it."

Camden just stared back at me. "You are in rare form tonight."

"And you're exactly the same as you always are," I spat back.

Camden looked like he wanted to say more, but instead, he slid his phone out of his pocket and responded to emails. I was dismissed.

I blew out a soft breath and straightened out. Camden didn't understand my socialite status. He didn't think that it was a real job. He'd made that perfectly clear the last year. That taking pictures and adding filters and captions to them was not in any way a real job. But I enjoyed it, and I always had. Even when technology hadn't been quite as convenient... or time-consuming. Keeping up with social media now was an all day, ever day kind of job. No matter what he said.

I returned to my followers and answered some of the comments from people that I immediately recognized.

Answering followers was easier than figuring out my marriage. I didn't know what to do about Camden. I'd walked into that dinner with my hackles raised. I'd been waiting for the other shoe to drop. And it had... just as I'd assumed it would.

But before that... he hadn't been so horrible. Maybe he'd even been trying to have a good night. That was the problem though. I didn't ever know which Camden I was going to get when we were together. More often than not, he was the one in "rare form," and I was the one left speechless and irritated. We were a hot mess.

If I wanted it to keep working—if I could even say it *was* working—then I was going to have to give a little tonight. Maybe if I let my guard down, then he'd drop the whole thing. Except that letting my guard down was the last thing I wanted. Not when I was used to getting stabbed in the back every time I let myself be vulnerable.

Eventually, the limo pulled up in front of Percy Tower, the flagship for the Percy hotel chain. Camden helped me out of the car and then silently guided me into the foyer. I never got tired of the beautiful, polished interior—the classic gilded look with marble floor and columns, all entranced with Christmas decorations and a floor-to-ceiling tree. We slipped through the crowded entrance filled with tourists here for the Christmas holiday, wanting to see the city at its finest.

It was both the best and worst time to be in New York. Christmas cheer was everywhere—from the tree at Rockefeller Center to the market along Central Park to Macy's *Believe* sign to the Rockettes *Christmas Spectacular* and *The Nutcracker* to ice skating. It had been my favorite time of year while growing up. My birthday was New Year's Eve—which was good and bad, depending on what age I was—

and so the Christmas season always felt like the buildup to my birthday.

I remembered one year, when I was about twelve, my father had gotten a horse-drawn carriage ride through Central Park for the family that ended with hot chocolate and the Rockettes performing just for *me* at Bethesda Fountain. The memory ached now. As all of my memories of my father were tinged with grief, for what he'd done and who he'd become. But I'd been a daddy's girl all my life and losing him had been a nightmare. Losing him and my brother's disappearance and my mother's utter denial all in the same week had been... too much.

I shook off the heavy memories that always came around Christmas and took the private elevator up to Camden's penthouse.

Thankfully, there was nothing Christmassy in sight. Unlike me during my childhood, Camden abhorred Christmas. He was glad that we were leaving the city and missing the worst of it. I'd never found out why.

"Drink?" Camden asked as I slid my jacket off and hung it up in the closet.

"Bubbly?"

He nodded and reached into the wine fridge, retrieving a bottle of Moet & Chandon Rosé. Maybe he *was* trying to woo me tonight.

I took out the box of diamond earrings from my pocket and carried it over to the bar. "My favorite," I said, taking the glass from him.

He poured himself a glass of scotch, neat. His eyes were on the box under my hand, watching me fiddle with the thing. But he said nothing. He was scariest when he was silent. His words sliced like knives, but his silence stretched like death by a thousand cuts.

Slowly, I set my half-empty champagne flute down and opened the box. I breathed out softly and then took out the pearl earrings I had been wearing, replacing them with the Harry Winston diamonds.

There. See. I was trying.

"What do you think?" I asked.

Camden took a step into my personal space. His hand cupped my jaw, holding me firmly in place. My heart stuttered at the command. For a fraction of a second, I'd forgotten how dominating he could be in one touch. How he could hold me like I was breakable and then enjoy watching me shatter.

He gently turned my head to one side, exposing the long column of my neck to him. I swallowed, telling myself that I didn't want this, nor did I fear it. I didn't know how much I lied to myself.

He moved me the other direction, examining the diamonds, controlling me with ease. I loved and hated how effortlessly he did it.

"They suit you," he said, turning my head back to look at him. "As I knew they would."

"You really picked them with me in mind?" I kept my voice low and silky. I hadn't believed him when he first said it. But now... maybe.

"I've always been a man of action," he said evenly. "I say what I mean with what I do."

It should have been reassuring. Instead, it felt like a gut punch. I knew the actions he'd performed. I knew what he'd done. And they hurt worse than words ever could. I took a breath. I wasn't here to argue. I didn't want to deal with another argument with him tonight. I just wanted to... *not* for one evening with him. Neither of us was going to move on from the past. But I'd rather be talking about this than what we'd been discussing back at the restaurant.

"Why don't we go for a swim?" I suggested.

"It's December."

"And? You have a hot tub."

"You want to get into the hot tub?" he asked incredulously.

"Is it on?"

"Yes," he admitted.

I stepped around him, plucked the champagne bottle out of the ice bucket, and headed toward the frigid night beyond.

"You know it might *snow* tonight, right?"

My hand slipped down the side zipper of my dress. I let the skintight dress slowly fall off of my shoulders and down around my hips. I heard his sharp intake of breath. At least he was predictable in *that* way. If nothing else.

I set the champagne down on the edge of the hot tub, shivering in the wind and cold. I hastily shimmied out of the rest of my dress, leaving me in nothing but a La Perla black silk thong and matching bustier. I was pretty sure Camden was going to owe me a new set. I sank down to my neck, taking pleasure in the heat.

Then Camden appeared in nothing but his black silk boxers. We matched. I would have laughed, but the heat in his eyes was enough to let it die on my lips. He looked... like a god. A Greek god leaving the trappings of Olympus to feast among and upon mortals. His dark hair was slicked back. His strong jawline cut like a razor. The six-pack that ended at the Adonis lines that made a perfect V, low, low, lower to what was hidden by a scrap of silk.

My mouth went dry.

I hated that I wanted him. I hated that we were so messed up. I hated that we were too proud to say any of that.

Camden stepped into the hot tub and sat on a bench in the water. He put his arms up on the edge of the pool. He watched me and waited. I sipped champagne, pretending to ignore him, but his gaze lingered. I determinedly sipped more champagne. I was definitely a little drunk now. I had to be to have even suggested this.

"Is this a game, too?" he finally asked.

I sighed. "It's not a game."

"I know you, Katherine. *Everything* is a game. And I thought that I'd made myself clear that I didn't want to be involved in your games any longer."

"If you think that's what this is, then why are you in this hot tub with me?"

His gaze turned lethal and heated. I could see through the water that my nearly naked presence had the desired effect on him. I knew why he was here.

"My wife is walking around in nothing but lingerie, and I'm expected to stay inside?" he asked.

I finished off my glass of champagne and then slid through the water to stand before him. I moved to straddle him, but his hands reached out and gripped my hip—hard.

"Uh-uh," he said, holding me in place. He ran circles along my hip bone.

"You don't want me?"

I knew that wasn't the problem. Camden had to be in charge. At all times. For all things.

He guided me forward, setting me down on top of him. His cock jutted up against my thin underwear. I fought to keep my face neutral, but I didn't think that I'd succeeded. Half of me wanted to tear our last bits of clothing off and let him fuck me bare against the side of this hot tub. And the other half of me wanted to slap him across the face for his need for dominance.

"Would you like to know a secret?" He held me firm and moved his lips to my ear. "*You*, my darling wife, want *me*."

It *was* a secret. One I never let anyone know. Not even my closest friends. Because Camden Percy was a means to an end. He was the man I'd married for money. He didn't love me. I didn't love him. Nothing in this world or any other could change that. But... I did want him.

"And you can't have me," he said, pushing me backward in the water.

3

KATHERINE

I stumbled to my feet, caught off guard by the abrupt change in direction. My pulse pounded in my ears and my cunt. Every place he'd touched me was super-heated.

I couldn't have him.

Yes.

That was true.

Another fact that I knew.

Even if my treacherous body didn't give a shit that I should stay the fuck away from him. That he only brought me misery. And bruises and welts and... all those delicious things I had somehow learned to crave. Not broken. *No.* Not like he wanted. I had too much fire in my veins to ever break before him. He liked me more as a wild mustang than a broken stallion.

"You're an ass," I spat.

He laughed once without mirth. "And you're trying to distract me."

"It was working."

"No, it wasn't." He leaned his arms back against the edge

of the hot tub and stared hard into my eyes. "We have to talk about this."

I poured myself another glass of champagne and guzzled it. "No."

"You can't escape it forever."

I knew that. But I could escape it as long as possible.

"You agreed," he reminded me.

"And things change," I snarled back.

He arched an eyebrow. "The contract hasn't."

"No, but we have."

"Have we?"

I bared my teeth at him before whirling away to look out across the Manhattan skyline. So much had changed. Before we'd gotten married, we'd been fucking. It was great. Even though I hated him. But *after* the wedding, everything had changed. We weren't the couple we'd been before saying *I do*.

I heard him shift behind me. His powerful legs moving through the water. Then his hands were on my waist under the water, running down my wet body.

"Katherine," he purred.

I forced my body still, refused to react.

His nose brushed against the space between my neck and shoulder. My body shuddered involuntarily.

"You have my money. That's what you wanted," he said, trailing his nose up my neck to my ear. He whirled me around in the water, dragging our gazes together. "Now, give me what I require."

I stared into his hungry eyes, saw the monster I'd married, and met him toe to toe.

"What if I don't?"

He released me, letting the mere inches between us feel like a mile. Then his hand went up to the diamond earring in my ear. "Then these will be the last payment you receive."

I reared back. "Payment?"

The word was horrific.

"What would you call it?"

"Yes, I sold myself for your money, but that doesn't make me a prostitute. I'm not subject to your whims. I'm *your* wife."

"Sure, Ren," he teased.

I clenched my fists at my sides. I seethed. "Don't you dare call me that."

"What? Only Penn can? Still pining after your long-lost love? Even after he married someone else? Your mortal enemy?" he asked with a sardonic laugh.

"I remember you making me attend their wedding reception," I said brusquely.

And how it had killed me to watch it and to see them happy together.

I'd liked Natalie once. Before she was a bet that I had to destroy. Before she stole the one pure thing in my life—Penn. I knew that he wasn't mine any longer, but I couldn't control how my heart had longed for him for more than a decade. I wasn't idiotic enough to try to continue the relationship with him though. He was out of reach now. I knew that.

"Then it shouldn't matter what I call you."

"You act as if you're a saint," I snapped back at him. "As if you haven't been fucking your side piece for the last year." He opened his mouth to say something, but I jumped right over his rejection. "I know you left with her at Halloween. I'm not stupid."

"I never denied that I left with her. You watched me do it and said nothing."

I rolled my eyes. "Are we done? I'm tired of this conversation."

"No, we're not done. You said that you would give me a baby. You signed it in ink, Katherine." He leaned forward. "I can promise that the practice will be enjoyable."

"I'm too busy."

"Busy?" he asked incredulously.

"Yes. Living my life."

"What life?" He huffed in disbelief. "All you do is work out and party. That's not a life."

"One, that isn't all I do. I'm a socialite. I run my social media pages all day. Plus, I help with the animal shelter charity."

"Your Ears and Tails thing?" he asked with a shake of his head. "We all know that's just a front, so you and your friends can have an excuse to wear lingerie in public. You don't *care* about it. You don't care about anything, except how you look and how many followers you have. You're a shallow, vapid Upper East Side princess, sweetheart, and everyone knows it."

I knew that I had poked the bear. That I'd provoked him into this, but it didn't make it any easier to hear. "Just because I'm not running a company doesn't mean that what I do is any less than your job."

"I employ thousands of people worldwide. I provide jobs. I provide shelter. I bring in billions of dollars," he drawled. "You have no ambition. You take some pictures and donate some money. You don't go to the animal shelter to help the dogs. You don't care about the charity for more than your party. You're about to turn thirty-one, and what do you have to show for it? A million followers? Who fucking cares? The clock is ticking."

"Fuck you," I said mercilessly.

The clock was ticking. Fucking fuck. How dare he!

I wasn't some ticking time bomb to use my body for motherhood. That wasn't how women were treated anymore. Women were successfully having kids in their forties. This wasn't the fourteenth century, where you needed to pop out ten in the hopes of raising five to adulthood. I had advanced healthcare on my side. I wouldn't even be considered at risk until thirty-five.

I trembled with rage. And he didn't even look like he cared.

This was Camden Percy. Right here in front of me. I needed to remember that the next time I considered letting my guard down. He knew how to walk right through my guard and take a machete to my feelings.

I stepped back from him. One step and then another.

"You know what?" I said as I stared back at him. He arched an eyebrow in question. "I was actually going to fuck you tonight. Good thing I didn't make that mistake."

Then I climbed out of the hot tub and into the cold. I wrapped a fuzzy robe tight around myself.

"Happy anniversary," I whispered.

I didn't wait for his response. I turned on my heel and walked back inside. I dropped the robe, slipped into my dress and heels, grabbed my jacket, and was out of the penthouse before he made it back inside. I took the elevator downstairs, still shaking from the cold... or from the conversation.

My body felt brittle. Like I'd break apart at any moment. It was a familiar feeling. I'd built up walls around myself. A bulletproof exterior to hide the little girl within who had been abandoned over and over again. If you kicked a dog too many times, you shouldn't be surprised when it bit back.

I flagged down a cab and headed up to my own penthouse. I left the dress, bra, and panties in a trail through the house before I stepped into my shower. I turned it on as hot as it would go and showered off any remnants of the night until there was nothing left. Not a speck of Camden Percy on my skin or on my heart.

But I didn't cry.

I seethed. I plotted. And I decided then and there how I was going to make him eat crow.

4

CAMDEN

It was three days later, and I was still pissed off.

Our anniversary had gone so wrong. So bloody wrong. It wasn't what I'd wanted to happen at all. I didn't know why I'd expected Katherine to react differently. We'd been at odds long before we got married. And we'd both made it worse over the last year.

I ground my teeth together and checked my Rolex for the third time. She was late. We were supposed to already be on the way to my father's annual Christmas dinner. My father hated when anyone was late. I'd hear about it.

Damn it, Katherine!

The whole thing gave me a headache. It wasn't as if we could just start over. She'd made that perfectly clear, and then I'd nailed the coffin shut when I pushed her away in the hot tub. I hadn't wanted to play her fucking games, but I sure as hell had wanted to fuck her. I knew she'd wanted me to fuck her. Still, I couldn't let her toy with me like she did everyone else.

Maybe it was control. Maybe it was the only way I could have Katherine, without pretense or bullshit between us. I just knew that my cock had stayed hard at the thought of her in lingerie in my hot tub until I jacked off to that image. My cock twitched again, just thinking about it.

This was my curse: I always wanted Katherine Van Pelt.

I wanted to stuff my cock down her throat everu time she mouthed off to me.

I wanted to teach her manners with my hand to her pert ass the next time she tried to play games with me.

I wanted to fuck her so hard that she couldn't walk to prove that she couldn't walk all over me.

But I reined it in. Always restrained myself. Never let her see the truth of how much I wanted to take the little perfect princess and break her. Because if she knew, she'd use it, use me. And above all, I could never let that happen. I had to maintain control.

These little indiscretions were enough to grate on my nerves as it was. Late twice in one week was enough to make me want to tie her to the bed until she begged for forgiveness. I'd never heard Katherine Van Pelt beg for anything. But a guy had to have goals, right?

The elevator doors slid open, and Katherine strode into my apartment. She looked like a knockout in a blood-red dress that hit just above her knees and a black fur-lined coat unbuttoned at her waist. Her lush, dark hair was piled high in an intricate design. I wondered how long it would take for me to rip every pin out of it. Her ruby-red lips were pursed, and she arched an eyebrow in my direction.

"Are you ready to go or what?" she asked, slipping her phone back into her leopard-print purse.

"Ready to go?" I asked dryly. "You're the one who's late."

"I was busy."

My anger unfurled within me. "Busy?" I seethed. "Doing

what? You knew precisely when dinner was. Same time ever year."

She shrugged. "Why does it matter? Let's go."

I stepped up to her, nearly touching her. "It matters."

"Whatever." She turned away from me. Without thinking, my hand darted out and snagged on her elbow. "What?"

"Where were you?"

"I was working," she said. Her eyes drifted to my hand. "Let me go."

"Work?"

She wrenched her arm out of my grip. "You know, taking pretty pictures and responding to followers," she said, her eyes slaying me. "Isn't that all you think I do anyway?"

"Fine," I ground out.

She never took anything seriously. It was all a joke. I knew that this socialite business was important to her. I shouldn't minimize it, but I knew how much *more* she was capable of. With that look alone, I knew that she could conquer the world. With an ounce of ambition, she could do literally anything she wanted. Why was she spending her time posting selfies? Especially when it only brought in about a million dollars a year? I knew she could go through a million dollars a year on *clothing* alone. My black card was smoking from her expenses.

We headed down to my limo and drove north through the Upper East Side. My family had lived in the same penthouse since the '40s when my great-grandfather returned from World War II. We'd slowly bought up all the other apartments that faced the park and torn down walls to make it larger and larger. Renovations were constantly ongoing. My childhood had been full of project after project within the Percy family home. I'd hated it. Not least of all because I had asthma and breathing in fumes and sawdust had made my childhood miserable. As soon as I could get my own place, I'd done it. I'd moved out of this hellhole and into the penthouse on top of Percy Tower at the ripe age of fourteen. Miraculously, my health issues all but evaporated overnight. All those years of my father calling me weak and trying to beat health back into me had been for nothing. Not that he'd ever once acknowledged that it was partly his doing.

My chest tightened as I directed Katherine into the elevator that would take us into the home that I loathed. She must have noticed I was tense because she stowed her phone.

"How long do we have to stay?" she asked.

"Let's try to make it through dinner."

She nodded. "There's a bright side to this."

I raised my eyebrows in question. "Is there?"

"No Christmas Eve mass."

I chuckled, surprised by the way she'd so easily defused the situation. "Two hours of midnight mass isn't your cup of tea?"

"I can think of other ways to use an altar."

I shook my head, trying to hide my delight. "Sacrilege."

She just winked at me and then faced forward as the doors opened. She had made me forget what we were walking into. This woman. This infuriatingly irritating woman. I never expected her to get me, but there were advantages to marrying someone in my social circle. We understood each other and how fucked up our childhoods had been.

"Shall we?" she asked.

I nodded curtly. Then we stepped into my father's home together.

The first thing I saw was a short incredibly tan woman

with a thick head of dark brown hair. I stopped moving at the sight of my sister.

"Candice?" Katherine asked in shock.

Shock enough for the both of us.

I hadn't seen Candice since the day I married Katherine. She was a bit of a holistic nutjob. The last I'd heard, she was in Bali, living a New Age Goop-esque lifestyle—vagina-steaming, bee-venom therapy, and fifteen-thousand-dollar sex toys. But before the wedding, she'd been in Dubai, living off of martinis, then Casablanca to soak up the essence of the '40s, and some private island off the coast of Morocco for a sex-healing treatment, which I could only guess consisted of nightly orgies.

She hadn't gone to Harvard, where our father had donated a small fortune to get her in. She had no degree. She'd never worked a day in her life. Not even as a socialite. Instead, she lived off her trust and flitted between one mind-less brainwashing adventure to the next. I'd once had to endure an entire conversation with her where she described in detail how she'd gotten with a "journey" group and done hallucinogens to open up her mind's eye.

Candice slowly turned, revealing her enormous stom-ach. "Heyyy," she trilled. "You made it."

She was pregnant. My cultist sister, who was high more than she was sober, was *pregnant.* Jesus Christ, who had been stupid enough to let that happen?

"What are you doing here?" I asked dryly.

"Nice to see you, too," she said with a wink, stepping up to us. "And your beautiful wife. How's the sex?" She pressed her hand to Katherine's stomach. "Still fucking like rabbits?"

Katherine stepped back, glaring down at Candice. "That's really none of your business."

"Oh, come on. Didn't you hear? I'm a certified sex therapist now."

"Certified by whom?" I asked with a shake of my head.

Candice waved her hand. "It was in Taiwan at this sex temple. I'll have to tell you the whole story."

"Please don't," I said. "I need a drink."

"Make it a double," Katherine said under her breath.

"Oh, but you shouldn't be drinking," Candice said gleefully.

Katherine shot me a pained look.

"Martini?" I asked.

She nodded gratefully.

I headed to my father's wet bar and poured her the dirtiest martini I could madke. I went for my father's scotch. As much as it upset me to admit it, he had an even more extensive collection than I did. I brought the martini back to Katherine, who looked like a fawn ready to bolt in distress. Neither of us had prepared for dealing with Candice on top of my father and his new family.

"Camden," a voice said behind me.

I turned to find my latest stepmother standing in the doorway to my father's sitting room. "Hello, Elizabeth."

I regrettably left Katherine to deal with Candice.

Elizabeth Cunningham was my father's fourth wife. They'd secretly eloped a month before my own wedding. I didn't mind her or her daughter, Harmony, who was Katherine's age. She was better than the last two. Candice's mother, Carrie, had despised that there was a child between Candice and the entirety of the Percy fortune. More recently, he'd married Jaclyn, a supermodel who was younger than me. She'd tried to fuck me once or twice. I'd almost done it out of spite, but I was certain my father might have actually killed me. Heir to his empire or not.

My mother was the only one he'd married for love. And

shortly after having me, she'd abandoned us both. Run out on him and only returned long enough to sign the divorce papers, refuse custody, and give up her claim to any Percy money. My father never let me forget that I was the reason she'd left. He never believed in love again after that. Drilled it into my head at a young age that marriages were business deals. Plain and simple.

"Come into the sitting room. Your father wants to speak with you," Elizabeth said with an easy smile.

My stomach hardened. Talking to my father alone was never a good idea. I was sure he was going to rail me for being ten minutes late to a dinner that had yet to be served. It wouldn't be the first time.

"Thank you," I said anyway and headed into the sitting room to find my father, Carlyle Percy, sipping on a glass of scotch. "Hello, Father."

"Ah, Camden, you finally made it."

I kept my face completely neutral. Nothing to set him off. "You asked to speak with me?"

"Yes, I wanted to show you the new construction on the old library," he said as he rose to his feet. He buttoned the top button of his suit and straightened. "We don't have time now since you were late but after dinner."

New construction. My throat closed as I imagined the fucking dust. Not that I could deny my father anything.

"Of course, sir," I said obediently.

I'd learned control from my lack of control as a child. And the tight fist of my father.

I knew what he'd meant when he said that he wanted to talk to me later. That I'd fucked up. That he wanted to wait until the ladies were otherwise occupied. It all spelled trouble to mend I knew there was no way to avoid it. The only way out was through.

5

KATHERINE

I couldn't believe that Camden had left me alone with Candice. She was two years younger than me, and we'd all attended the same prep school. I'd been a terror in high school, but Candice was her own brand of horrendous. And one of the last people on the planet that I wanted to be left alone with.

Especially with her giant belly and her pseudo-science sex therapy. I needed no help with my sex life, thank you very much.

"So, tell me everything," Candice said with a glint in her amber eyes. "Does he go down on you? Have you experimented with toys? What's working?"

I downed half of my martini in one long gulp. I needed to be hammered to endure Candice the rest of the night.

She didn't wait for a reply. "You know what the key to long-lasting pleasure is?" She leaned in as if she were imparting some secret wisdom. "Giving your partner full access to all holes."

"And you learned this in Taiwan?" I choked out.

"Oh, well, I already knew that bit," she said with a wink.

"I just like to share it in the States because everyone here is such a prude. Like, you'd think they'd be a little more open after having a stick up their ass for... ever."

"I'm not sure I'm comfortable discussing my sex life with... you," I told her as delicately as possible.

"Why not?" she asked, clearly mystified.

"Well... I'm married to your brother."

Candice waved the comment away. "I'm not afraid of sex. If he isn't pleasuring you fully, it's my duty to help."

I opened my mouth, uncertain what was about to come out of it. I usually tried to rein in my outrage when I was around Camden's father. Without fail, he always did something that made me want to stab him in the eye. I'd prepped myself for that. But god, I didn't want to deal with Candice.

Then another woman walked into the room. It was the first time in my life that I was happy to see Harmony Cunningham. Elizabeth's daughter had been my enemy since high school when she tried to sink her claws into Penn. But I would do anything to get out of this conversation with Candice Percy about my holes and sex life.

"Harmony," I said in greeting, hoping my voice didn't betray how much I wanted an escape.

Harmony's nose crinkled. "Katherine, what a pleasant surprise."

"Oh, Harmony," Candice said in delight. "I was just helping Katherine with her sex problems."

Harmony raised one eyebrow and tucked a lock of her platinum-blonde hair behind her ear. "Problems?"

"Candice-invented problems. She's a sex therapist, didn't you hear?"

"I did," Harmony said in a way that said, *Unfortunately.*

"I've been psychoanalyzing her relationship with Kurt," Candice explained.

"Kurt?" I asked in surprise. "Kurt Mitchell?"

"The one and only," Harmony said with a shrug.

"I didn't know he was in New York again."

Kurt was old Upper East Side money, but he'd been such a fuckup that his parents shipped him off to boarding school. He'd gotten kicked out of a half-dozen of them in Europe and continued his bad-boy ways when he returned for college. I knew that he'd had a fling with my bestie, Lark, but he'd been off my radar since then.

"He's cleaned up and working for his daddy in investing," she said.

"Too bad."

She narrowed her eyes at me. "Why is that?"

"Bad boys have more fun."

Harmony actually laughed. We'd spent so many years fighting each other over Penn that we weren't going to suddenly be friends. But I'd rather talk to her than deal with Candice, which said a lot.

"And what are you up to?" I asked Harmony, cutting Candice out of the conversation.

"I started designing for my mom. Cunningham Couture's latest visionary," she said with a shrug. "Mom thinks it's a good angle."

"It is a good angle," I admitted. "I didn't know that you had interest in designing."

Harmony and I had competed for more than just Penn's heart. Up until this latest endeavor with design, she had also been living her life as a socialite. She modeled, especially for her mother's line, which I'd also done for a time. I'd never thought that she'd willingly give it up.

"Designing is more... stable," Harmony admitted.

Which really meant that women over thirty didn't usually model. Not unless they were superstars. Not when fashion designers could get size double-zero twits fresh out of high school. Eternal youth.

The thought made my stomach twist. I had my name and notoriety, but I wouldn't always have my looks. I couldn't compete with fresh-faced eighteen-year-olds. I was down a dress size from my new workout routine, but I'd never be a double zero again.

As much as I hated to admit it, the vile things Camden had said on our anniversary weren't entirely... wrong. I enjoyed the life that I lived, and I'd never much cared about anything else, but this job wasn't forever. I'd wanted to prove him wrong enough that I'd reached out to a friend who ran a charity to see how else I could get involved. I didn't want a job, but I might need a purpose beyond my status in society.

"Sex therapy is stable, too," Candice cut in.

Harmony and I exchanged a look. It was strange to detest someone for so long and then have her understand me so completely.

"Maybe you could help my mom with that," Harmony said, biting her cheek to keep a straight face. "Unless it's weird to talk to her about your dad."

Candice made a contemplative face. "In the interest of medicine, I could help her."

Then Candice beelined for Elizabeth, leaning against the sitting room doors.

Harmony and I turned away at once. Both of us trying to conceal our laughter.

"She is the worst," Harmony whispered.

"Completely oblivious to the world and a danger to herself and everyone around her," I said.

"If I had to hear her talk about how vagina-scented essential oils had changed her life one more minute, I was going to blow my brains out."

"I am so glad I missed that," I muttered. "She was educating me on the proper use of all of my holes for pleasure."

Harmony groaned. "I can't."

"Not even a little."

Harmony laughed and then gestured between us. "This is weird."

I nodded. "Yeah. A bit."

"Go back to hating each other after she's gone?" Harmony asked, holding her hand out.

I put my hand in hers and shook. "Deal."

"God, has she started telling you about Lars yet?"

"No. Who is Lars?" I asked.

"Her husband."

I sputtered in shock. "Candice got married?"

Harmony shrugged. "Apparently. And he's some Swedish prince or something. I'm not clear on the details. I tried to get away as quickly as possible."

"Jesus. I thought she had a sperm donation. Monogamy never seemed like her thing."

"Oh, they're not monogamous," Harmony clarified. "They met in an orgy and decided their souls were bonded or something. After that, she said their genes needed to procreate." Harmony wrinkled her nose again.

"Well then," I muttered, "is he here?"

Harmony nodded. "He's supposed to be here for dinner tonight."

"The night keeps getting better."

"Tell me about it. I just want to get this over with, so I can head over to Kurt's."

"How did that happen anyway?"

Harmony flushed, her cheeks reddening. "Uh, well... it might or might not have started as a one-night stand."

I chuckled. "Of course it did."

"Anyway," Harmony said with an eye roll, "I don't know where it's going, but I'd like to see."

I watched the eager light in her eyes. The first flush of love that came with a new relationship. The hope that this time, this person was *the one*.

I'd felt that way before. My heart panged as I remembered the scant few months this spring when I'd thought it was happening with Camden. We'd come back from our honeymoon aflush with new... well, if not feelings, at least respect. We agreed not to see other people. I'd made the mistake of thinking he was serious. That this could go somewhere. But there was no *the one*. There was just the person you ended up with, and you made it work. It wasn't a romantic ideal. But I wasn't a romantic at heart. While things weren't great... or even good with Camden right now, I knew where we stood. It was safer.

Speak of the devil, my husband appeared out of his father's sitting room with a cloud over his face. I knew how much he enjoyed seeing his father.

"Ah, look who found each other," Camden said, sweeping past Candice and Elizabeth, who looked like she desperately wanted to escape, and coming over to where Harmony and I stood together.

"Camden," Harmony said stiffly. "What a pleasure to see your face here."

"I'm sure, sis," he said with a quirked eyebrow. "Making friends with your enemy?"

"We came together under common ground," I said, gesturing to Candice.

"So, Candice brings you together when Penn always split you apart."

Harmony and I glanced at each other. There was

nothing shared in that look. Neither of us had Penn. Would ever have him again. And still, that animosity lingered.

"Don't be an ass," Harmony told him.

"It's in his nature," I said.

"Just trying to lighten the mood," Camden said.

"No, you're not," Harmony spat.

"Illuminate the truth then," he suggested instead. "Perhaps you can inform me what's so special about Penn Kensington. Katherine has never been able to explain it."

Harmony glared at him. "Maybe he's not a total fucking douchebag, like you."

She whirled on her heel and stalked away from us. Truce broken.

I deflated slightly in her absence. It hadn't been horrible to have an ally in this room. Where everyone else was at each other's throats.

"Why do you have to do that?" I hissed at him.

"What?" he asked with mock innocence.

"Take your anger toward your father and abuse everyone else around you with it?"

He had no answer for that. Perhaps I had illuminated the truth in the same way that he had.

I didn't wait to see what else would come out of his mouth when he was in this mood. I headed deeper into the living room and found Elizabeth Cunningham excusing herself from Candice's presence. She drew me into a hug.

"Katherine, it's wonderful to see you," Elizabeth lied.

Our mutual connection to Percy men had made us work together for a time. I'd been the socialite always in her couture, but Harmony's grudge had ruined that as well. She'd designed my wedding dress. After that, we'd parted ways. It hadn't been mutual. Though I'd never tell her how much it had wounded me. I'd been vulnerable about it all once, just once. My armor had hardened around it since. Otherwise, I wouldn't be able to pretend in this moment, and most of my life was pretending.

"You look as fabulous as ever," I told her.

Elizabeth's smile didn't reach her eyes. "Thank you, dear."

Just then the elevator dinged again. We all turned to find a man striding into the penthouse. He was exceedingly tall, as pale as fresh snow, with wheat-blond hair to his shoulders. His blue eyes were piercing against his pale skin, even from a distance, and his smile was the most genuine thing in the room.

Candice squealed and launched herself across the apartment. "Lars!"

Ah, so *this* was her husband, Lars.

They started making out in the foyer, and the rest of us quickly turned away from the display. If Camden's father, Carlyle, hadn't entered the room at that moment, they might have started fucking right then and there.

Carlyle cleared his throat, and it sent a shiver through everyone present. Even Candice wasn't immune to it. She wrenched back from her husband, and a hesitancy flickered through her features. One I hadn't been sure she had in her.

"Dinner," Carlyle suggested sternly.

Candice and Lars hastened to catch up with the rest of us. Elizabeth entered the dining room with Harmony.

Camden touched my arm to hold me back. "Another drink?"

"God, yes," I told him.

He nodded and headed toward the wet bar. I moved toward the dining room, passing Carlyle with his eyes fixed uncomfortably on me.

"Evening," I said, keeping the bite from my voice.

"Katherine," he said.

His eyes roamed up and down my body as if I were a piece of meat that he had purchased at the market. As if I were his for the taking.

It was not the first, nor would it be the last time Camden's father looked at me like that. But the way his gaze fell on me... I knew that look in his eye. I had seen it on dozens of men. I knew their licentious thoughts.

For a long time, I'd hoped I was imagining it. Then we'd been out at a company function. Camden and I were in a fight. We were always in a fight. When his father approached me, I wasn't on my guard. When his hand slid to my ass, I realized what was happening. I spilled my drink down the front of his tuxedo and rushed away. He'd never brought it up again, but I knew he remembered and I knew to keep my guard up around him.

I gave him my best blasé look and strode past him as if I didn't give a shit that he was eye-fucking his daughter-in-law. I never told Camden. He'd likely go ballistic... or not care at all. I couldn't decide which would be worse.

6

CAMDEN

I needed more alcohol to survive this fucking dinner.

My father had been droning on about his latest golf partners and asking Lars pointless bullshit about Sweden. I'd discovered halfway through the conversation that he was *not* an actual prince. Though Candice called him that. He just smiled sheepishly and let her. I still didn't know what his official title was, but apparently, he was part of the nobility, whatever good that did him.

The biggest surprise was that Katherine remained silent through much of dinner. She poked around at her food and ate a measly few bites. It was a miracle that she could hold her tongue that long. Usually, she was full of quips and jabs aplenty. I didn't know what was going through her head right now, but I was more concerned with the conversation I was going to have with my father *after* dinner.

I wanted to avoid it. Even more than this dinner.

If I could have caught Katherine's eyes, I might have been able to have her fake an illness, so we could leave early. But she didn't look up at me. Not *once*. I was going to have to fix that. Even if every time I tried, it backfired in my face.

She and I needed to have a conversation. A real one. Not one where we screamed at each other. As it seemed to be the only way we communicated in our stalemate.

By the time dessert came and went, anxiety had settled itself into my stomach. I didn't show it, of course. My exterior was as hard as diamonds. I would never, ever let my father see that he affected me again. But I was not looking forward to our conversation.

Finally, Katherine looked up. She hadn't touched her dessert. I hadn't seen her eat dessert in months. Not with her crazy diet she'd been on since getting that new trainer.

She startled when she looked at me. "Are you ready to go home?"

She asked it as if she had been living with me these last couple of months instead of in her own penthouse.

Home. With me.

"We have a big day ahead of us," she remarked faintly with a sly smile.

"What are your Christmas plans?" Candice chimed in.

"We're going to a private island off of Puerto Rico to test out the new St. Vincent's Resort," Katherine said. "It's going to be like reliving our honeymoon."

She made that sound like a good thing. Though fucking her on our honeymoon was one of the best things that had ever happened to me. No games. No people. Just me and her for a month.

"Honeymoon sex." Candice all but swooned as she looked up at Lars.

Lars blushed the deepest, darkest red.

"Unfortunately, I have to steal my son for a minute," Carlyle said, pushing his chair aside. He winked at Katherine, who retreated from that look. "It won't be long."

Katherine looked like she wanted to bark back at him.

So, I hastily rose to my feet. No point in letting her take the brunt of his anger. It was always reserved for me anyway.

"By all means," Katherine said.

"Don't smoke those disgusting things in the house," Elizabeth said, wagging a finger at my father.

Carlyle shot her a devilish grin. "Of course not, darling."

Then he tipped his head to the side, and I followed him out of the dining room. As soon as we were away from everyone else, my father produced two cigars and a lighter. He lit them as we headed toward the library that was currently under renovation.

"Well, son," he said as he pulled open the door, "what do you think?"

I forced my face into neutrality. I'd liked the old library. It had been a refuge for me, growing up. I had no idea what he was doing to the room with its floor-to-ceiling built-ins and thousands of books.

I stepped inside with a sinking feeling in the pit of my stomach. He'd gutted the room. No bookshelves. No books. Nothing cozy about it any longer. It used to have just one window with a cushioned bench. Now, there were enormous windows covering the entire wall. It must have cost a fortune. But the room wasn't finished yet. It was still empty, except for the dust and construction work. I wondered how long I could hold my breath in here.

"It's great. What are you putting in here now?" I asked, bringing the cigar to my lips.

"It's a new studio for Elizabeth," he explained. "She wants a design room."

Of course. She already had a studio in Midtown and a store on Fifth Avenue. Not to mention, the upstairs room she had renovated into an enormous walk-in closet for her designs. Now, he was stripping out the one room in this place I'd ever liked to give her a studio.

"I'm sure she will like that."

"She will," he said. "It's my anniversary present to her."

I took another pull on the cigar and said nothing. I would have much preferred this was a joint. I needed to mellow the fuck out after all this shit.

"This wasn't the real reason I brought you here though, of course," he said, turning to face me.

Of course.

"How long will you be gone on this little jaunt to the Caribbean?"

"A week," I said with a shrug. "Maybe longer. We'll have the jet."

"You'll not be on vacation," my father growled.

No. Aside from my honeymoon, when had I ever gone on vacation? "Of course not."

"This Ireland deal is finally falling into place. You will need to be available at all times for meetings and conference calls. Have your phone with you and your iPad."

"Already planned to," I agreed. "I want this as much as you do."

I didn't know how many fucking ways I could prove that to him. Nothing I did mattered. I'd graduated top of my class at Harvard, top of my class for my Harvard MBA, and worked relentlessly for the company. I actually loved the work despite the crazy hours. I was damn good at it, too.

My father looked inscrutable in the soft light. "If we lose it, it will be because of your ineptitude."

I clenched my jaw. "We're not going to lose the deal. We've been working on it all year. We're going to put a Percy Tower in the heart of Dublin. I won't miss a thing."

"Well, we'll see," my father said, little faith in me.

"They're going to come into the city after the New Year."

"I'll be prepared for that, as always."

My father just looked at me and shook his head. "You'd better be. We wouldn't want Candice's chump prodigy taking over."

I ground my teeth together. "She got married without telling anyone and is claiming to be a sex therapist. I don't think anyone has anything to worry about with Candice."

"And why isn't Katherine pregnant?" he demanded.

I had no answer to that. None that he'd want to hear.

"We've been trying," I lied.

"Not hard enough apparently. You're going to lose that girl, and all of it will be down the drain. She's just like your mother," he said harshly, "She never loved you either."

He was trying to get a reaction out of me, but I was numb to that particular pain. My mother had left me. She'd left me with this monster... who had then made me into a monster. I didn't need love from someone like that.

Nor Katherine's love. She had given it away once. She would never give it to me. I'd never deserve it anyway.

I met my father's anger with a flat stare. "I am not going to lose Katherine. Our marriage was not built on love. It's a mutual understanding. You were the one who helped create this. Surely, you see that we have time. You're just mad about Candice."

My father just glared at me. I never knew why he hated me so much. I was his only son. The only son of the woman he had loved... the woman who had left. I didn't know if he saw her in me somehow. But no matter how much of a perfect son I was, he would always look at me as less than.

"You're not getting any younger."

"I'm well aware."

I didn't need to hear this shit. I knew everything he was

going to say. I'd heard it all before. This was how I'd been raised. To believe that love wasn't a good enough reason to get married, that money was what was important, and to keep the family name and old money and virtues in one place. I still couldn't believe he'd even approved of Katherine, considering her father had bankrupted them. But her name got her by.

I'd done my part. And it still wasn't enough.

"If Candice can have a brat in a few months, you'd think that you could honor the agreement and secure the Percy line."

I wanted to snap back at him. Anger burned through me. He ignited it like no one else. Not even Katherine with her brash behavior and smart mouth. My father lit me like a fuse dipped in lighter fuel.

My blood boiled, but still, I tried to rein it in. Knew he wanted it from me. "If I said that we were practicing quite frequently, would that satisfy you?"

"Just don't fuck this up, too."

Too.

The word made me tremble with barely suppressed rage. I'd never fucked up a goddamn thing.

"Fine," I ground out. "I'll go home and get started right now."

I pushed past him and out of the claustrophobic construction zone. As soon as I was out, I felt like I could finally breathe again. If I wasn't careful, I'd have a goddamn asthma attack. I hadn't had one in fucking years. No way was I going to let it happen in front of my father.

I needed to get out of this house. Get away from my father. Get away from... everything.

Maybe then it would be far enough.

But knowing my father... probably not.

7

KATHERINE

Candice droned on and on and on about her sex therapy work. My ears were going to start bleeding. Elizabeth had excused herself from the conversation, but somehow, Harmony and I had been roped into staying and listening to her.

I'd pulled my phone out after Camden disappeared and started texting Lark with an SOS. She had responded with a picture of the sunset on the water and the message:

Merry Christmas Eve! See you tomorrow. Love you!

The rest of the conversation was her sending me picture after picture of all of my friends having the time of their lives while I was stuck... here. She could have at least had the decency to call and help me get out of here. Not that I could leave without Camden. Well, I could... but I wouldn't.

Footsteps down the hallway indicated someone was returning. I breathed a sigh of relief.

"Finally," I muttered.

I swiftly rose to my feet. Harmony looked up at me with a pained expression.

"Weren't you saying that you had to meet Kurt?" I suggested to Harmony, giving her a way out.

She stood up so fast that she nearly knocked the chair back. "Right, Kurt. I almost forgot."

"Oh, do you have to leave already?" Candice asked.

"Unfortunately so," Harmony said.

"Well, maybe we could meet up this week while Lars and I are still in town."

"Maybe," Harmony offered reluctantly.

Then Camden stormed into the room with all the force of a hurricane. He had a cigar in his hand, which he promptly put out in a tray by the wet bar. He tipped back the rest of his discarded drink, and then his eyes found me. "Time to go."

I nodded and hurried after him as he darted toward the elevator. I barely had time to retrieve my coat and purse before following after him. The doors almost closed before me.

The air was heavy between us. Charged with energy and anger. He smelled like cigar smoke and scotch and after-shave. I should have been irritated with him, but I wasn't. I knew what it was like to have to deal with difficult family members. I hadn't seen my father in prison in years. My mother treated me like everything was perfectly fine, even when it wasn't... especially when it wasn't. I had a brother who had literally changed his name and disappeared to Texas to get away from us. I'd learned that my friends were my family long ago, but it didn't mean that my family didn't still bring out the fire in my veins. When it happened to Camden, it somehow made him so much more... human.

He'd hate for me to say it, but the height of his fury with

his father was also the height of his humanity. A part of me just wanted to help. Not that he'd ever let me help. It was a festering wound that revolted when touched.

So, I held back. I waited and debated on saying anything. It wasn't like I was the queen of dealing with my issues.

And yet...

And yet...

It wasn't until we were back in his penthouse that I worked up the nerve to say something.

Camden was angling for the wet bar, rolling his sleeves up to his elbows as he went. I saw a bender ahead of him.

"What happened back there?" I asked.

He wrenched the top off the crystal decanter. "My father."

"Well... obviously," I said softly as I breezed toward him.

He poured himself a knuckle's worth of liquor. Drained it and then poured another.

"Do you want to talk about it?"

"Do I look like I want to talk about it?" he snarled.

I ran a hand down his arm. My nails grazed his forearm. "Tell me about it."

"He's a prick. What more do you need to know?"

"I know what it's like," I said gently. "My father isn't exactly a dream come true."

"Yeah, well, you're lucky he's locked up then."

I flinched at those words. My father was a monster but a different kind than Camden's father. Mine loved me... in his own way. He'd spoiled me. But he'd ruined everyone he did business with to get there. Camden's father just hated everyone who stood in his path and didn't buck under the force of his personality.

"Don't take this out on me," I told him. "I just want to

talk about it. You were mad when you came back out the first time. That's why you snapped at me and Harmony."

"Katherine, tonight is really not the night."

"Why won't you talk to me?" I demanded, unable to keep the edge out of my voice. "Must you cut me out of everything?"

His eyes found mine. But instead of the fire that usually burned there, it was just emptiness. There was nothing looking back.

I swallowed at that look and brought my hand down to rest on his. "I know what your father is like. I understand that he's an asshole."

"You have no idea," he muttered.

I sighed. "I never wanted to tell you."

"Tell me what?"

"I know how bad your father is because... he came on to me."

Everything about Camden stilled in that moment. "What?" he asked, his voice lethal.

"It was at a company event this summer. He'd always... looked at me like that. Like I was eye candy. But you and I were fighting, and you left with..." I didn't say her name. "And your father approached me."

"What happened?" he asked, low and brutal.

"Look, I handled it. He touched my butt, and then I poured my drink on him. He's never done it again. But I know the kind of person he is."

Camden looked like he was about to explode. "And he's never going to do it again because I am going to kill him."

I squeezed his hand and held him in place. "Camden, no, please. I don't want you to do anything. I never told you because I knew this would happen. I knew you'd be mad." Or he wouldn't care. Though I couldn't bring myself to tell him that I'd thought it was a possibility. "I don't want or need you to defend my honor."

"Katherine, he touched you."

"And?" I demanded, holding my ground. "For one, I told you that to explain that I understood your anger and that you could tell me what was going on. And two, why do you even seem to care?"

"Fine. He was pissed about Candice coming home pregnant. He wanted to know why we weren't pregnant. Suggested that I wasn't doing my duty," Camden told me.

I winced at the words. The ones we had been arguing about before his father went and spit on him about it. It wasn't Camden who wasn't ready to have a baby. It was me. And I could see that written on his face.

"I see," I whispered.

"Yes, so do you see why I didn't tell you about what he said? You'd just get more pissed off that I was bringing this shit up to you."

"Fine," I said, straightening my spine and letting the rest of it drop. "But you didn't answer my second question. Why did you get so mad? It's not like we're *together*. Not like that. We haven't been for a while."

"You are my wife," he said fiercely, as if that explained everything.

Considering the fact that this had all been arranged and Camden never seemed to care one way or another that I was his wife, it didn't feel like enough of an answer. Was he mad because it was his father? Was he mad because it was me? It didn't make sense. Not with how we'd been together for *months*.

"So?"

"What do you mean, so?" he asked. "You're my wife. If

another man touches you—I don't care who the fuck he is—
I'll kill him."

I froze at those words. I wanted to relish them. I hadn't
been with another man other than my husband, but that
didn't mean that he had been similarly faithful. Not that
either of us had made promises to each other. Not for a long
time. He could do whatever he wanted. And he did.

"I don't see why," I told him.

He just shook his head. "It's been a long fucking night. I
don't want to talk any more about this. I want to get drunk
and forget this night ever happened."

"I could drink with you," I offered.

"No, forget it," he said, pushing away from me and
heading toward the door.

"Where are you going?" I asked, following him.

"Out. I need to blow off some steam."

"Camden, we're leaving in the morning. Just stay here
and get drunk and sleep it off."

He'd already grabbed his coat and pressed the button
for the elevator. I couldn't believe this was happening. What
the hell had really happened with his father that made him
react like this?

"Should I go with you?" I offered in vain.

His eyes lifted to me. "I wouldn't have even had this
conversation with my father if you'd held up your end of the
deal."

I took a step back in shock. "Are you saying this is my
fault?"

"Isn't it?"

"Your father is a dick. That has nothing to do with me."

"Sure, Katherine."

Then he stepped into the elevator and left me behind in
his apartment. I stared at the closed doors in shock. Camden

and I had our differences. We yelled at each other and hurt each other. This should have been par for the course. Especially after how I'd acted on our anniversary.

This was why I didn't put myself out there. He had accused me of being the problem, of the things that his father was responsible for. Nowhere in the contract did it say that I had to be pregnant in the first year. It just said *have a baby*, for fuck's sake.

I stormed away from the elevator and went into the extra bedroom where I'd stashed my suitcase for the vacation tomorrow. I'd planned to stay here so that I wouldn't have to wake up and get over here before we headed to the airport. I was regretting that now. It would be nice not to sleep under the same roof as him.

When I checked my phone, Lark had gone silent. My friends English and Whitley, who were also at the beach with Lark, had picked up the thread and sent obscene pictures from a beach party. What I should do was call Lark and vent to her.

Instead, my finger hovered on Penn's number. It wouldn't be strange for me to call him. He'd been in my life since I was little. He'd always been the person to pick me up, even more so than Lark. And yet, this felt like a betrayal, even to the man who had just abandoned me.

Ignoring my phone, I opened my email instead, resisting the temptation. I just needed a Xanax and to go to sleep.

As I absently scrolled through my email, a new email popped up from the contact at the charity. We'd met this afternoon, which was the real reason I'd been late to meet Camden, and she'd said that I'd hear from her if something came up. I opened the email and scrolled through the information for the children's charity along with a date to meet the kids after I got back.

A part of me wanted to be so pissed at Camden and cancel it. I didn't need to do more work, and I'd only decided to do it to prove myself. But what did I have to prove when he was off doing who knew what with who knew who?

Lies. I knew exactly where he went when he needed to "blow off steam." He'd gone to Fiona's. I knew it for certain. As much as I knew that he'd be furious if I called Penn. My own Achilles heel.

But maybe I'd still go through with the charity, not to prove it to Camden or to make myself look good, but maybe just... for myself.

8

CAMDEN

My head was fuzzy as I crashed back into my limo and told my driver to drive. I knew it was the alcohol and the cigar, but it was more than that. My lungs felt tight. It was hard to breathe, and I wasn't getting in enough oxygen. As I sucked in another breath, I placed my hand on my chest and wheezed. My lungs rattled.

Fuck. I knew what that meant. Fucking fuck.

I leaned forward, swiping open the compartment in the limo where I kept emergency supplies. "Where are you? Goddamn it."

I scooted past bottles of booze, a box of condoms, and a collection of chocolates that must have belonged to Katherine.

Then I saw it. "There you are." I grabbed the inhaler.

I shook it a few times, brought it to my lips, and pressed down on the top, inhaling deeply. I leaned back against the leather seat and waited for my breathing to even out, for the tightness to leave my lungs. It took a few minutes before everything began to return to normal.

That could have been bad. As Katherine and I argued

upstairs, I'd felt it coming on, but I'd ignored it, willed it away. Not that it had ever fucking worked.

Alcohol, cigar smoke, and construction dust were not a winning set. Not even close. Fuck, it was amazing how one little life-saving bit of medicine could make me feel like such a fucking failure. Millions of people used inhalers to control their asthma, but somehow, it made *me* a freak to have to use medicine because my lungs couldn't properly function.

There were very few people who knew that I needed to use it. Besides my father and Candice, if she even remembered, I could only think of my closest friend, Court Kensington. He'd never bring it up, but we didn't hide from each other. We knew all the dark and nasty sides that we kept from everyone else. I actually wished that he were here tonight instead of in Puerto Rico already with his girlfriend, English.

But he wasn't, and I'd just snapped at Katherine. There was no one else in my life to be with. I just needed to get away.

I knew exactly where I should go.

It was an hour later when I showed up outside of Hank's, a run-down billiards hall on the wrong side of town. One night about two years ago, I'd stumbled across the place with the police chief, José. I'd needed an escape, and despite the fact that most people thought I had him in my pocket, we actually enjoyed each other's company.

He'd suggested Hank's. After he'd seen how I played, he'd regretted bringing me. Pool was my sport of choice. Unsurprisingly, as a kid who had suffered with asthma, I hadn't been too fond of most outdoor sports, but pool was a game of math, strategy, and skill. A game I had gotten really good at while secluded in my father's home, growing up.

I'd shown up to the pool hall dressed as a nobody, and life had faded away. I was still Camden Percy. I couldn't escape who I was, not even in this shithole, but no one treated me differently for it. After a few months, I'd purchased a condo down the street for nights when I got too fucked up or I just wasn't ready to go back. It was a refuge from a world that never knew I needed one.

I changed into jeans, a T-shirt, and a leather jacket at the condo before heading into Hank's, which was surprisingly packed with customers on Christmas Eve. I recognized a few of the guys playing pool.

"Hey, Camden," Ricky called as he leaned over a pool table. He had a wiry mustache and potbelly. The guy was from Texas and wore a cowboy hat every day of the year. In New York City. Baffling.

"Ricky," I said, shaking his hand.

"You up for a game after I crush Big Al?" Ricky asked.

Big Al was actually a scrawny twenty-something, who wore a white sleeveless shirt and low hung jeans. He sometimes worked as a bar back for Monica, when she let him.

"Hey, I'm going to clean up," Big Al said before missing his next shot.

I laughed. It came out effortlessly. None of the pressure from real life here. "Maybe next game, Ricky."

"Sounds good."

I passed them by and headed straight for the bar. I really fucking needed a drink. I needed to drink and not remember anything that had happened tonight. My father, Candice, Lars... even Katherine. It was all too much of a goddamn nightmare. And maybe if I let Monica liquor me up, I wouldn't have to think about anything for a few hours.

"Camden," Monica said, already reaching for her top-shelf liquor as I slid into a seat at her bar. They'd only started carrying it once I became a regular. "You look like shit."

Monica was in her fifties and could scare the piss out of any man in this establishment. Everyone said that she had been a knockout in her youth. I didn't need to see a picture to imagine it. She was still beautiful now. Only about five feet tall with dark brown hair and green eyes, and a total hard-ass. She didn't take anyone's shit, which was probably why I liked her.

"Thanks, Monica," I said, passing a hundred-dollar bill into the tip jar.

"At least you tip well," she said. She dropped a glass of scotch on the rocks in front of me.

"And a shot of tequila," I added. "For you and me."

She shrugged and reached for the Patrón. She poured us each a shot and held it out. "What are we toasting to?"

"No toasting," I said. "Just drinking."

I clinked the glass against hers, and we both downed the shots. She didn't even blink as she got back to work.

"Well, what brings you in on Christmas Eve?" she asked. "Don't you have family to see? Your pretty wife?"

"Yeah. That's why I'm here."

"I hear you," she said, pouring a pitcher of beer.

Monica rarely saw her family. She and her husband were separated. She'd said that her son didn't live nearby and he was busy a lot. She claimed that the bar was more her family now.

"Just keep 'em coming," I told her.

"You going to clear out Ricky before Christmas? I don't think his wife will much appreciate that."

I shook my head. "I'll just play. I only try to hustle the new guys."

She snorted. "I remember the first time you came in here with José and cleaned the entire place out. He was spitting mad at you. I'd never seen him so pissed off. Then you bought the entire bar drinks the rest of the night. They begrudgingly liked you after that."

I shrugged and shot her a lopsided smile. It was a good memory. I had definitely hustled them that night, but they'd come to accept me after the drinks.

"It's how I knew you weren't a complete shit."

I snorted. "Like the rest of the Upper East Side?"

"Wouldn't know anything about that, but I can tell that you're down tonight. Worse than normal. Tell Mama Monica what's been going on," she said, leaning into the bar and flashing me a smile.

"I don't know," I said, downing the scotch and passing it back to her for a refill. "My father is a dick. He's pressuring me to get this deal done, but he's pissed off because my sister came home pregnant."

She arched an eyebrow. "That's a bad thing?"

"To him, yes. She's pregnant before my wife. He doesn't like the competition."

She rolled her eyes. "That sounds stupid."

"It is," I agreed. "It might have all been okay if I'd ignored him baiting me, but he gets under my skin, and things aren't great with my wife."

"Katherine, right?"

"Yeah, Katherine. I fucked up our anniversary. We're supposed to try to have a baby, and she got mad at me for bringing it up."

"Why?" she asked.

"She's maybe not ready."

"And you're pressuring her? Did you talk about this before you got married?" Monica asked, sinking into one hip and giving me a look. "Because, you know, pressuring a woman to have a baby is the dumbest thing you can do. She's the one who has to carry it for nine months and birth the damn thing. Then she's mostly in charge of raising it. She either wants it or she doesn't."

"Yeah, yeah," I said, waving her off. But she was right. I'd come at it all wrong. How could I expect Katherine to want to have a baby when we were in such a shitty place anyway? "We talked about it before getting married, but we're in a rut. We're going away for a week, and we can't seem to do anything but bite each other's heads off."

Understatement.

"You want some advice, kid?" she asked as she wiped down the bar.

I laughed. "Do I have a choice?"

"Nope," she said with a smile. "You need to call a truce."

"A truce?"

"Yep. Call a truce with your wife. You need to talk it out, but right now, you're both too hardheaded to do that. You need to relax and forget about your problems, you know?" She passed me another shot of tequila. "Once you come home, things will be better, and you can talk this shit out. It'll help."

I shrugged, uncertain if any of that was true. Katherine would never let me call a truce. I knew her too well. She thrived on arguing and conflict. What would we even be like without it?

"Just think about it," Monica said as she held up her shot of tequila.

I clinked my shot against hers and then tipped it back. Maybe I'd think about it. Tomorrow. After I got rip-roaring drunk and forgot about everything that had happened tonight.

"Thanks for the advice, Mon," I said with a head nod. "I'm going to go beat Ricky."

"Good luck."

I came to my feet. Wobbling from side to side, I realized how drunk I already was. Well, fuck. This was going to be interesting.

"Ricky, you ready for that game?" I slurred.

He took one look at me and dropped a twenty on the table. "I think I can finally beat you, pretty boy."

I matched his bet and grinned slyly. No one ever beat me.

PART II

THE TRUCE

9

KATHERINE

The sound of the elevator dinging open woke me the next morning. Camden had never come home last night. He'd stayed out all night with Fiona. Merry fucking Christmas to me.

I pulled the pillow over my face and screamed into it. Not until I was completely exhausted did I toss it aside and slip out of bed. I couldn't even handle him right now. I trudged through the bedroom, stripping as I went, and then stepped into the shower.

We had to be at the airport in a matter of hours. I needed to find a way to look fucking presentable. I had to be Katherine Van Pelt today. The cool ice princess of the Upper East Side who never let a goddamn thing bother her. Not the pathetic girl who had stayed up way too late, waiting for her husband to come home.

"Katherine!" Camden called up the stairs.

He could go to hell as far as I was concerned. I ignored him and focused on my beautiful, long hair. I lathered it up with shampoo and then conditioner, taking time to thoroughly rinse it all out. Then suddenly, there was a person in front of the glass shower door.

I screamed on instinct. My heart fluttered as I realized it was Camden standing on the other side of the steamed-up glass door.

"What the hell are you doing?"

But as the words fell from my lips, he pulled his button-up over his head, stripped out of his slacks and underwear, and yanked open the door. My eyes went wide with shock.

"Camden, stop," I commanded, stepping deeper into the shower.

He didn't. He stepped into the spray and came toward me, pinning me back against the stone wall. My heart thudded in my chest but not from fear any longer. From that look in his eye. The one that said he wanted me.

His lips crashed down on mine, and his hand slipped over my wet skin. I gasped against him, caught off guard by his need for me. He tasted like whiskey and smoke and unbridled desire. Our bodies collided. His hand jerked my leg up around his hip. His cock pressed hard between my legs.

And then last night flashed through my mind. Me standing there like a fool, watching him walk out of his penthouse. Me waiting up, hoping he'd return. Me finally passing out from exhaustion. Now, he was back after staying out all night, doing who knew what. I might want this—I loved having sex with him—but I was not pathetic enough to accept this.

"Stop," I said harder this time, pushing against his chest.

He stumbled back a step into the water, soaking his dark hair. His brown eyes were nearly black in the low light. He looked feral and dangerous.

"Where were you last night?" I demanded.

"Out."

"Not good enough," I said.

"Katherine..."

"You don't get to do this," I told him. "You don't get to come back like nothing happened."

"Nothing did happen," he said, swaying slightly on his feet as if he was still drunk.

I glared at him. "That isn't an apology."

"I don't apologize," he growled.

Which was true. I'd never heard him apologize. Not to me. Not to anyone.

"We have a flight to catch," I told him, pushing past him in the shower. "You need to sober up."

I stepped out of the shower, grabbed a towel, and walked away from him. My chest ached with every step. A part of me wanted to go back there and claim that vicious man as my own. The rest of me knew that walking away was the only option, and that this vacation was going to be a nightmare.

Two hours later, I was in a sundress with a full face of makeup, cherry-red lipstick and all. The nude Christian Louboutins on my feet were the final pieces of my armor. I needed that armor to survive the next week.

Camden appeared in a three-piece suit, decidedly more sober than he had been two hours ago. Though clearly hungover from however much fucking alcohol he had consumed last night. He didn't say a word to me as our luggage was taken down to the limo, and then we traveled out to his private jet.

Silence was my ally in this. It was easier to text Lark,

English, and Whitley about how excited I was about coming to see them than it was to pretend to be happy to be going with my husband. We made it to the airport in record time and out to the plane even faster. It was a miracle.

Camden looked like he wanted to say something to me when we were boarding, but I shot him a glare and then hustled in front of him, so I wouldn't have to hear it. Wasn't it bad enough that he had been out all night with Fiona? Then he'd had to come home and try to fuck me, too? I couldn't *deal* with him right now. I wanted to be in the sun with a drink in hand, lying by the pool and working on my tan. That was it.

I sank into the first available seat, texting away with Lark as the pilot prepped for takeoff. To my dismay, Camden took the seat next to me.

"Do you mind?" I asked pointedly.

"Katherine, can we talk?"

"No," I spat.

He put his hand to his head and winced once. "God, it's bright in here."

"That's what you get," I snapped.

He just groaned. "Maybe I can ask them to dim the cabin lights."

"Oh, just sit there and suffer."

"I know that you're pissed at me for leaving last night, but do you mind bringing it down an octave?"

I shot him another glare. "Mad at you for leaving? No, why ever would I be mad that you disappeared in the middle of an argument to go see your mistress instead of having a normal conversation with me? So, you might find that I really *don't* want to talk today. Nor do I care about your hangover."

He straightened at that. Some part of his bad mood dissolving. "Wait, you think I was with Fiona?"

"Why else would you stay out all night?" I mused rhetorically and went back to my text messages.

"I wasn't with Fiona," he said.

"And why should I believe you?"

"Because," he said, pitching his voice low, "I'm not a liar."

My eyes swept up to his. He wasn't a liar, but his response didn't make any sense. Why would he have been out all night? Where the hell had he gone?

"Fine," I muttered. "You weren't with Fiona. Hooray for one day of mildly good behavior. Do you want a gold star?"

"Katherine," he said softly, "I don't want to fight."

I whirled on him. "Then maybe you should have thought about that last night. Go back to nursing your hangover. I don't want to talk to you the rest of the way to Puerto Rico. I'm going to pretend that you're not here."

Camden seemed to turn into a statue for a moment, as if processing my seething in anger. Then he nodded once and took a different seat.

He must have fallen asleep because he didn't stir again until we were up in the air.

A catnap seemed to have rejuvenated him. He grabbed a bottle of water and then opened his laptop. He typed away at it for a few minutes distractingly before seeming to come to a decision and closing it.

I nearly groaned when he headed back toward me. He crossed his arms and waited for me to look up. I took my sweet time.

"What?" I finally asked.

"The company is brokering a deal to get a tower into Dublin," he told me flatly. "My father took me aside last night to tell me that I wasn't allowed to take a vacation. I have to be on call and available at all times while we're away. That if it falls through, it's all my fault."

I straightened in surprise. "Why are you telling me this?"

"You wanted to know what had happened last night. That's what happened. Along with blaming me for Candice being here and pregnant, for us not being pregnant, and for my mother abandoning me as a child."

"But none of that is your fault."

"Obviously," he said stiffly. "But he's a giant jackass when he decides to start blaming me for my very existence, and I admittedly don't take it very well."

"You should tell him to go fuck himself."

"I would love to if I didn't think he'd kick me out of the company."

"He can't do that!" I blurted.

Camden raised his eyebrows. "Are you certain?"

No, I wasn't. I could see then all the weight on his shoulders. He loved his job. He loved the company. Despite his father and all the pressure he put on him, Camden truly enjoyed the work. He never complained about not getting time off or having to always be available. The thought of his father taking that away from him made me furious.

"I'm not," I admitted. "But... why didn't you tell me this last night? Why run off in the middle of the night?"

"I was angry. I wasn't thinking. I just needed to get away," he said. "But I wasn't with another woman." He paused, as if contemplating that. "Unless you consider Monica getting me back to my bed."

"What?" I asked with wide eyes. "Who is Monica?"

"She's a bartender."

My eyes widened further.

"No, not like that. She's older than me." That wasn't helping. He sighed when he saw my expression. "Like, twenty years older than me. She's not..." He shook his head. "She's just nice. It's not like that."

"Okay."

"I went to a bar and had a few drinks. I needed to clear my head."

"Blow off steam," I suggested.

"Yes. I actually meant that last night."

"Then you came home and decided to jump in the shower with me?"

He shrugged. "I admit to being a bit drunk, and I wanted to fuck my wife."

I kept my face neutral, even as desire flared through me. "You can see how I was angry about that, considering I thought you'd come from Fiona."

"I can see that," he admitted.

"I still don't understand why you're telling me this," I whispered softly.

Camden didn't explain himself. He didn't think about my feelings in the matter. He wasn't like that. I knew that he cared in some infinitesimal way, but it wasn't enough for an explanation. Not for the wife he'd acquired through an arrangement.

"Because," he said, running a hand back through his perfect hair, "I want to... call a truce."

He looked uncomfortable, saying those words. Or almost... nervous? That couldn't be.

"A truce?" I asked uncertainly.

"Yeah."

"What does that mean, Camden?"

"It means that I'm tired of fighting."

I looked up at him in shock. "Since when?"

"Since now," he said sternly. "This is the closest thing I'm going to get to a vacation for a long time. Can't we just enjoy it?"

"I don't know. You're the one constantly acting like a grade-A asshole."

"Look, I'm not the only one," he said pointedly.

"Fine. What would a truce even look like?"

He seemed surprised that we'd even gotten to the part where I'd ask him that. Maybe he hadn't really thought this through.

"We agree to no arguing for the week we're gone."

"There is no *way* you can abide by that."

"I can... if you can."

"No arguing? No fighting?" I laughed and shook my head. "Might as well say that we won't bring up our pasts or any of our issues right now."

"All right. Then we won't."

"What?" I asked in surprise.

"I won't bring up Penn. You won't bring up Fiona."

"Or the baby," I added hastily.

"Or the baby," he agreed. "One week in paradise. When we go home, we can go back to arguing all we want but a truce while we're gone."

I stared at him, waiting for the catch. Why was he even doing this? It made no sense. It wasn't Camden Percy to want something like this. Half of our foreplay was arguing with each other. But I looked into those dark eyes and saw sincerity. He was serious about this. He wanted to call a truce. No more fighting. What the hell would we even say to each other?

"Do you think we can do it?"

"I'm willing to try," he said.

And he sounded almost... earnest.

What did I have to lose? A week in paradise with my husband with no fighting. It could be perfection or destruction. But either way, it would be a new challenge.

"All right," I finally said.

He held his hand out. "Shake on it."

I shook my head in disbelief as I slipped my hand into his. It was warm as it engulfed my small palm. He tugged me up off of the couch and into his arms.

I arched an eyebrow at him. "What are you doing?"

"Sealing it with a kiss."

And then he did.

10

KATHERINE

We landed in Puerto Rico a few hours later. Gone was the New York bitter cold, and in its place was beautiful eighty-degree weather and ocean as far as the eye could see. I hadn't realized how much I'd missed the sunshine until we landed in a tropical paradise. I shucked off the jacket I'd been wearing inside the cabin and exited the plane in a sundress and Tory Burch sandals, leaving my Louboutins in my oversized bag. I might be an ice princess, but I thawed in the summer with the best of them.

Camden was still in a suit as he followed me down the stairs and onto the runway. A car service waited for us nearby. I headed toward it while our bags were delivered to the trunk.

Our driver opened the door to the backseat. "Welcome to Puerto Rico."

"Thank you," I said and slipped into the interior.

Camden followed a minute later, stowing his phone in his pocket. "Jesus, it's a thousand degrees outside."

"Isn't it great?" I said with a rare smile.

He tugged at his suit collar. "Not exactly."

"I told you to change out of that thing. You have a spare pair of clothes."

He opened his mouth, clearly to argue with me, but then just shrugged. "Oh well. I'll do it when we get there."

A thrill hit me in the stomach. He was actually serious. He was going to have a real truce here. No arguing, like we did every second of every day. I was excited and nervous and wondering what the hell was going to come from this. Would we leave this island better or worse for it? Only one way to find out.

Camden tugged his phone back out and returned to work. I knew that he didn't mind that he had to work while he was on this trip, but I felt a little bad for him. I didn't know how he'd managed to get the time off for our honeymoon. I hadn't realized quite how impossible it must have been for him to be without his work while gone... and how freeing.

My eyes fell on the landscape as we drove inland toward the resort. Everything was green and lush and vibrant. So different than a New York winter. It was almost easy to believe that I could leave all my problems back in the city. That Camden and I could be a happy married couple here in this world. It was probably a lie, but sometimes, it was easier to believe a lie.

We pulled up in front of St. Vincent's Resort, which was a gorgeous sprawling complex of buildings surrounding eight enormous pools with swim-up bars and poolside restaurants. From what Lark had explained, the resort had two dozen private, beachside villas. Our party had taken up eight of them before they were offered to other high-end clientele. Unofficially, the property had opened for family, friends, and business associates of St. Vincent's Enterprise just after Thanksgiving. But the resort itself wouldn't open up to the general public until after the New Year. So, the entire place was only other people in high enough positions to gain this kind of access. It was an Upper East Side dream come true.

We had virtually checked in to the resort on our flight, and a gentleman was waiting for us as the car pulled up to the resort. He was probably in his early thirties with sunbaked brown skin and floppy brown hair. He seemed particularly effusive.

"Hello, and welcome to St. Vincent's Resort: Puerto Rico, Mr. and Mrs. Percy. I am Paulo, your personal guide for the remainder of your stay. Should you need anything, I will assist you."

Camden shook Paulo's hand but flashed me a look, as if waiting for me to correct him. I hadn't changed my name from Van Pelt and had no interest in doing so. Camden had never seemed to care. Normally, I hated when someone called me Mrs. Percy and quickly corrected them. In the interest of not arguing, I let it pass.

"Hello," I said genially and shook Paulo's hand.

"We're thrilled to have you on our wonderful island and hope that we can show you everything that we have to offer —from original food, a unique cultural experience, the beautiful rainforest, and bioluminescent bays to our incredible nightlife and alcohol selections." His smile only widened. "Allow me to escort you to your private villa. Right this way."

It was a short walk to our villa, which was an enormous one-bedroom suite, complete with a private pool with in-water beach chairs and a hot tub. The inside was sleek and modern and stunning. An enormous king-size bed took up much of the space with a desk against one wall and a mounted eighty-inch television. A bottle of champagne chilled in a bucket next to a plate of fresh strawberries.

I picked one up and nibbled on it as I moved into the bathroom. It was like walking into a dream. The space had a waterfall shower and a large free-standing tub with an assortment of salts, bubbles, and oils. Even for someone with my expensive taste, it was above and beyond.

"Is everything to your liking?" Paulo asked, hovering near the open-air doorway.

"Superb," I said honestly.

Our luggage had already been rolled in and deposited near the bed. I didn't know how they had beaten us here, but the service was to my liking.

Camden nodded and passed him a twenty.

Paulo pocketed it without comment. "If you need to reach me, dial 1 on the hotel line or use my personal number." He gave Camden his card. "I hope you enjoy your stay with us at St. Vincent's Resort."

He ducked out of the room.

I arched an eyebrow at Camden. "Well?"

"I have a conference call in an hour. How drunk can we get before then?"

I shook my head. "Aren't you still drunk from last night?"

"I think I sobered up too much on the plane." He reached down and grabbed the champagne, which I realized was a Yellow Label Veuve Clicquot. He popped it open and poured us each a glass. "That was a mistake."

I took mine from him and drank deep. "Well, let's get into bathing suits and find our friends, shall we?"

"I had other ideas," he suggested.

"Oh?"

"We could finish this bottle and fuck instead."

"So eloquent," I said, taking another sip.

He shrugged, downed his champagne, and poured another. "I'm a man of simple tastes."

"Liar."

His smirk was particularly deadly. "Fine. I'm a man of expensive tastes. We're in a grand villa thousands of miles away from home. I want to get you naked and spread you like a feast on that bed."

My blood heated at his words.

We hadn't been intimate in... months. After the honeymoon, things had been great. But then Camden found me in Penn's arms at Natalie's party. Nothing had happened, but it didn't matter. Something intrinsically broke between us. The feeble trust we'd had shattered. He'd returned to his old ways, and I'd been left bereft. It would be so easy to fall back into how things had been. So easy. But a part of me resisted. A part of me feared what would happen if I gave that small bit of trust to Camden Percy. Would he break me with it again?

"As appetizing as that sounds," I said, glad there was no waver to my voice, "I think I'll have to take a rain check."

He seemed unsurprised, turning away from me as he said, "Then get dressed, and we'll go find Lark."

I didn't know why it sounded like he was disappointed. Camden was the one getting plenty of ass. It was *me* who wasn't sleeping around after all.

Still... his disappointment made me wonder why I'd refused.

A half hour later, after I put on my dark purple cheeky bikini and lathered myself in sunscreen, Camden and I departed the villa. He'd changed into cerulean-blue board shorts that stopped a few inches above his knees, revealing his muscular legs and six-pack. The only thing Camden did other than work and play pool was work out. Apparently, it was the only way for him to release his anger... and he was still a raging jackass most of the time.

Lark had texted me her location, and we found our friends seated around one of the large pools in front of the swim-up bar. Of course.

Anna English saw us first and jumped up from her beach chair, where she had been leaning into her boyfriend, Court Kensington. English was our resident Hollywood babe with long platinum-blonde hair and a rocking bod.

"Katherine," she cried, throwing her arms around me.

"Hey, English," I said. I dropped my beach bag next to an open seat as Lark and Whitley hurried over to me.

Camden touched my wrist before they could bombard me. "Drink?"

I nodded. "Anything with a fucking umbrella."

He grinned and yanked me forward into a kiss. "I can do that."

I pulled back, flushed, as he strode away. As if he hadn't just pushed me off-kilter with that kiss.

Lark raised her eyebrows when she got to me. "What was that about?"

"Nothing," I said at once.

Lark didn't look like she believed me. Well, that was fair. I didn't believe myself.

"So, you're finally here," Whitley Bowen said. Her hair, which had been blood red at Halloween, was now a caramel color. She was the resident pixie of our group, not even reaching five feet tall, but unequivocally with the biggest personality.

"I made it," I told her.

"Do I have a story for you."

"Oh god," I muttered. "Do I even want to know?"

"Yes," Lark said at the same time English said, "No."

They all laughed. Whitley was known for outrageous dating stories. But I'd thought that was temporarily behind her since she started dating Robert Dawson. My eyes glanced over all my friends in one place. Court Kensington, Sam Rutherford, and Gavin King were at the bar, talking animatedly to Camden. But, hmm... Robert wasn't among them.

"Maybe I do want to know," I conceded.

"We'll tell you later," Lark said, pulling me away to grab a beach towel as she dragged her ginger-red hair up into a high ponytail.

God, it was good to see Lark not working. The last year, she had been dedicated to Mayor Kensington's reelection campaign. Of course, it had been worth it for more than the fact that they'd won. She'd met her boyfriend, Sam, on campaign, and he was the best thing that had ever happened to her.

I grabbed two towels and laid them out next to the girls' chairs. Then I plopped down next to them.

"How was the flight?" English asked.

"Fine." Of course... it had actually been one of the strangest moments of my life. But no one needed to know that. I turned to Whitley. "Where's Robert?"

"That's the story!" Whitley said.

Lark rolled her eyes. "It's not as dramatic as usual."

"Well, you didn't put glitter on his ceiling fans, did you?"

"That was one time!" Whitley cried. She grinned. "And he had it coming."

It was still probably my favorite Whitley story. How she'd found a guy was sleeping around and to retaliate she'd put glitter on all of his ceiling fans in the middle of the summer. So, when he came home, he'd turned on the fans. *Poof.* Glitter everywhere!

"Well, tell me. I thought things were going well with Robert. Wasn't he supposed to be here?"

Whitley nodded. "Yeah. I guess, like, ten days ago, he heard that he wasn't going to be able to take the time off. His company needed him to stay on through the holidays."

"That's bullshit. You broke up with him because he couldn't come with you?"

"No," she said fiercely. "I broke up with him because... I think he just... likes me more than I like him."

"Story of your life, huh?" I asked.

Lark huffed. "She did it because she was scared."

"I was *not* scared," Whitley said.

"You had feelings for someone for the first time maybe ever, and you ran away," Lark said with raised eyebrows.

"Damn, Lark," English said. "Get straight to the point."

"I did have feelings for him," Whitley admitted. "He didn't care that I liked my space. He wasn't clingy. He thought my strange relationship quirks were adorable. But... he didn't challenge me either. I could walk all *over* him. The only time he ever had to stand up to me was about this vacation. And you know what I felt when he said that he couldn't come?"

"What?" I asked.

"Nothing. I wasn't even sad. I was like, 'Okay, bro. Maybe next time.' Is that normal?" Whitley shook her head and then drank from her piña colada. "I don't think so."

"Maybe you should talk to him about that," English suggested. "Maybe, when you get home, you should sit down and have a real conversation with him. He might have been acting like a pushover because he thought you'd run scared otherwise."

"Yeah... maybe. I don't know. I'm not going to think about it. We have another week here. I'm augmenting some rich girl's tits," she said, making light of her job as one of the top plastic surgeons in New York City. "Maybe I'll find an uncomplicated girl to hook up with while I'm here."

"Didn't you *just* say, like two months ago, that girls were more complicated than guys?" Lark asked.

"Hmm," Whitley said. "Maybe you're right. I do love eating out though... but dick is nice, too."

"You are one outrageous person," I commented with a smirk.

Whitley was an acquired taste. I'd thought she was crude and extreme the first couple times I met her. We clashed like oil and water, but she'd grown on me... kind of like a fungus. Now, I enjoyed her crazy tales and wild personality.

Camden returned with my piña colada, complete with a pineapple slice and umbrella.

"Thanks," I said, taking it from him.

He leaned down then and cupped my chin in his hand. I was so startled by the contact that I just saw the hint of his smirk before he claimed my mouth. When he pulled back, my heart was fluttering.

"You're welcome."

He strode back over to the bar, leaving all of my girls speechless.

I took a sip and avoided their gazes. I had no explanation for that. Camden wasn't... like that. He was a hard man. That was what I'd come to expect. What had our truce *done*?

"What was that?" Lark asked.

"Um... a kiss?"

"Yeah, no shit," Whitley whispered. "He just fucked your mouth in public."

English shrugged. "Even I can admit, that is not normal behavior from Camden Percy."

I sighed and leaned in closer to them. "Well, we have a sort of... truce."

"Truce?" Lark prompted.

"Yeah. We're not going to argue at all while we're here. Going to just... see how it goes."

Lark opened her mouth to clearly speak the disbelief that was evident in her green eyes. But then she looked up over my shoulder, and her smile ignited. She waved. "Penn, over here!"

My body seized. I felt frozen in place. But slowly, I loosened enough to turn around to see none other than Penn Kensington strolling over to our party.

11

CAMDEN

I closed my eyes and breathed out slowly. My grip tightened on my beer. I had one hour. *One* hour where I could be out with my friends before I had to take my conference call back in our villa. The last thing I wanted to deal with was Penn Kensington.

Court put his hand on my shoulder. He didn't have to say anything. We both knew that this wasn't good. It was ironic really that my closest friend was brothers with the man I despised the most. Of course, up until recently, Court and Penn hadn't gotten along either. It had been easier for me that way.

"Just let it go," Court finally said.

But I couldn't. I couldn't just let it go.

I turned and found Penn striding toward my wife. *His* wife, Natalie, was nowhere to be seen. Convenient. I didn't trust him. Not an ounce. And I couldn't see that I ever would.

"It's not worth it," Court continued.

Gavin laughed next to him. "I mean, I would like to see who would win that fight." Court shot him an exasperated look. Gavin held his hands up. "What? They should get it over with."

Gavin was our resident instigator. He didn't take much seriously. Not even the work he did for his family's oil company, Dorset & King. But he reaped the benefits. I'd begrudgingly learned to like him when he was at Harvard with Court and me. I didn't mind when he spoke to my baser instincts.

"They should *not* just get it over with," Sam said automatically.

He was the newest member of our group. In fact, he hadn't even been born Upper East Side. He had come from some small town in North Carolina. It was amazing that I even tolerated him. But the first time I'd met him, he'd hustled all three of us at poker. It had been a big enough jackass move, clearing out thirty grand from the lot of us, that I decided he could stay.

I gritted my teeth. Penn had finally reached the girls. He smiled effortlessly, like he had not a care in the world. Katherine was looking up at him. I couldn't see her face, but I could picture it. I'd seen her stare at Penn Kensington enough to know what she looked like around him.

"Why do you even care so much?" Gavin asked.

"That's his wife," Court said.

"And? It's a contract, right? You and Katherine got, like, an old-fashioned arranged marriage. You can both fuck whoever else you want."

Sam frowned, always so solemn. "I don't think it works like that."

"Yeah, but Fiona..."

"We're not talking about Fiona," I growled.

"All right, all right. I was just asking," Gavin muttered.

"Well, don't ask," Court said. "It's complicated."

I didn't know how to explain any of it to Gavin. Let alone myself. I'd wanted Katherine long before I got her to agree to marry me for my money. And I'd hated her relationship with Penn even longer. The way they fed off of each other. Hurt each other. Abused each other. All in the name of love. I didn't miss the irony, considering my relationship with Katherine now. But it didn't mean I liked seeing her around Penn either.

Before I questioned what I was doing, I pushed away from the bar and headed toward where Penn stood with my wife. I could feel Court follow behind me, there to intercede if need be.

Penn looked up at my approach, and his mouth turned down in a frown. He did *not* look pleased to see me. Not one bit.

Katherine and Lark rose to their feet. I saw that they both looked unsettled by my approach. But neither said anything. What would they say? They were crew. The core group of people that Katherine had grown up with—Larkin St. Vincent, Penn Kensington, Lewis Warren, and Archibald Rowe. They were her family as much or more than the people who had raised her. They protected their own.

"Percy," Penn said with no love lost in his voice.

"Kensington," I said with the same tone, only harder, rougher.

Katherine cleared her throat. A little cough and a pointed look in my direction. She crossed her arms over her ample chest. My eyes flicked down and then back up at her. "Camden..."

Fuck.

Oh fuck.

The goddamn truce. Why had I suggested that?

When Monica had mentioned it, I'd never thought that

Katherine would agree. It had seemed out of the realm of possibility. But now, we were here, and we'd both agreed not to argue or fight for the next week. I'd meant with each other, but if I laid into Penn right here, would it be any different?

No.

I ground my teeth together. I couldn't say a damn word that I wanted to say. I had to bite my tongue. Even though it was the last thing that I wanted to do. I wanted to tell Penn how much of a self-righteous prick he was and to stay the hell away from my wife, but it wouldn't even matter. Katherine wouldn't listen. She and Penn circled each other. It was inevitable.

"Hey, man," I said finally, releasing my anger.

As much as I hated him, I was not risking this chance with Katherine.

Penn startled, as if surprised that I'd said anything else to him. That I'd said something pleasant and not bitten his head off was even more of a shock.

"Uh, hey..." Penn said.

His eyes darted to Katherine's, and he raised his eyebrows in confusion.

She shook her head, just barely perceptible.

Court stood next to me, his mouth hanging open. Then he shook himself out of it and held his hand out to his brother. "Hey, bro."

"Court."

"Where's Natalie?" Court asked.

Thank fuck for Court Kensington. Way to bring everyone back to the real matter at hand. Penn was married. To Katherine's enemy.

"She's back at the bar with Addie and Nicholas," Penn

said, pointing across the property. "They've abandoned Lewis and Rowe. I was coming to check on you all."

Because he couldn't do it with his wife in tow. There was a schism in their crew. Natalie had broken something that had been impenetrable for decades. I wasn't saddened by it.

"We'll come over later," Lark told him quickly.

Katherine nodded. "I want to see Rowe in board shorts. He hates them."

Penn laughed, clearly forgetting for a moment that I hovered over them. "He really does, but it's too hot for pants." He shrugged. "I'll catch you later." He nodded to the girls and his brother, skipping right over me before disappearing the way he'd come.

Good riddance.

Court jerked me back from Katherine, who shot me a small smile. It felt like a victory. Even if it tasted like ash.

We headed a few feet away. Not quite back to Sam and Gavin, but far enough away from the girls. Court's gaze was skeptical. Even more so than the surprise his brother had given me.

"Okay. Who are you, and what have you done with Camden Percy?"

"Very funny," I said dryly.

"No, seriously. Did you just say something *nice* to Penn?"

"I said something neutral."

Court shook his head. "When have you ever been neutral with my brother?"

"I'm not," I said darkly. "It took all my self-control not to call him the bitch that he is."

Court snorted. "Well, I can't really deny that. He's family, but god, does he know how to brood." He eyed me again. "I didn't know you had said self-control."

"How do you think I survive a boardroom?"

"Fair," he said. "I've never known you to use it outside of that. Does this have something to do with the business?"

"No." Then I relented, bringing Court in on my plans. "Katherine and I have... an arrangement."

"Well aware of that one."

"A new arrangement," I told him. "We've agreed not to argue or discuss our issues while we're here."

Court raised his eyes. "That's great. To what end? Are you finally going to admit that you're in love with her?"

I blew out an exasperated breath. "No."

"If not that, then why bother?"

"You always think I have to divulge every explanation for everything that I do, don't you?"

Court grinned like the Upper East Side prince that he was. "You just answered my question with a question. Oh, you're in deep."

"I no longer wish to discuss this." I pushed past him and returned to the bar... and my drink. I downed a large gulp of my beer and flagged down the bartender for another round.

Gavin leaned into the bar, seemingly oblivious to all that had happened a minute prior. "You know, I think I really want to get laid tonight."

Sam rolled his eyes. "Dude, you want to get laid every night."

"Who doesn't?" Gavin asked with a laugh.

Court returned then. He eyed me warily. Perhaps he'd hit too close to home. Not that I was in love with Katherine, but I did feel as if I was in too deep with her. I wanted to figure out a way to navigate our relationship if this was going to continue, and I couldn't do that if we were down each other's throats every minute of every goddamn day.

"I'm the only guy here without a girlfriend," Gavin

pointed out. Then he gestured to me. "Or wife. All of you have to fucking wingman for me."

"No," I said at once.

Sam shook his head. "Pass."

"Court?" Gavin asked hopefully.

"I think English might chop off his balls and feed them to him for dinner," I mused.

Court laughed. "You are not wrong, sir."

"Fuck, fine. I'll convince Whitley to do it," Gavin grumbled.

My eyes narrowed. "That doesn't seem like a hardship."

"Well, she's probably better at it than all of you shits. Women aren't put off by her at least."

Sam laughed. "Keep telling yourself that."

"Yeah, dude," Court continued, "you've had a thing for Whitley since day one."

Gavin's eyes rounded. "What the hell are you all talking about?"

"You believe that you are subtle," I told him. "I don't think that you are."

"Look, it's not like that. She just got out of a relationship with *our* friend. Even if I wanted to, I couldn't do that to Robert," Gavin said valiantly.

"If you say so," Court muttered.

Sam looked unconvinced. And I had no doubt that Gavin King, the infamous flirt, would move in on Whitley if she gave the slightest indication that she was interested. The problem had always been that she was *not*. Whitley was easily distractible and flirted even more than Gavin. They were a match made in hell. Two people who refused to settle down. Gavin was setting himself up for failure with those feelings.

But who the hell was I to talk? My gaze shifted to my

wife. She'd nearly finished her piña colada, and she was leaning back in her chair, soaking up the sun. Weren't we also a match made in hell? Wasn't that what I had wanted?

"I have to go," I said, pulling my gaze from her.

"Go?" Court asked.

I nodded. "I have a conference call. Unlike you lucky fuckers, I still have to work."

"That blows," Gavin said.

"Sorry, man," Sam said.

They had no idea.

I strode away from the lot, taking my beer with me. Working wasn't the problem. In fact, it gave me the out I needed to escape. The problem was Katherine Van Pelt wearing nothing but a tiny bikini where her pert ass was all but hanging out. And that look. The one of approval. That made me want to scoop her up and carry her back to the villa. To hear her approval ring through the room again... and again... and again.

12

KATHERINE

Camden didn't return the rest of the afternoon. I didn't know how long his call was supposed to be, but I hadn't thought it'd be three hours. What the hell was his father making him do while here?

Granted, it was just our first night. He'd probably have more time to enjoy the beach. But I still didn't like it.

I extracted myself from my friends, promising to meet them for dinner before heading back to my villa. It was a short walk, and I was already anticipating what I would find when I entered. Would Camden still be working? Would I be interrupting? I could never predict his mood. Even though we'd agreed not to fight and he had held up his end of the bargain with Penn, which I was still shocked by, I didn't know if he'd be upset that I was barging in on him.

I softly crossed the threshold. "Camden?"

No response.

I narrowed my eyes and continued inside. Past the bubbling hot tub and the desk where his computer was shut down and then past that to the enormous bed. To my surprise, Camden lay completely naked, passed out in the massive bed.

Oh. He'd barely slept the night before, and had only taken a small catnap on the plane. But I'd never seen Camden Percy actually... nap. Not in the middle of the day. He was so strict about his schedule.

He looked so... peaceful. I'd forgotten how human he could look while he was sleeping.

My foot stubbed on the bed, and an *oof* fell out of my mouth.

Camden jolted, jerking upright in bed. His chest was heaving as he assessed the room, as if anticipating a threat.

"Sorry," I muttered. "I didn't mean to wake you."

He didn't immediately deflate when his eyes adjusted and found me standing nearby. "What are you doing here?"

My first response was to tell him to go fuck himself. That I was fucking staying here, too. He had no right to question me. But I let the anger pool out of me and land like a puddle at my feet. Maybe the truth might be better than my deflection.

"I... came to check on you," I admitted.

He shifted, revealing the full length of him to me. My gaze snagged on his cock, unable to look away. He was hard. At full mast while he had been passed out, asleep on the bed. Heat settled in my core. What exactly had he been dreaming about?

Camden said nothing before he dropped to his feet and tugged boxer briefs on. It barely obscured that he was rock solid and straining against the material.

God, I wanted to ask... I probably shouldn't. But I fucking wanted to.

My eyes shot back up to his, and there was nothing to

indicate whether or not he wanted me to say anything. So, I arched an eyebrow. "Having fun while I was gone?"

Tension coiled through his muscular shoulders, and he took a dominating step toward me. "Would you like it if I was?" Then he tilted his head. "Or would you prefer to join me?"

I swallowed, feeling the tension snap taut between us. I knew this game. We had played it for so long, but the rope between us had frayed and then snapped. I wasn't sure we could knot it back together to keep playing.

"Maybe," I whispered throatily.

He took another step toward me until his fingers pushed up into my dark hair and bared my throat to him. My limbs were tight as unease and anticipation both managed to wind their way through me. I couldn't do this. But... I could. I *could* do this.

His lips landed on the soft spot between my neck and shoulder. My legs nearly buckled under the force of that one kiss. The possessive way he held me and owned me in that touch. Camden Percy did something to my body that I could never explain. He could make it war against me. He could make it succumb to him. He played a pied piper, and I danced to his tune.

And yet, the thought... scared me. To be that vulnerable with him again. To give him the chance to break me again.

So, I took a step back. Enough for him to release me and not meet my questioning look with an answer.

"We're going to the resort club tonight," I told him, offering an olive branch. "Maybe... you could meet me."

I hadn't used those words with him in months. He knew what it meant. How it used to be between us. Camden and I never showed up anywhere together. Recently, it had been out of necessity. I hadn't been able to stand being in his presence for much longer than necessary. But before... when things had been more open between us... when he found me, he could claim me.

Recognition sparked in his dark eyes.

"I think I should do that," he said with a smirk.

Before we went dancing, I'd met the girls for dinner at a local restaurant that Paulo had recommended. We went all in, ordering the local pork mofongo, which was delicious. Though I could barely touch it or the flaky passion fruit pastry dessert that English had ordered for the table.

Nerves bit into me. What was I thinking? Did I really *want* to start a sexual relationship with Camden again? I wanted to have *sex* with him. But sex wasn't just sex with Camden Percy.

Sex was control. Primal, passionate, and addicting. It wasn't just a fling in the afternoons after the pool. It would never, could never be something that flippant. I'd known it before I'd married him. But I hadn't *really* known. Not until our honeymoon when I'd left the Maldives with welts on my legs and ass and my pussy aching for more of whatever he'd give me. The sweet torment of his touch and his absence. Something that should have made me run the other way but somehow felt... safe.

I shook my head out of my thoughts of those weeks of blissful sex. I didn't have to decide right now. I could figure it out as I went. It was a lie, but I held on to it for dear life.

Lark nudged me as we headed toward the club. "You barely touched your food."

I bit my lip. I hated to admit this, but it was *Lark*. "I'm actually... nervous."

"About what?" she asked with a laugh. "You're on vacation."

"I invited Camden tonight."

"So? Wasn't he already going to meet us with the rest of the guys?"

"Yes," I said softly. "But I invited him to meet *me*."

"There's a distinction?"

I nodded. "I don't know. Maybe I'm overreacting."

"Just be careful," Lark said softly. "I remember how you were after you and Camden... stopped." She didn't have to remind me. I knew the shell of a person I'd been. "I don't want you to go through that again."

"Me neither," I whispered, but the words were drowned out by the pulse of the nightclub as we stepped inside.

English wove us through the crowd to an unoccupied booth nearest the DJ. Latin music blasted through the speakers with an intoxicating beat that made me want to move my hips. Couples ground against each other on the dance floor, just like back at home, but there were enough who were spiraling together, as if their movements were a choreographed salsa routine, and it was hard to pull my eyes away from them. They were fantastic and utterly sexual. Foreplay in the form of a dance. Erotic in nature but with rules unlike most of what I saw in America. It was a nice change of pace for our usual haunts.

Rum was the drink of choice. Some I'd heard of, like Bacardi, but others had names that I'd never seen—Palo Viejo, Don Q, and Ron del Barrilito. Our bartender was a saucy woman with long black hair nearly to her waist and a smile that made Whitley lean in. She poured drinks that were fruity and delicious and *strong*. So strong that my head was fuzzy after just one. Fuck, I really must not have eaten much at dinner.

I watched a couple dancing like they'd been born for it. I'd wanted to dance so freely once. Not any form of ball-room, of course. But I'd done ballet growing. I'd always been tall and willowy, and ballet had suited my frame. It had been years since I'd longed to put my pointe shoes back on. Even though Lord knew my ankles were not ready for that anymore. I would have never given it up if I hadn't ended up in the hospital right after graduation. That had changed everything.

I shoved aside the bad memory and was startled to find the man striding toward me. He must have seen me watching him. I straightened at once, fear coiling in my stomach, though I looked cool on the outside. I always did.

He held his hand out to me. "Dance?"

"Oh, I don't know how," I said automatically.

He laughed. "You don't need to know how. I will lead. You will follow."

He was so damn sure of himself that, without thinking about it, I put my hand in his.

"What are you doing?" English hissed behind me.

But I was gone before I could answer.

And he was right. He *did* lead. I had enough rhythm to follow wherever he led me. It was fun. *Really* fun. A laugh erupted out of me. Real and genuine. I didn't know when I'd last laughed like that.

"You lied," he breathed into my ear. "You do know how."

"I haven't danced like this in a decade," I said.

"Your body doesn't forget."

He wasn't wrong. He pulled me through another series of movements. My hair flew out behind me. I turned in place, and then he pulled me back into his arms. He was strong and sturdy. It had seemed so sexual when I watched others, but there was nothing sexual here with this man. Just the joy of dancing.

He meandered us back over to my friends and spun me one more time when a shadow descended over us. Camden. I stopped in place. The man I'd been dancing with glanced over at Camden as if realizing he'd intruded.

"Feel free to cut in," he said, offering my hand to Camden, who took it.

Then the man was gone. I'd never even gotten his name.

I was breathing heavily as Camden tugged me against him. Sweat dampened the back of my neck, but my eyes and heart and soul were alight as I looked up at him. The dance had knocked out all my nerves and fears. Reminded me what it was to be alive. So, I just stood on my tiptoes and pressed my lips to my husband's mouth.

After the rejection earlier this afternoon, he seemed surprised that I'd offered him that... anything. But then his hands slid around my body, pulling me tight to him. He deepened the kiss, his tongue stroking down into my mouth. He tasted me. Really tasted me. As if he were a man possessed. As if he had been waiting all this time for a *yes* from me. And I offered it now greedily.

When he pulled back, his hand moved down the length of my spine to cup my ass. "You were dancing with another man."

"Yes," I said breathlessly.

I couldn't tell if my heart pounded in my chest from the dance or that one heart-stopping kiss.

"I don't like to see you with anyone else."

"Is that so?" I asked coyly.

His hand tightened on my ass. He didn't have to say the words. I could see them in his eyes. *Possession.* I was not an object to be controlled, but in that look, he owned me.

"You invite me here, and then I find you with someone else. Is this a game to you?"

"What if it is?" I countered. My hand trailed up his suit coat. I grasped the lapels in my hands.

"I do not play games, Katherine."

My body trembled at the way he'd said my name. "You play them better than almost anyone."

"Not with you. Not like this," he growled.

I leaned up, brushing my nose along his jaw. My lips lingered at his ear. I let one free hand roam to the front of his suit pants. I dragged my nail down the length of his cock. "What if I want you to play a game with me?"

He jerked me against him—hard. Desire blasted out his pupils. We'd crossed a line, and I wasn't sure if it was smart. No, I was sure it wasn't. Giving Camden my body was one thing, but offering him *me* was asking for him to hurt me. Not physically... just emotionally and mentally, down to the hardened shards of my soul.

And yet, I offered myself up on a silver platter anyway. We had one week in our bargain. It might be worthwhile to see where the week took us.

"Then I believe we should leave," Camden said hoarsely.

I nodded. "After you."

He took my hand in his. Without a backward glance for our friends, I followed him out of the nightclub.

13

KATHERINE

When we returned to our villa, even the air was charged between us. I felt reckless, and I was not known for being reckless. How much rum had I had? It didn't feel like enough to be walking into a dimly lit room with my husband, knowing what I'd proposed.

The heady relief of the dance had evaporated by the time we were back inside. A fresh bottle of champagne was chilling in a sweating bucket. As if Paulo had known we would need refreshments for the night. I moved toward it to give my hands something to do.

Camden said nothing as I uncorked the champagne and poured bubbles into two flutes. I drifted back over to him, passing him a fizzing glass.

"You seemed so confident in the club," he said. "I forget sometimes that so much of you is bravado."

My eyes narrowed. We'd agreed not to argue. Under normal circumstances, I would have bitten his head off for that comment. I was *not* all bravado. Even if so much of me was in this moment.

"What does that mean?" I asked instead.

He set his glass down without taking a sip. "It means usually you are yelling at me. So, I can't see that something else is lurking beneath."

"I don't know what you're talking about." I finished my drink and discarded it on a nearby table.

"Oh, Katherine," he said faintly, sending a chill down my spine as he came to stand behind me. His hand ran down my vertebrae, one after the other after the other. "Underneath your hard exterior, you *want* me to take control."

I swallowed. "Is that what you think?"

"No." His hands moved to my shoulders, placing light touches across them and down my arms to my wrists. He grasped each of them, pulling my shoulder blades together and drawing my hands tight behind my back.

My breathing hitched. Oh god.

"It's what I know," he whispered against the shell of my ear.

He put both of my wrists in one of his large hands and then used the other to cup my chin and turn my head to the side. I could just barely look at him. I was caught in his embrace, completely at his mercy, and my entire body was singing.

"What are you doing?" I breathed, my voice betraying my desire.

"Giving you what you want."

"What if I say no?"

He arched an eyebrow. "You and I both know that is not the word you have chosen."

"I didn't agree..."

"Do you not agree?"

I swallowed. That was the question. Did I want this? Did I agree? I'd given this to him once. Enjoyed his command in the bedroom. And then my trust had been shattered. Irrevocably. Was I willing to try to repair it? Would this even fix it?

And yet, I couldn't say no. I didn't *want* to say no, for fuck's sake. My thong was already soaked under this minidress. He'd discover it soon enough. We'd been tiptoeing around our desire.

If I gave in now, it wouldn't be a promise of forever. It would be a promise of for *now*.

I could always back out. I had a word for that. A safe word I'd never used. But it was there all the same.

"Yes." My voice was rigid with emotion. "Yes, I agree."

"Oh, how I do love to hear that word out of your mouth." He drew his thumb along my bottom lip. I struggled slightly against where he held me, and his eyes darkened. "Don't fight me."

I stilled. My body reacted to him wholly. In a way that I never would react out of the bedroom. Usually, we were so at each other's throats that the idea of submitting to his demands was impossible. But here... right now...

His thumb continued its perusal of my mouth. Gently stroking back and forth against my bottom lip before venturing in, parting me. I flicked my tongue out, caressing the tip. His hand tightened on my wrists, almost to the point of pain. I squirmed against him, but he held me firmly. A warning. Which only made me want to squirm more.

He continued pushing his thumb inside of my mouth. "Now, suck."

I swallowed at the command and closed my lips around him as he withdrew slowly. His eyes were on fire as he removed his thumb from my lips, no trace of my blood-red lipstick on him.

"There. You do remember how to take direction," he said with a faint smirk on his lips.

Something ached in me to lash out at that comment. Every fiber of my being wanted to fight him. And yet, I said nothing. Bit the inside of my cheek to keep from saying exactly where he could shove his directions.

His smirk widened into a smile when I remained silent. He surely could see the fire lit in my eyes.

"I think it's time that I took care of you," he said, finally releasing my wrists.

My shoulders ached as my hands returned to my sides. "Take off your dress."

I eagerly reached behind me to pull down the zipper.

But his eyes narrowed. "Slowly."

I huffed slightly. His hand found purchase on my ass. A not-quite-gentle smack that sent my entire body reeling. I could barely keep from moaning as remembered welts melded together with orgasms in my mind.

It wasn't that I necessarily wanted him to spank me again. It was humiliating. And somehow, desire pooled even deeper into my core. My body pulsed with it as I slowly, ever so slowly, dragged the zipper of my dress down. When I finally reached the base, I let the straps fall from my shoulders, baring my breasts before sliding over my narrow hips to puddle at my feet.

Camden moved to stand before me. His eyes roamed me, assessing. A look I never would have tolerated. And now, I found only intense hunger.

He stepped forward, bringing his fingers down over the curves of my ribs before lightly running them over the underside of my breasts. And then up and around until his thumb flickered across my erect nipple.

A sigh escaped me at the contact. I was so sensitive. I always had been. And he knew it as he pinched the nipple between his fingers, twisting slightly. I arched into him. My eyes fluttered closed. Another soft exhale released from me.

"Eyes open," he commanded.

And so I did. I stared right back at him as he pulled and tugged and twirled my nipples between his fingers. Until they were sore. Until I felt like I could release right then and there.

Not that he would have let me. He wasn't ready for me to come. Not just yet.

One hand traced down my stomach and then fingered the front of my thong almost absentmindedly. Except I knew he managed my reactions with keen focus. Just as he managed the company. Just as he did everything.

He almost slipped inside, and it took everything in me not to urge him onward. But he moved over the silk material, dipping his index finger across the front and slowly, slowly, slowly to the point where I wanted him. He pressed harder against my clit and I couldn't make myself stop. I moved into him, eager, wanton.

He pulled back. Because, of course. I wanted to grumble. Instead, I bit my lip.

He smirked. "Do you want me?"

"Yes," I whispered hoarsely.

"Show me where."

I froze in place. He arched his eyebrow expectantly. I pushed my pride down to the back of my mind and gestured vaguely to my underwear.

"Walk backward to the bed," he told me fiercely.

I nodded primly and stepped back in my Louboutin heels until the back of my knees touched the bed. His finger hooked into my underwear and unceremoniously yanked them down to my feet. He pushed me down until my back was against the soft comforter. My legs were squeezed tight together.

"Now, *show me*."

I knew what he wanted. What he wanted me to do. Goddamn this man. He knew exactly what buttons to press.

I pulled my heels up onto the edge of the bed and spread my legs open before him, baring myself to his gaze. Then with a deep inhale, I let my hand fall between my legs and moved it over my own slickness to the apex and down to my waiting pussy.

Camden bent down and gingerly picked up my discarded thong. "If this is any indication, then you must be soaking wet for me. Are you?"

My fingers stilled. "Yes," I all but moaned.

"Would you like me to find out?"

"Yes." I hardly recognized myself.

Right now, I could focus on nothing but Camden Percy kneeling between my legs. Camden Percy. Kneeling. Fuck.

He placed his hands on my knees, spreading my legs wider and wider. Until I was fully exposed before him. I tried to pull my hand back, but he grasped my wrist.

"I like the idea of us getting you off together," he mused. My body responded in kind, and he laughed gently. "So it seems, as do you."

I wanted to reply with something particularly venomous, but he took that moment to bring his tongue down onto my clit. And I was pretty sure I lost consciousness. His tongue laved over me, brushing against my fingers and my clit, tasting all of me at once.

He released my wrist when he seemed certain I wouldn't move it and slid that hand down my exposed inner thigh. I trembled under his machinations, knowing exactly where he was headed. And fuck, was I already so fucking turned on that the thought of him driving into me made my pussy clench again.

His hand slipped upward, trailing gently over my ass and then between my legs to where I really wanted him. He hesitated—or really forced me to wait for him—just hovering over my opening, as if he expected me to beg for it. Which I would not do. There were lines even I wouldn't cross. Katherine Van Pelt did not beg.

Even if, right now, I really, *really* wanted to beg him.

He flicked his tongue again, his eyes on me. But I pressed my lips together. There was no way.

He pressed his finger down on my opening, running it along the inside of my lips, sliding down and almost touching me. Teasing me but not entering me. And god, I wanted more. I wanted him inside of me. I wanted to beg and plead. But I couldn't. I wouldn't.

Just when I felt my walls webbing with cracks, my orgasm, which had been just out of reach, hit me full tilt. My body bowed off the bed, and I cried in pleasure as the culmination of all of his teasing arrested me.

One digit slipped in just barely as I came hard and then back out.

"Next time," he told me and stood.

I lay back, my eyes finally opening and my chest rising and falling with my pants. He smiled like a Cheshire cat, clearly loving the effect he had on me.

"Camden," I purred.

"Yes?"

"Fuck me."

He smiled then, eyeing my body, primed for the taking. "I think... I'll make you wait."

"What?" I gasped, coming up to my elbows.

He narrowed his eyes at me. "Are you not satisfied with what I provided?"

"I... I am," I stammered out. "But don't *you* want..."

"Don't presume to know what I want," he commanded.

I slumped back on the bed. My legs were still spread. I was still dripping wet. I was an offering on a platter. Everything he could want. He strained against his suit pants. He *did* want me.

But he wanted the control more. It was clear in his dark eyes. He wanted to make me beg before he gave me what we both wanted. And I wouldn't beg.

And he knew that. He was patient. He could wait.

"I'm going to take a shower," he said, striding out of the room. "You can imagine me fucking you while I get off."

I groaned at his words and wondered why the fuck I couldn't swallow my pride. He'd made me come by barely touching me. I would find a way to get him inside of me without begging. He couldn't hold out forever.

14

KATHERINE

The next couple of days, I ignored the questioning looks from my friends and the desire that flared between Camden and me. I tried to ignore it all and enjoy myself. Not that it was easy, sleeping next to Camden and not fucking him. When all I wanted to do, now that he had denied me, was fuck him.

I was glad when Lark suggested a spa day without the boys. It was harder to pretend that nothing was happening between us when Camden was around. We weren't arguing and there was a new heat between us. One that everyone seemed to be stepping around.

No Camden for a day would be for the better.

Lark had gotten us all the full-day executive treatment—massages, facials, salt scrubs, body wraps, mani-pedis, plus use of the sauna and salt pools. With a famous Cortes chocolate martini in hand, I stepped into the salt pool for our first thirty-minute relaxation period.

"This drink is out of this world," Whitley said.

"It's like if a Frosty had a baby with an alcoholic Frozen

Hot Chocolate," English said, taking another sip of the delicious concoction.

"What's a Frosty?" I asked.

All three girls turned and stared at me.

"What?" I asked, wide-eyed.

"God, you were sheltered as a child," Whitley said with a laugh.

"I started drinking wine at, like, eight," I told her.

"Fine. Maybe *sheltered* is the wrong word."

"Wendy's just not proper enough for you?" English asked, stifling a smile. "Only Serendipity will do?"

I rolled my eyes. "I don't eat fast food."

"Are you eating anything at all?" Whitley quipped. "Look at how fucking skinny you are."

Lark frowned. "You do look very trim."

"You look amazing," English said. "What are you doing? Tell us your secret. I wouldn't mind losing another five pounds."

"Shut up," Lark said, swatting at her. "You do not need to lose weight. None of you do. You're all perfect exactly as you are."

"Okay, Mom," Whitley said with an eye roll. "If everyone thought they were perfect exactly how they were, I wouldn't have a job."

We all laughed. It was a fair point, coming from a plastic surgeon.

"So, apparently I don't need to lose five pounds," English said, rolling her eyes at Lark, "what are you doing?"

Katherine shrugged. "I got a new personal trainer. He works with dancers from the New York City Ballet. He's all about building lean and toned muscle and keeping dancers fit for their grueling jobs."

"And you need that... why?" Lark asked. Her eyes bored into me, asking so much more than the question conveyed.

"Hey, don't knock it," English said. "It's clearly working."

"Anyway, it's not that I need it. But you know, my face and my body are part of my public persona. I'm a socialite by trade. It's no different than a model trying to stay in shape. I'm not eighteen anymore, and I'm competing with those skinny twits."

"I'm glad you're not eighteen anymore," Lark said pointedly.

I frowned and looked away from her.

"God, aren't we all glad not to be eighteen anymore?" Whitley said. "I was not doing this kind of shit at eighteen."

"No shit," English said with a laugh. "I was blowing up-and-coming rockstars and working as a bartender in the Valley."

"Speak for yourself," I said. "Lark and I were doing precisely this at eighteen."

"Depends on when. We didn't leave Manhattan the summer after graduation," she said through clenched teeth.

Before I could respond, two women appeared at the edge of the pool.

The first one said, "Whitley?"

"That's me," Whit said, scampering back out of the pool.

"I have Anna," the second said.

"I go by English," she said as she followed Whitley out.

"Your therapists will be with you two shortly," the first woman said and then smiled politely before leading our friends away.

Lark whipped around on me as soon as they were gone. "What are you doing?"

"I don't know what you mean," I said primly, finishing

my martini and setting it aside. Normally, I wouldn't drink something so sweet. The calories were killer, but it was vacation after all. I could burn it all off when I got home.

"Is it happening again?" She sounded sad and resigned.

"Is *what* happening again?" I really did not want to have this conversation.

"I was there when you were hospitalized after graduation, Katherine," Lark said mercilessly.

My whole body shuddered. I didn't want to think about that. I'd fought so long not to think about that summer. I wished that she'd let the whole thing drop.

"I'm only asking because I care about you," she whispered. "I don't want you to become that person again. It was horrible. We were all so worried. I thought you were past it."

"I *am* past it," I snarled more forcefully than I'd intended.

"You've barely eaten a thing since we've been here."

"I just downed that entire martini."

"Liquid calories are not the same thing, and you know it," Lark said.

I turned away from her. Why did she have to bring this up? Couldn't she see that I was better? I'd beaten the illness. I'd... I'd recovered.

Yes, when I was eighteen years old, my entire world had fallen apart. My father was arrested for fraud. He went to prison. My inheritance was shot. My brother disappeared. My mother became a walking zombie.

And me? Who cared about little old me?

So, I slowly drifted away, too. Even as I drifted, I fought to stay the same. To still be the impenetrable Katherine Van Pelt. The most formidable bitch on the Upper East Side. And the only way to do that was to keep looking the part. To be skinnier, prettier, larger than life. My appearance was all that mattered. Because if I looked better than everyone else, then no one would notice that I was empty on the inside.

And no one did notice. Not for a long time. Not until it was too late.

Then I ended up in the hospital.

Anorexia.

That was the label they put on my file.

It had taken me weeks to believe the word applied to me. Months of therapy before I acknowledged that was what I'd been doing. And still, years later, I didn't even want to face it.

That was the past. I wasn't there again. I wasn't.

And I would never, ever be in that hospital again. Not ever. The very thought scared me more than anything else in my life.

"I'm not... anorexic," I whispered the pained word. Lark looked at me with raised eyebrows. "I'm not."

"Okay," she said softly. She reached out and took my hand. "I know that times have been rough between Penn and Natalie getting married and the rift in our crew and then... Camden. But you're my best friend, and I don't want to lose you to that illness again."

"You haven't lost me," I told her more gently. "I'm right here. We can even have another martini."

Lark nodded. But I could see that she wasn't convinced. I didn't know how to convince her either.

We lapsed into silence, which was promptly broken by our masseuses arriving. I was whisked into a small room that smelled of valerian root and hops aromatherapy. The combination nearly put me to sleep as I was pampered into submission.

The spa was a dream. Lark's family had not spared a

single expense on this resort. Even I was impressed, and I was a tough sell.

By the time I was through with the spa services, I felt relaxed and positive. The conversation from earlier had completely fled my mind. And Lark, English, and Whitley seemed equally tranquil.

Paulo appeared after our services were complete and ushered us to the nearby restaurant for lunch. He spoke speedy Spanish to the hostess, who took us to a prime table overlooking the water. Paulo had apparently ordered for us, and out came pernil, which was a slow-roasted pork shoulder marinated in sofrito and served around the holidays.

I had been skeptical, but I shouldn't have been. Every bite was absolutely delicious. I didn't even have words to describe the spices and how succulent the meat was. We must have a place like this in the city, but I'd never had anything like it.

Lark kept a close eye on me while we ate. I tried to ignore her and just enjoy the meal. I was *eating*. I didn't want my entire vacation monitored. I gave her a pointed look back as I put another piece of pork in my mouth.

She laughed softly and turned to English. "Hey, no boys!" she said with a laugh. "Girls' day out, remember?"

"Yeah, yeah," she muttered, putting the phone away. "I wasn't messaging Court anyway. It was Winnie. The company is getting off its feet after the holidays."

"Gah, next week already?" Lark asked.

English nodded. "Now that Margery is out of the picture, we're free to start our own publicity firm." She smiled brilliantly. "Signed the paperwork before we left. Just have to open my office in the city and start collecting clients."

English had left her old PR firm in LA to start over here after she and Court got together. Her old colleague Winnie had left the firm, too, and they'd decided to branch out on their own. One firm, two offices—New York City and LA.

"Are any of your old clients coming with you?" I asked.

"A few, but a lot of them are staying with Winnie. I'll have a different client base here in New York."

"Makes sense."

"Speaking of new ventures, I'm excited and nervous to start my new job with the mayor," Lark admitted.

She had recently been appointed as Mayor Kensington's chief of staff. It was a huge honor, and she had gotten it all on her own merit. Not because she was Upper East Side. Not because she was close to the mayor's son. I was so proud of her. Even if I thought her talents were wasted, I knew it made her happy.

"You're going to do great," English told her.

"I know that I've been working with Leslie a long time, but it's still something new."

"If she gives you any shit, sic Penn on her," I suggested.

Lark laughed. "Yeah, right."

"What about you, Whitley?" English asked.

Whitley looked up at English, then to Lark, and then finally me. She quirked a smile. "I'm happy not to talk about work, thank you."

I chuckled. "Oh, Whit."

"Don't use that tone with me," Whitley said with a wink. "We're here on vacation. I hardly get any time off, and I had to move clients around to even get here. The last thing I want to talk about is my latest face lift."

"Fair enough," English said. "What about you, Katherine?"

"What about me?" I asked in confusion.

"Tell us about being a socialite," Whitley encouraged. "What fancy parties and premieres and events do you have coming up? Isn't Fashion Week soon?"

"It is," I admitted.

Though I hadn't been thinking about it much. Last year's party had been such a disaster that I'd put it out of my mind. I'd acquired a designer for my dress, but I'd been more hands off about this than any other Fashion Week. To the point where... I didn't even want to talk about it.

"But you know, actually, I'm more excited about this charity that I'm going to start helping."

Lark's eyes widened in surprise. "What charity?"

"ChildrensOne," I told her. "They work with the local children's hospital to get volunteers to help when they can. They plan events for the kids—carnivals and game nights and dances. And when I spoke to the director, I offered to help fundraise for the cancer wing."

"Wow," English muttered.

"Wait... there are carnivals at the hospital?" Whitley asked. "That sounds badass."

Lark just smiled faintly. "Are you going to throw a gala for the charity?"

Something clenched within me at the suggestion. I couldn't help but think about what Camden had said. That I did charity work for me. So that my name could be on it. I didn't want to do that for this.

"That's a great idea," English said. "You could invite all your friends and get them to donate money."

"I'd go," Whitley agreed.

"Oh, yeah, I don't know yet," I told her, reaching for my water and taking a sip. "We're still discussing it. I'll meet with her and visit the hospital once we get back."

"You're a great party planner," Lark said. "I'm sure it would be a hit."

"We'll see. There are other options, too," I said. "But mostly, I'm going to meet the kids first."

I didn't admit to them that I was nervous. I knew what it was like to be hospitalized for an illness that I couldn't control. It wasn't the same as what these children were going through. But I didn't know how much of what I'd gone through would come back to haunt me once I got there. Maybe if I faced my fear, I could finally put the hospital behind me.

"All right, I'm thinking, beach time," Whitley said, standing as our plates were being cleared away.

"I'm down," English said.

"Me too," Lark agreed.

I opened my mouth to agree. We'd done nothing but hang out at the pool and beach since we'd been here. I was itching to get back out there, but I'd left Camden that morning with a dozen calls he had to make and some report he needed to write up. I wondered how far along he was on that. If he was going to spend the entire day inside.

"I think I'm going to check on Camden first," I told them instead.

Whitley winked. " 'Check on Camden.' " She made air quotes around the words.

I laughed. "He's still working while he's here. I need to get him outside for a bit. We'll meet you at the beach."

English grinned. "Have fun."

I shook my head, and Lark squeezed my hand.

"No, really," she said as Whitley and English linked arms ahead of us, "have fun. It's good to see you two getting along. To see you happy again."

"I wouldn't go that far," I said.

"I would," Lark said and then traipsed off after the girls.

Huh. Happy again. Had it been so long since I was happy that I didn't even remember what it felt like? Was this new thing with Camden... happiness?

I didn't know. But I was prepared to find out.

15

CAMDEN

"Yes, we already discussed that," I said gruffly into the phone. "Of course I would be willing to look at the details one more time."

I rolled my eyes and stared out the open villa door. This was taking all fucking day, and it was only my ninth call. There were still three more scheduled. I was going to have to move some shit around. My irritation level was off the charts. I didn't even understand why I had so many calls the week between Christmas and New Year's. Normally, most other businesses were shut down that week. It was usually my down week.

This had to be my father's meddling. He always pulled this kind of shit. It wasn't enough that I was precisely the heir he wanted for the company or that I worked my ass off. Somehow, I was still a failure in his eyes. And when he thought I was slacking, like by taking a fucking needed vacation with my wife, he piled shit into my schedule.

"Yes, I'm free to meet face-to-face after the New Year," I told the man on the other end of the line.

I half-listened to what he was saying. My eyes were still

locked on the waves crashing against the surf nearby. And then my wife trod up the beach, carrying her sandals in one hand. Her long, tan legs were visible in her too-short shorts. An inch of her stomach showed beneath the little blue crop top. Her hair was piled high on her head. She glowed as if the hours at the spa had been exactly what she needed. My cock twitched at her approach. I was definitely going to have to reschedule the next call.

Katherine attempted to get the sand off of her feet as she dropped her sandals at the door. She strode right up to me with a coy smile on her face.

"How's your meeting?"

I muted the phone. The guy was still rambling. "A huge fucking bore."

"Are you going to be free soon?" Her eyes were wide and inviting.

"I'm going to cancel my next call."

She nodded and took a step away. I reached out and wrapped my fingers around her wrist. She looked back at me in surprise.

"Stay," I told her.

"You're on your call," she reminded me.

"So?" The word was short and abrupt, powerful. I knew the effect it had on her.

She swallowed and walked back toward me. I pulled her into my lap, and she sank down onto my ever-growing erection. Her eyes widened again, and then she shifted, rubbing her ass against my cock through the thin linen shorts. I pressed her down harder.

Fuck, I wanted to fuck her.

If it were only that easy with Katherine. I couldn't give her everything she wanted. Not when our relationship hung in the balance. I needed her to want to keep coming back.

"You're hard," she murmured, suggestively shifting again.

My hand slid across her hip bone and down between her legs. I pressed against the front of her shorts, spreading her legs apart with my knees. She gasped lightly.

The man on the other end of the phone tried to get my attention, but it was already lost.

I clicked to unmute the call. With my other hand, I massaged Katherine. "Yes, I'm still here. Absolutely. Why don't you go through the full review of the plans again? If I have questions, I'll chime in."

The man began what I was sure would be a long rant about something we had already discussed. I put him back on mute.

"I can't believe you're doing this while on a call," she muttered.

"This seems to be a much better way to spend my time."

"I don't know that your business associates would agree."

I sucked her earlobe into my mouth and gently bit down on it. "I think they might agree... if they knew."

She laughed softly, and the sound went straight to my balls.

"I want you on your knees," I told her.

She stiffened a bit and then looked back at me. "Oh?"

"On your knees." My voice dipped down. A command. No longer a request.

Then Katherine Van Pelt slid off of my lap and dropped to her knees before me. It was a fucking beautiful sight. Her following my orders. Her patiently kneeling before me. No fire in her eyes, just... curiosity. Oh, yes, I fucking liked this.

I stood from the chair so that I was towering over her.

She looked up at me with her big brown eyes and fucking licked her lips. Goddamn, she would be the death of me.

Without prompting, she unbuttoned my shorts, sliding them down my legs. Then she took my boxers and pulled them over my cock. It jutted toward her, hard and ready.

With my clothing discarded, I took a seat back in the chair and gestured her forward. There was that fire. There and gone in a split second. If I hadn't been watching for it, I never would have seen her anger boil to the surface by one simple gesture. But I was in charge here. Whether she admitted it or not, she wanted that.

She ran her red-lacquered nails along my thighs before taking my cock in one hand. My head dipped back at the pressure, but I still held the phone to my ear, barely listening to a word he was saying. Not while Katherine stroked my cock, lingering at the tip before going back down to my balls.

She drew in closer until her breasts were pinned between my knees. Her gaze came up to mine just once. Not asking permission, but seeing whether or not I'd have to tell her what to do.

I arched an eyebrow that said, *Suck it.*

And she did.

Katherine lowered her mouth onto my cock. Her tongue flicked out, laving across the tip. Then she sank down, getting nearly the entire length of my cock in her mouth. She hesitated for a breath and then seemed to put her gag reflex aside before pushing further until she had all of me in her mouth.

My hand laced into her hair and held her head there for a second longer. Taking me all in was impressive, and fuck, she felt incredible.

The guy on the line was asking my opinion of something. I unmuted the conversation as my wife began to move up the length of my cock and then back down.

I watched her suck me off as I answered, "Sure. That sounds good."

The man said something else that I had to concentrate to hear as Katherine swirled her tongue around my dick.

"Yes, run me through the numbers one more time."

Fuck, her mouth. Her fucking mouth.

I put him on mute again and leaned back in the chair. I wanted more. I wanted harder. I wanted faster. She was taking her time. Getting me riled up. Jesus Christ, I was going to have to fuck her face.

"Katherine," I said, running a hand down her spine. "That feels so fucking good."

She hummed in approval.

"Going to fuck you now. Stop me if it's too much."

Her grip tightened on my thigh as my hand slid back into her hair. I held it like a rope, tight enough to hurt, and she stilled completely. Then I thrust up into her mouth. I was using her mouth as my fuck toy in the dirtiest possible way. She had no way to escape, but she didn't protest or try to stop me. She just held on as I drove deep into the back of her throat, imagining sinking into her pussy.

I was getting close. Really fucking close. Her mouth was so hot and so wet. I wasn't going to be able to hang on. I gave no warning as I emptied myself into her mouth, holding her down around my cock. A grunt exploded from me as I finished.

She gagged once, but when I released her, she pulled back, looked me in the eyes, and swallowed. Tears glistened in her beautiful eyes, and I leaned forward to brush them away with my thumb.

"Good girl," I breathed gently.

A smile cracked her features at the compliment, and a flush suffused her body.

I unmuted the conversation. "Hey, that all sounds good, Brad. Send over the final numbers for consideration. Thanks for the call."

Then I hung up unceremoniously.

I discarded my phone on the desk and pulled her to her feet. I replaced my boxers, stepping out of the shorts entirely. I pressed a kiss to her lips. Her eyes drifted to my boxers, and a little pout settled on those perfect lips.

Something in me darkened. "Are you pouting?"

"I..." she began and then saw my expression. "No."

"You don't want me to wear these?" I asked. She could hear the note of disapproval in my voice.

"I..." She fell silent after that. As if she didn't know what was the right answer.

"Tell me," I commanded.

"I wanted you to fuck me."

"And so, now, you're pouting because I'm not?"

She bit her lip and then shook her head.

"You did good," I told her. She brightened. "And now, you're being bad."

"Camden, I didn't mean..."

"Oh, I know," I told her.

Then I bent her over at the waist, laying her across the desk. She whimpered a little in protest, but she didn't actually try to stop me. Her legs already shook in anticipation.

I reached around her body and unbuttoned her shorts. Then I dragged them down her legs along with her underwear. She stepped out of them, and then I nudged her legs further apart.

"Do you think that you've earned the right for me to fuck you?"

She froze like a lamb anticipating the slaughter. I could see from where I stood that her pussy gleamed. She was so fucking turned on that I could barely touch her and she'd come for me right here and now.

"No," she whispered.

"That's right. And is pouting about it tolerated?"

"No," she said again.

"No," I agreed and then slapped her ass with my open palm.

She yelped softly at the first touch. Her eyes rolled into the back of her head, and a quiver ran through her.

I spanked her again. She was silent this time, but I wanted her whimpers and moans and cries. I wanted them all.

"How many do you think that you deserve for pouting?"

A flush ran up her back. Anger mixed with desire. But she didn't answer me.

"Katherine," I commanded.

"Ten?" she said more a question than a statement.

"Twenty," he corrected.

She whimpered softly and I grinned. There it was.

I started over, alternating the spanks from her bottom to thighs and back. Her ass was high and rosy. Her whimpers turned into cries and then into moans. Her pussy was so wet, I could have slid right into her. And I fucking wanted to. By the end, she was so near to begging for me. I could have pushed further, given her a few more spanks just to hear her beg for me to stop... for more... for me inside of her. I was here to push her, but not too far. She wasn't ready. Not yet.

"Twenty," she whispered as I finished her punishment.

"Good," I finally said, rubbing her red ass gently. "That's good. I think you understand now."

"I do," she said hoarsely.

"Think I should finish this for you?" I asked as one of my fingers touched her swollen clit.

"Yes." The word was a moan.

My other hand slid up her back, pressing her chest harder into the desk. Then I slipped two fingers into her wet pussy.

"Oh god," she groaned at the first feel of me penetrating her.

"Not God," I corrected. "Just me. Say my name as I make you come, Katherine."

"Camden," she whispered.

I pumped in and out of her, hard and merciless. My fingers wet with her desire. Her body trying to hold me inside of her.

Fuck, I wanted my cock in her. I wanted it so fucking bad that I was already hard again. It would take no effort to wrench off my boxers and plunge deep into her. It took every ounce of my self restraint to hold back. I would give her this, and we would get to fucking when she was ready.

She was close. I could feel it. Her back flushed with pleasure. Her breathing more of a pant. Her pussy tight with need. I wanted her to come so hard that she blacked out. She was almost there.

"Oh fuck," she cried out as I finished her off. "Camden. Fuck, yes, Camden."

Her pussy tightened all around my fingers and then pulsed in the aftermath. A pulse I could feel all the way to my balls. The way she'd said my name nearly made me come a second time. She was more compliant. She wanted this. Even if she still had that vibrant anger at her core. But the pleasure... fuck, the pleasure was unlike anything else. We both knew it.

I finally released her, drawing her up from the desk. Her

knees buckled, and she nearly collapsed. If I hadn't been holding her, she would have.

I kept an arm tight around her waist and brushed a lock of hair behind her ear. "You should always say my name when you come."

She smiled. Her eyes were still glazed over from the force of her orgasm.

"I'm not going to be able to sit down the rest of the day."

I arched an eyebrow. "And whose fault is that?"

She bit her lip invitingly. "Mine."

"That's right."

"When will you fuck me?" she asked baldly. No trace of the woman who had screamed at me on our anniversary.

Right now, was what I wanted to say. I wanted to throw her on that bed and fuck her all day and night long. But instead, I said, "When you've earned it."

"For my birthday?" she asked.

It wasn't so much a plea as a request. We'd get there.

"If you're lucky," I told her.

She smiled devilishly, and I saw the scheming girl underneath it all. "Oh, I will be."

And fuck, I wanted to believe her.

16

KATHERINE

By the time my birthday arrived, my ass finally stopped hurting. I'd had a fun time explaining to my friends why I didn't want to sit down. But fuck, it had been worth it. Every smack on my ass had been like a fire I'd never be able to douse. When I sat and it still stung, the residual pains heated me through again. I wanted more. His fingers had done the job, but they weren't enough. And I was damn well going to get the rest of him tonight.

He'd said maybe. But a maybe on his lips meant yes.

He was not a man of maybes.

I still didn't know where we stood, but that was part of the point of the truce. No discussions of the past and no fighting. It was much easier to be physical with him when we weren't ripping into each other. But there were buried issues. Things we'd have to discuss. I didn't really want to think about it. Not yet. Not when things were actually going well for once. I could pretend we had no issues for a little bit longer.

At least through my birthday party tonight.

It felt strange, getting dressed for the event and knowing

I wasn't going to be wearing heels. They were a staple of my closet, but not at a beach party. Bare feet and sun-kissed skin and wind-tossed hair were the requirements for my birthday this year. And cake, of course.

"Will there be cake?" I expectantly asked Lark as we took the path down to the beach.

"God, you are impatient. Can't you wait and see?"

I gave her my best look of disbelief. "Do you know me at all?"

"Right. Surprises aren't your thing."

"I don't mind a really good surprise, but I'm a planner. The details are important."

"Let me handle the details for a change," Lark said. "Also, I have English on it, too. If I can manage the mayoral reelection campaign and English can run an entire PR firm, I think we can handle one birthday party."

"Maybe," I conceded.

Lark laughed and looped our arms together. "You're going to love it." She looked over at me shrewdly. "How are things with you and Camden? Will he be your midnight kiss this year?"

I shrugged, nonchalant. "We're good. It's fake, of course. But good so far with the truce."

"Why does it have to be fake?"

"Because it is. If we never discuss our issues, they don't just go away. We're just ignoring them right now."

"So that you can have sex?" Lark asked with a grin.

"No... actually, we haven't had sex... yet."

"What?" Lark asked in confusion. "Then what about..." She gestured behind me.

Okay, so maybe I hadn't been so great about hiding why I couldn't sit down.

"We've been... intimate," I amended. "But, yeah, no sex."

"That blows. Well, let's hope he gets his shit together for your birthday. You deserve to get laid."

I grinned ferally. "Let's hope."

"Aw, look, you want to sleep with him. That seems like an improvement since last fall. And the fact that you even want to be anywhere near him is a huge improvement since when you got married. Maybe it will only keep getting better from here."

I thought that was a bit optimistic. Camden and I were not a straight line. We didn't start at one point and end at another with a happily ever after. We were the road less taken. We meandered, found our way back to each other, and diverted again. I wished that things could stay like this forever.

But eventually, we would have to leave paradise behind and return to the real world.

I was not certain where the road would take us from there.

Lark and I stopped at the edge of the beach where the resort had set up their first New Year's Eve bash. Since it was also my birthday, we were commandeering it for my party. A two-in-one, as most of my birthdays had always been. Only my daddy had ever made it so that my birthday was its own separate event. No black, gold, and silver events, and only I had been allowed to wear a tiara. But those days were long over.

And now, I enjoyed when everyone was required to wear black, gold, and silver to events. So, when I showed up in my signature red, I stood out as the guest of honor.

Whitley and English loped across the sand with wide

smiles on their faces. I realized that Lark *had* paid attention to the details. While Lark was in gold, highlighting her burnished hair, Whitley was dressed in silver, and English was in black. With my red dress, together, we were a set. Just how I liked it.

"Happy birthday," English said, pulling me in for a hug.

Whitley was there next. "You look beautiful, you lucky bitch."

I laughed. "You're ridiculous."

"As ever," Whitley said with a spritely curtsy.

Then she grasped my hand, and we traipsed across the sand.

The sun had already set, and bonfires were burning bright on the beach. Bars had been placed outside with bartenders mixing drinks for the crowd dancing to the music the DJ spun on the stage.

All of my friends were in attendance, save for my husband, who was conveniently absent. I wasn't surprised. I knew he had work engagements. Though I couldn't even begin to understand why someone would schedule that on the last day of the year, let alone on my birthday. But he'd show up when he wanted.

Lark had somehow managed to create a beachside pillow fort for our group. There were expensive, plush blankets laid out, topped with a mountain of pillows for lounging. We had our own bartender, who prepared fruity drinks, complete with umbrellas, for the lot of us. Though the boys were unsurprisingly drinking bourbon.

Everyone wished me happy birthday as I joined the group and took my drink. This was the first time in a very long time that I hadn't designed my own birthday party. And it was kind of... nice not to have to be in charge. Something I never would have guessed before.

"Let's dance," Whitley said, downing her drink like a champ. She pointed at Gavin.

He arched his eyebrows and gestured to himself. "Me?"

"Yeah, you. Come dance with me."

He laughed, but there was something else in his expression as he stepped across the blankets toward her. "All right, bossy."

"Bossy girls are just leaders who didn't stay down when boys told them to be quiet," Whitley said defiantly.

He smirked then, roguish and handsome in the firelight. "By all means, lead then."

She winked at us and then dragged him into the crowd. What a pair.

English was already pulling Court away. Sam looked reluctant as Lark tried to get him out in the crowd.

"Come with us," Lark told me.

I saw Penn walking toward me, alone. He was handsome, dressed down in a linen button-up rolled to his elbows and khaki shorts. His eyes were the same brilliant blue, and he had a half-smile on his face.

"Can I have a minute?" he asked.

I swallowed. Warning alarms went off in my head. This was a bad, bad idea. Camden was surely on his way here. It probably wasn't a good idea for me to incur his rancor. Not today. Not with what was on the horizon.

"Later," I told him, letting Lark drag me out into the sticky, sweaty crowd.

Penn's face disappeared in the chaos, and I breathed a sigh of relief.

I wasn't sure that I'd ever denied Penn anything. I'd toyed with him and teased him and purposely riled him. But it had never been real. Not like this.

I lost myself to the music then. Lark, English, and

Whitley came to dance around me. Our hands were raised high in the air, and we dizzily sang along to the pop song. Even with the noise, it was a little unfair how good Whitley was.

"Do you sing?" I yelled over the crowd. I didn't think that I'd ever heard her sing before.

Whitley shook her head. "No!"

"You should!" English shouted.

Lark agreed vehemently. "Seconded."

"You can't even hear me!" Whitley said with a laugh.

"What I heard was great."

Whitley just rolled her eyes. She grabbed Gavin's shirt in both hands and dragged him against her. But she didn't sing again. It was odd for someone who was always the life of the party to now be so silent.

I shrugged it off as a pair of hands came to rest on my hips. I knew those hands. I tipped my head back against Camden's shoulder and looked up at him.

"You made it," I said into his ear.

"Of course I made it," he said gruffly.

I shivered as his hands slid down the side of my dress and then around back to cup my ass. I tensed just slightly. His hands there brought back memories from the night before.

"Sore?" he asked.

I shook my head.

"That's a shame," he breathed. "Going to have to fix that. I liked the way you had to shift every time you sat down."

I nearly groaned at the words. I wanted that. I wanted more than that.

I turned in his arms and pressed myself flush against his chest. Our hips moved to the thrum of the music. My fingers tangled up into his dark hair. He leaned down then and kissed me. It was not gentle. It was possessive. I dug my toes into the sand as desire shot through me.

"Happy birthday," he said against my lips.

"Am I going to get my birthday wish?" I asked as my eyes fluttered open to look at him.

"Right now?" he asked. "Here, in the sand?" I softly shook my head, but he just smirked. "You don't want to be watched?"

I swallowed. "No."

He nipped at my earlobe. "Liar."

I closed my eyes again and leaned into him. "Maybe..." I amended. "Like... not completely public, but we could get caught..." I trailed off.

"You have a filthy mind." We swayed from side to side, dancing in the moonlight, as the party went on all around us. "I do enjoy it."

Our friends closed in around us, hips grinding and music pumping. Everything felt right. It might be a truce, but a part of me liked having him here rather than always a source of contention. Never knowing which side of his personality I was going to get. Maybe he could take his anger and just use it in the bedroom. Maybe it could always be this way.

Eventually, my friends all left the sand and flopped down on the blankets. Lark *had* procured a cake—a huge cake with frosting that swirled from blood red all the way up to the lightest pink. It was beautiful, and there was one tiara-shaped candle at the top.

I moved to stand before it as my friends all sang "Happy Birthday" to me over the noise from the party. I smiled so hard that my cheeks hurt. This was how it was supposed to be. And as the song came to an end, I stared into that one flame.

"Make a wish!" Whitley cried.

Gavin nudged her, and she laughed, leaning into him. He slung a casual arm around her waist. But I couldn't think about what that meant for them at this moment.

Just the candle before me. The one wish I had for my birthday. My eyes met Camden's over the flickering light. And I knew just what I wanted to wish for.

I closed my eyes and blew the candle out.

17

KATHERINE

A waiter came by to cut the gorgeous vanilla cake with raspberry cream layers and dish it out to the rest of the partygoers. It looked delicious, but I couldn't even eat a bite. I was so fired up from the party and the wish and the magic of our last night on the beach. I wasn't even hungry.

I just wanted more dancing and singing and a kiss at midnight. Then Camden and I could finally finish what we'd started. The perfect birthday.

I walked around the others who were enjoying the cake and to my husband's side.

He tugged me in close. "So, what did you wish for?"

"If I told you, it wouldn't come true."

He arched an eyebrow. "But what if I guess?"

"I can neither confirm nor deny," I said with a wink.

"I'm a very good guesser," he breathed into my ear.

"Oh, I bet you are."

"Was it to have my cock inside of you later?"

My body tensed with anticipation and need. Fuck, I wanted that. But that hadn't been my wish. He could think that was it all he wanted. I wouldn't mind. I wouldn't tell him what it actually was. I'd never let myself be that open, not when so much was still on the line.

"Would you make that wish come true?" I purred.

"I would consider the matter."

"Well," I teased, trailing my nail down his jawline, rough with stubble, "I will let you know when it comes true."

His phone buzzed in his pocket then. Loud and insistent.

I sighed. "Another call, really? Are you *ever* going to get a day off?"

He frowned. "I wasn't expecting another call."

He removed his phone from his pocket and turned it to face him. His frown deepened, but I didn't see the name on the screen.

"Who is it?" I asked.

"No one. I have to take this. I'll be right back."

"Camden, it's nearly midnight."

His voice hardened. "I'll be right back."

"Okay," I muttered, but he was already walking away across the sand.

My stomach tightened in worry. I didn't want to feel anything at all about who could be on that line. But if he hadn't been anticipating another call and he hadn't shown me who was on the line or told me, I had only one guess who it was.

Fiona.

I needed a drink. A stiff drink. No more umbrellas. Shots would do.

I stomped back over to the empty pillow fort. All of my friends had returned to the dance floor. The countdown was drawing ever nearer to midnight. And here I was, taking shots, alone, on my birthday. Fabulous.

Then there was a body next to me.

I looked over in surprise to find Penn Kensington. "What are you doing here?"

"Well, you've been avoiding me like the plague," he said with that signature smirk.

"Don't you think there's a reason for that?"

He took the shot out of my hand and downed it himself. "That's your third. I think you're a bit drunk."

"So what if I am? It's my birthday."

"And you can cry if you want to?" he asked imperiously.

I glared at him. "Could you cut the shit, Penn? You're here. Risking the ire of my husband and your *wonderful* wife. What could you possibly want?"

He sighed and motioned for the bartender to pour us each another shot of tequila. He held one out to me and took the other in his hand. "I'm here to wish you happy birthday."

I took the shot and sighed. I was taking my anger out on him. Not because he'd actually done anything wrong. I was mad at someone else, and Penn just happened to be here.

We lifted our shots and then downed them, as we'd done hundreds of times together. I swallowed the burning liquid and smiled up at my partner in crime. Exactly where he had always been—at my side.

"Thank you," I said, dispelling my irritation. "I'm not mad at you."

"I know."

"So, what are you *really* doing here?"

"I actually wanted to wish you happy birthday. And... I saw you taking shots all by yourself. Didn't seem right."

"So, you wanted to be chivalrous?" I admonished.

He shot me a look that I'd seen a million times. One that said he could be nothing but who he was.

"Of course you did," I muttered.

"You know, just because things are different between us doesn't mean that I stopped caring about you," he said softly. "You're still one of my closest friends. We're still crew, Ren."

I waved him away. "I really don't need to hear it."

He frowned but stayed resolute. He'd always been comfortable with the worst parts of my personality. They used to mirror his own. Before he'd gone all moral.

"And I brought you this," he said, holding out a red box with a gold ribbon.

I stared at it. My heart tripped over itself. I knew what was in that box.

"You didn't," I whispered.

"I missed last year. We were..." He trailed off.

He didn't have to say it. Besides the fact that I had been on my honeymoon, Penn and I hadn't been talking a year ago. But every year before that, every year since my father had been arrested and thrown in prison, he'd given me one of these little red boxes.

"I thought you'd forgotten."

He gave me a half-smile. "How could I forget?"

I didn't want to accept it, but this wasn't about Penn Kensington. It had nothing to do with us at all. This was about the little girl I'd been once upon a time. The girl who had believed in love at first sight and big, romantic gestures and happily ever afters who had never thought she'd ever love a man as much as her daddy—the one person who had sworn he would always be there. And I'd believed him. To my own detriment.

I took the box from Penn's hand, tugged the gold ribbon off, and slowly peeled away the red wrapping. I popped the lid on the box, and nestled inside on red crushed velvet was a small silver ballerina charm. The same exact brand and style of bracelet charm that my father had given me every single year on my birthday. Every year until we'd all discovered the truth about what a vicious liar he was.

Penn, in his unending goodness, had known how much those charms meant to me. He'd given me a new one every year since then, save for last year.

"Thank you," I whispered, my heart in my throat as I clutched the box to my chest.

He pulled me in for a hug, planting a faint kiss on the top of my head. "You're welcome."

"What's this?" a voice sneered nearby.

I jerked back from Penn's touch at the first sound of Camden's voice. He strode across the sand back toward us. His eyes darted back and forth between us, alone on the beach.

"Nothing," I said, mirroring what he'd said to me when Fiona called on *my* birthday to talk to him.

"*Nothing*," he said, disbelieving. "It's always nothing with you two, isn't it?"

"I was simply wishing her a happy birthday," Penn said. He shook his head at Camden. "I'll go now."

"Oh no, stay," Camden growled. "By all means, wish my wife a happy birthday."

"Camden," I said in distress, "it wasn't like that. He just gave me my birthday present."

"Of course he did." Camden snatched the box out of my hand. I made a sound of protest, but he was already opening it. "Let's see what lover boy got you."

"Stop it," Penn said in frustration. "What is wrong with you?"

He plucked the charm out of the box and held it aloft. "I think it looks a little cheap, but what do I know?" Camden asked. His eyes were straight fire. The brown so dark that they were nearly black in the flickering light. Anger swept his body like a tornado, wrecking everything in its path. "Who knew you'd like this better than diamonds? But it comes from *him*. So, of course you do."

"The truce, Camden," I reminded him. Tears were brimming in my eyes.

This wasn't supposed to happen. He wasn't supposed to be doing this.

He dropped the charm back in the box, closed it, and tossed it back to me. I fumbled the box and barely caught it.

"Fuck the truce." He stepped forward, dangerously close. "Just when I thought that I might be able to trust you again."

"Leave it, Percy," Penn said. "Can't you see that you're hurting her?"

Camden grasped the front of Penn's shirt in his hand. I thought Camden was going to punch him.

"What are you doing?" I gasped.

"You should get the fuck out of here, Kensington," Camden growled.

Penn pushed him off, straightening out his shirt. "Yeah, I'm going to go, and I'm taking Katherine with me. I don't trust you not to hurt her."

"My wife is not going with you."

"Both of you, stop it," I said, pushing my way between them. I turned to Penn. "Just go. I'll be fine. He's not going to hurt me."

"Only if you ask me to," Camden said low.

Penn's eyes were pained. He didn't want to go. Not because he was in love with me, but he was my closest friend. We'd been through everything together. He'd defend me to his last breath, but he couldn't defend me against this. We both knew it.

"Go to Natalie," I said, jutting my chin toward where she

stood, her silver hair glowing in the moonlight. She was watching what was playing out. I could practically see the calculus running through her mind about whether to come over or not. "*Go.*"

"Fine. But if he lays a hand on you... I swear to god."

"He won't. He's never hurt me," I assured him. "It's not like that."

Penn shot one more furious look at Camden, and then walked toward Natalie.

I could hear her voice rise up out of the crowd. "What's going on?"

He wrapped an arm around her waist and just shook his head. I didn't hear his response. I probably didn't want to anyway.

I whipped around then. My own gaze now simmering with anger. I needed off of this beach. I needed to be somewhere alone to release all of this. I didn't want to have the rest of this argument in front of my friends and a party full of strangers.

"Walk with me," I snapped.

Then I set off across the sand with the box clutched in my hand. My knuckles were white with strain. I didn't wait to see if he followed me. I had no doubt that he would. I heard his feet behind me, but he made no move to catch up. I walked until my legs ached and I could go no further. Our villa was mere feet away, but I couldn't go back inside either.

I waited for him to reach me. My chest rising and falling with a growing fury. I had put everything aside for him this week. I'd ignored all the problems we had. I'd done *everything* so that we could start fresh, just like *he* had asked. He had wanted this truce between us. And then he'd thrown the whole fucking thing in my face. My hands trembled at my sides.

Camden finally came to stand before me.

I lifted my gaze to meet his. "What the fuck was that about?"

He laughed once sardonically. "You have to ask?"

"We were on a truce!"

"That doesn't mean you can go and fuck with Penn Kensington and I'm going to ignore it!" he shouted back.

"Penn and I aren't together! We haven't been for a very, very long time, Camden. He's with someone else. And he... he doesn't *want* me."

"But *you* want him."

"Maybe I did, but not anymore."

He laughed, but it was a cruel thing. "I don't believe you. I saw you two together."

"You saw what you wanted to see. I don't even know why I have to justify myself to you. You were the one on the phone with Fiona."

"So what if I was?" he asked, uncaring.

"It's my birthday," I snarled. "You talk to your fucking *mistress* and then have the audacity to blame me for having a conversation with my best friend. You need to get the fuck over yourself, Camden Percy."

I pushed past him, prepared to walk the beach until I felt calm enough to go back to my party. But he reached out and grasped my wrist, pulling me toward him.

I tried to yank away, but he held me firm. "Let me go."

"You know, I was going to ask that we keep this truce going," he said, low and urgent. "I was going to say that maybe we should go home and try this out again. Try to be together. But we can't even make it a week without tearing each other apart."

"*You* can't make it a week," I yelled at him.

He arched an eyebrow. "You fell into his arms as soon as

my back was turned. You're never going to change, Katherine."

I shoved against him, but he still didn't release me. "Let me *go*."

Finally, he did. My momentum pulled me backward, and I toppled over, landing hard in the sand.

"I was going to grant you your birthday wish," he said with narrowed eyes. "But we both know that you haven't earned it."

Then he strode off toward our villa, leaving me still seated in the sand. Tears burned my eyes. I put my elbows on my knees and my hands on my forehead. With a deep shuddering breath, I tried to hold the tears at bay. I could hear chanting in the distance.

"Five, four, three, two, ONE! Happy New Year!"

Yeah.

Happy New Year.

PART III

BACK TO NORMAL

18

KATHERINE

I'd flown back to New York with Lark.

I hadn't answered any of her questions. So, she stopped asking them. But I had seen the looks she was giving me. They were the same ones she'd given me in the past. She was worried. I supposed... she had every right to be.

I'd canceled my meeting with ChildrensOne when I got home. I didn't have the headspace for anything else in my life. The director, Deborah, had been understanding, but insisted I call her when I was ready to reschedule.

Mostly, I tried to go back to my normal life. Thankfully, I'd already scheduled my social media accounts with content ahead of time. So, I didn't have to really pay attention to them. Though I couldn't ignore the volley of comments asking where I was and why I wasn't responding as often. Social media was a blessing and a curse.

I'd gone back to personal training with Rodrigo. He'd bumped me from four times a week to five and recommended his nutritionist. In two weeks, I was back down to pre–Puerto Rico weight, and I could see the tone in my muscles again. I was healthier than ever... physically.

My mental state was another thing.

It must have been bad because even my *mother* noticed.

Never a good thing. She rarely saw anything that wasn't right in front of her face.

That was how I'd ended up here, in a carefully selected black dress and my favorite fur-lined jacket. My mother preferred Manolo Blahnik. So, even my shoes had been picked with her in mind. Conservative yet stylish. The crux of Celeste Van Pelt.

I stepped into the private tea room, used only for select company on the Upper East Side. It was my mother's favorite establishment. She came here at least twice a week with her friends for high tea and even higher gossip. I found her seated at her usual table with tea already in front of her along with a glass of champagne. Celeste Van Pelt never thought it was too early to start drinking. She was scrolling an iPad, likely reading the gossip column.

"Hello, Mother," I said, pulling my chair out and having a seat.

"Hello, Katherine." She looked up from her iPad and perused my outfit. "Is that new?" She gestured to my dress.

"Yes. Cunningham Couture. It's part of Elizabeth's new line. It won't even reveal until Fashion Week next month."

"Sensible for her," she said. "Isn't she usually a bit more... daring?"

I shrugged. "Depends on the line. I think Harmony is taking over the more daring side of the industry."

"Ah, her daughter is designing with her?"

"Yes," I told her. Though I was sure she'd already known that.

"Interesting." But she said it in a way that made it seem not at all interesting.

A waitress appeared then, depositing a tray of finger sandwiches and little pastry delicacies. She poured our tea and asked if we needed anything else. My mother waved her away. She must have been accustomed to my mother because she left without another word.

Finally, my mother put her iPad down. "Have you heard from your brother?"

"Not really," I told her, adding a bit of milk to my tea before taking a sip. "How is Sutton doing with the pregnancy?"

My brother, David, lived in middle-of-nowhere Lubbock, Texas, where he was the CFO for Wright Construction, one of the largest construction companies in America. He'd moved to San Francisco after college to escape New York. And then Lubbock to escape San Francisco. He'd promptly fallen in love with a Wright and decided to stay permanently. Sutton was pregnant now, due sometime next month. David had never really been loquacious before he left. He didn't talk to me much now that he was thousands of miles away.

"Going wonderful. It's her second, so she seems confident."

"Do they know if it's a boy or a girl?" I asked distractedly.

"A girl. They haven't told me her name yet."

"Smart."

My mother arched an eyebrow. "And why is that?"

"Because if you don't like it, you can't say anything about it if it's already the kid's name."

She relented and reached for a small cucumber sandwich. "Anyway, I thought that you and I could go down there when the baby is born."

I nodded. Though I didn't particularly want to fly to Texas right now. But I wanted to see David. I wanted to meet my niece. It would be a welcome distraction from my life on the Upper East Side.

I picked at my food, finishing off my tea and champagne as my mother droned on about her life. She didn't ask me about mine. Which was just fine by me. I didn't want to talk about it. She hadn't batted an eye at my arranged marriage. I doubted she would bat one now at the circumstances.

"Katherine, are you listening?" she asked.

I blinked and looked up. I had completely lost the thread of the conversation. My head was a bit fuzzy from the champagne. I'd had a second glass when offered.

"What were you saying?"

She sighed in disappointment. "I had a call from a friend."

"Oh?"

"Deborah Morrison."

"Oh," I said again.

"She runs that charity foundation, ChildrensOne."

"I know," I told her.

She was the director that I'd blown off when I got home in such a spiral that I was able to do nothing but work out and sleep.

"She mentioned that you had spoken with her but that you canceled." My mother's voice dipped into a tone of disapproval.

Following through on promises had been the cornerstone of my upbringing. I hadn't wagered that Deborah would know my mother. But of course, Celeste Van Pelt knew everyone who was anyone.

"Yes, I have been... under the weather." It wasn't a lie. But it wasn't the truth either.

"You don't seem sick now," she mused.

"No," I said softly. Not precisely the truth either.

"Well then, I suppose you can let her know that you will make time again."

"I cannot believe that she called you about this."

"Why ever not, dear? She's a close friend. She was worried about you," my mother said. "You were taught not to break commitments. Hasn't the Van Pelt name been dragged through the dirt enough?"

I took a deep breath and then released it. "Of course."

There was no point in arguing.

"Should I reach back out to her?"

"That's not necessary. I'll go see her as soon as we're done."

"Excellent. Glad to clear that up." She raised her hand for the check. "Also, have you lost weight?"

I stilled in my seat. Was this a trick question? I didn't know the right answer. Not here with my mother. She played more head games than even I did.

"You look great," she added.

I relaxed. Okay. She wasn't going to say something negative or make it into an issue.

"Thanks," I said with a confident smile. "I'm working with a personal trainer and a new nutritionist."

The waitress dropped the check off.

"Well, whatever you're doing, it's clearly working." My mother gestured to the check.

Oh. Right. I pulled out the Percy black card and placed it on the check. My mother had her own money that my father hadn't been able to drain away. Her maiden name was Cabot, and the Cabots were an old-money family that had essentially died out with my mother. So, now that my grandparents had passed, my mother had the reins of it, but so much of it had been squandered that it wasn't enough to live as she once had. Just enough to stay comfortable. I shouldn't have been surprised that she'd wanted Percy money to secure us further. She'd wanted the arranged marriage maybe more than I had.

Once the check was paid, we both stood.

"Excellent," my mother said. "Wonderful to see you, dear. Do let me know if you need any other help with the charity."

"I will," I lied.

"You know, you should plan a party for them," my mother suggested.

I soured. Why did everyone think the only thing I was good at was party planning? "Maybe. We'll see what they need from me."

"I'm sure your contacts would be sufficient." She laughed. "Nothing brings in money like a party planner on the Upper East Side."

"I'll think about it," I said, hedging the conversation.

My mother kissed my cheek and then disappeared through the room with her iPad back in her oversize bag. I followed her out, taking the Mercedes uptown to Deborah's office, which was across the street from the children's hospital. I texted her to let her know that I was incoming.

"Katherine!" Deborah cried when I stepped into her office thirty minutes later. "I'm so glad that you could join us."

I didn't mention her subterfuge. I just smiled genially. "It's good to be here. Last we talked, you were going to show me around the facility."

I wasn't particularly looking forward to it. I'd never been a fan of hospitals. Not since I'd been stuck in one for six weeks.

But Deborah rose quickly to her feet. "Yes, of course. Do you have time for that now? I could take you around the children's ward. Let you see why we do what we're doing."

"I'm free for a while. I have another appointment in an hour."

She smiled. "Plenty of time. Come on."

We walked out of her office and across the street to the hospital. My throat closed as we crossed the threshold. I'd thought that by volunteering for a children's hospital, I'd be able to overcome my fear. That I'd realize it wasn't the *place* that was the problem but rather that I had been locked away against my will. But now that I was here, my body didn't seem to care about the difference.

The hospital I'd been in for my anorexia was nothing like this, of course. It was a top-of-the-line private facility that my mother paid a fortune for. We didn't have the money at the time, but she still paid it. And she'd paid to expunge the records so that no one would ever know her daughter was sick.

Deborah didn't even seem to notice my discomfort as she walked me through the halls, explaining volunteer schedules and treatment areas. I took in what I could, even though I felt the beginning of a panic attack coming on.

I just remembered waking up in a strange room and being told that I couldn't leave because there was something wrong with me. I had been kept in that room for six straight weeks with only time out for one-on-one and group therapy. Of course, they said it wasn't a psych ward, but I did have a mental illness—anorexia—and I would be kept in the private center with other eating disorder patients until I was well enough to enter society again. They monitored everything I put in my mouth including the medication, which made me feel worse rather than better.

It'd saved my life. That was what they'd said.

But I'd never really been able to shake my fear of being forced back here. That if they could do it once, they could do it again. I'd never expressly trusted hospitals since then.

"And this is the cancer ward," Deborah said as she led me down the hallway.

My hands shook at my sides. This wasn't the same hospital. It *wasn't* the same. And yet, the anxiety crawled up my throat and burrowed in my skin.

"Is there a restroom nearby?" I asked, swallowing down bile.

"Oh, sure. Right down the hall, to the left. I'm going to check in on a patient. You can meet me when you're done," Deborah said.

I nodded and hastened into the restroom. My already-pale skin was pasty white. I looked like a ghost. I needed to get it together. I splashed water on my wrists and the back of my neck and tried to remember the meditation exercises to calm my breathing. In my mind, I repeated the soothing words over and over that I'd used after therapy.

This doesn't control me. I control it. No one will ever force me back here. Not ever.

After a few minutes, I felt more composed and stepped out of the restroom. I didn't know which way Deborah had gone. She'd said she was seeing a patient but not mentioned which one.

"You look lost," a small voice said behind me.

I turned around and found a little girl with tan skin in a hot-pink dress, pink flip-flops, and a hot-pink wrap around her head. "Hi," I said to her. "I am a bit lost. I came here with a friend, and now, I don't see her."

"Are you looking for Miss Deborah?" the girl asked,

dramatically putting her hand on her hip and then sinking into it with extra force.

"I am," I agreed.

"I know where she is. She's with Patricia. I can show you the way. What's your name?"

"That would be nice. My name is Katherine. What's yours?"

The girl abruptly turned around with all the flare of a dancer and gestured for me to walk with her. "I'm Jem. Do you know that you look like a Disney villain?"

I laughed. "Do I really?"

"Uh, duh. Have you looked at yourself in the mirror? You're dressed in all black. You're wearing high heels and red lipstick. Your hair is dark. You're pale and pretty," Jem said. She arched her eyebrows. "Villain."

"Well, maybe I am a villain," I told her.

"Hmm," Jem said, narrowing her eyes. "Does that mean I'm going to have to fight you in a battle to the death?"

I couldn't stop the smile that stretched on my face. "That sounds very serious."

"It is," Jem agreed. "Okay, here we are. Miss Deborah is inside. But, Katherine," she said, raising her finger and pointing it up to my face, "I'm keeping my eye on you."

I stared down at this little pip-squeak of a child. She was in the cancer ward, and she had more oomph than most of the people I knew in my life. More life and vibrancy. More color—that was for sure. And she had completely obliterated the nerves that jumbled inside of me. That quick, and I'd forgotten why I was afraid. Maybe if I'd had my own Jem when I was hospitalized, I wouldn't have even felt like this.

"That sounds okay to me," I admitted. "Jem, do you mind if I come visit you again?"

Jem crossed her arms. "Depends on if you show up in all black again, missy."

"I can probably find another color."

"Pink," Jem insisted. "It's my favorite color."

"I would have never guessed."

"Okay. Sounds good. Bye, Villain Katherine. I'll be here when you come back." Jem turned and skipped down the hallway.

Deborah appeared then with a laugh as she pulled Patricia's door closed. "I see you met Jem."

"I sure did."

"She's a handful. They can never keep her in her room."

"I think I'll do it," I told Deborah. "I'll help out. I can volunteer here at least once a week, and I think I can plan a party to raise money for the hospital."

Deborah's face split in two. "Oh my god, really? That would be so amazing, Katherine. We would just love to have you on board."

And for the first time in a long, long time, I felt like I was really doing the right thing.

19

CAMDEN

Every Monday at three o'clock in the afternoon, I left work early and went in for my weekly meeting at the gentlemen's club, Height. It was a members-only bar and lounge for the most elite in the city. People jokingly referred to it as a secret society, but that was just the mystery surrounding it. So far, I hadn't been inducted into a cult... as far as I knew. Not that any of us said anything to dispel the notion. It gave us credibility.

I flashed my member's card—a thick, clear card with a skyscraper etched in twenty-four karat gold, an *H* the only indicator of what it was for.

The female attendant allowed me to pass, and a second took my coat with a timid, "Welcome back to Height, Mr. Percy."

I knew it wasn't *that* sort of gentlemen's club. Though nothing was far from our fingertips if we so much as asked. I had never asked.

I strode through the long burgundy-carpet-lined hallway and up a short flight of stairs to the main sitting room, complete with a dark mahogany bar that only served top-shelf and exclusive imported liquor. There were a dozen men in equally tailored business suits scattered about the room.

While I went to Hank's to be invisible, I came to Height to be seen.

The bartender poured a glass of scotch before I even had to ask for it.

"Mr. Percy," she said, passing the drink to me.

"Thanks," I said. I didn't even know her name. They changed much more frequently than at Hank's.

I shook hands and made small talk with the men here. I knew them all. Though none of them all that well. That was the way of this place. Court could have come here, but he found it too uptight and oppressive. Gavin hadn't been inducted yet. There was no hope for Sam. None of my friends would be here. Just business associates and potential business associates.

Phones were supposed to be off when we entered the sanctum, but it was the one rule that no one adhered to. None of us could afford to be unavailable.

So, when my phone buzzed in my suit pocket, no one blinked as I pulled it out and excused myself. My father's name appeared on the screen. He knew I was here. Why the fuck would he be disturbing me? Yes, I was always supposed to be free, but this was the one time that he usually let me be. He knew it was good for the company for me to be seen among the wealthiest in the city in whatever way that came to be.

I stepped aside and answered the phone, "Yes?"

"What did you do?" my father asked, his voice cold and menacing.

I thought of all the things that he could be referring to. The fact that Katherine and I were definitely not trying to have a baby. The flight I'd put my sister on to get her the fuck out of Manhattan for a while. Or worse. Deep down, there was something much worse. Something he'd never forgive. The reason I had befriended the police chief in the first place was to locate my mother. I'd never found her. Everything had led to a dead end. As if Helena Percy had just disappeared off the map.

It wouldn't matter to my father whether or not I'd found her. Only that I had been looking. But I didn't know *how* he could have discovered that. It was just latent fear bringing the thought to the surface. It had all ended almost two years ago. There was no way he would know that *now*.

"I don't know. What have I done this time?" I asked him.

"You *ruined* the deal."

My heart stopped. "What do you mean, I ruined what deal?"

"Ireland," he spat at me. "It's done. Gone. They pulled out this afternoon."

My stomach dropped out of my body. Fury singed through me. "They did what?" I shouted, ignoring the looks from the other men in the room. "How the fuck is that possible? We already finished negotiations. We were just waiting for them to fly into New York to sign the paperwork. I laid that in your lap."

"It seems you didn't do a good enough job," he said. "Or else they wouldn't have told me that they couldn't work with you. That you didn't seem fucking competent enough for the job. That they wouldn't risk this property on someone like *us*."

My head spun. No. That made no fucking sense. I had been dealing with these guys for months. There had never once been a time where I thought that they were going to bail out of this. Not because of me certainly.

"They said that?" I said in disbelief.

"Yes," my father ground out. "So, congratulations, Camden. We're out a hundred million dollars with the loss of this deal. Do find a way to make that up."

And then he hung up on me.

I stared down at the phone in shock. Then I hurled my scotch across the bar where the glass shattered against the wall. The nearest waitress flinched, but no one else even looked half-surprised. Did they know what had happened? Was I the last to know?

I was of half a mind to call up the guy I'd been working with in Ireland and find out what the fuck had happened. No, better yet, I'd fly my ass to Ireland and demand answers. No one bailed on a fucking hundred-million-dollar deal after jerking me around for months on end.

Fuck *that*.

With my fury barely contained, I stormed back down the stairs and toward the exit. The attendant retrieved my jacket. I snatched it out of her hand and dashed out the door. My driver waited nearby and whisked me back to Percy Tower.

I was a thundercloud as I took my private elevator up to the penthouse on the top of the tower. The only thing between me and the heavens was Club 360, one of the hottest elite clubs in Manhattan. I raced up the flight of stairs that led to my bedroom, my steps echoing in the empty house. I yanked out my suitcase and began to pile clothes inside it. I was nearly finished when I heard the downstairs elevator ding open.

"Camden?" Court called out from downstairs.

I snarled something unintelligible and zipped the suitcase closed. I heard footsteps on the stairs, and then Court peeked his head into the room. He took in the sight before him.

"Going somewhere?"

"Ireland," I said, jerking the suitcase to standing.

"What for?"

"The deal fell through. I'm going to go fix it."

"Oh," he said. "That explains a lot. Someone at Height messaged me. You broke a glass?"

"They sent you to check on me?" I asked, my voice dangerously low.

"Well, one, you have a notoriously brutal temper. And two, they know we're friends. I came to make sure that you weren't going to do anything stupid," Court said. He gestured to the suitcase. "Like that."

"This is the only way to fix it." I brushed past him and carried the suitcase down the flight of stairs.

Court followed behind me. Not stopping me, but not letting me go either. "Why don't we back it up a few steps? Why did they back out of the deal? This was the one you were working on when we were in Puerto Rico?"

"Yes."

Then I stopped in my tracks. It was the one that I'd been working on in Puerto Rico. The one that I'd been working on when my head was so full of Katherine that I let her blow me while I was in the middle of a conference call. "My father said they backed out because of me."

"That sounds unlikely."

"It does," I said.

"Can we go have a fucking smoke and chill before making any rash decisions?" Court asked. He reached in his pocket and pulled out a pair of joints.

Fuck, I could use a joint. Everything was just anger and madness and the desperate need to prove that I could make this right. But maybe I needed to stop for a minute. I had the private jet. I could take a red-eye when my head was a little clearer.

"Fine," I said, snatching one out of his hand.

I left the suitcase in the middle of the foyer and strode into the recreation room. My pool table took up the center of the space along with a pool table opposite it. I sank into a large black leather chair and reached for a discarded metal lighter. I flipped the top open and lit the joint. Then I took a pull on it, letting the pot do its job.

Court took the lighter from me and lit his own, sitting opposite me. "So, what do you think is the real reason they pulled out?"

"My father said it was because of me. That I lost a hundred million dollars."

"And you believe him?"

"No," I snapped, "I don't."

"But it's what he believes, which means the dick is going to punish you for it."

I brought the joint back to my lips and sucked in deep. "Yep."

"Fuck."

"Yep," I repeated. "The worst part is... he's not wrong. I wasn't in it a hundred percent."

"I don't believe that. The Camden Percy I know doesn't do anything less than a hundred percent."

"I was distracted. My focus was on Katherine," I admitted. "My head wasn't in the game. It was in *her* game. I slipped up."

"Whoa, whoa, whoa," Court said. "You cannot blame Katherine for this. You were less of a jackass while we were away *because* of her. This is not her fault. It's not your fault. It just... happened."

"Nothing just happens," I told him. "Something caused this."

"Then figure out what it was. But you don't actually believe that it's your fuckup. Camden Percy doesn't fuck up, even when his head is more interested in getting laid than the business."

"And I didn't even get laid."

Court choked on his next inhalation. "What the fuck, dude? You two were alone for a week! How hard was it to get in her pants?"

I didn't explain it to Court. He didn't need to know my particular proclivities. Not when it came to Katherine Van Pelt. The truth was... it would have been easy to fuck her. Fuck her until she couldn't walk and do it again day after day after day. It was what I'd wanted to do, but it wouldn't have kept her. She needed more than that. She needed handling. And I enjoyed handling her, but then she'd gone and fucked it all up royally. Just when I'd been ready to give her what she'd been all but begging me for.

Court shook his head at my silence. "You know that she doesn't love Penn, right?"

I narrowed my eyes at him. "You didn't see them together."

"I don't have to. I have eyes. I see Penn with Natalie. I see Katherine with you. There's no comparison, man. You two are the only ones who don't see it."

"I'd still like to kill him," I told Court.

He snorted. "Yeah, well, it should say something that you want to kill him and *not* her, you possessive jackass."

I shrugged. "I need to be focused on work right now, not Katherine."

"Wrong. You need to focus on your wife," Court said. "Or else you're going to lose her for good this time."

His words chilled me. Katherine and I had gone back and forth for so long. It didn't seem possible that this would ruin everything. We were bound for life. She wasn't getting out of this contract, but that didn't mean that we had to be together. We'd spent the last six months seeing each other only in public when we had to. I didn't fucking want that. It was why I'd offered the truce in the first place. Then I'd gone ballistic at the sight of them together.

Fuck, maybe I'd have to call her. She was likely still furious with me. She hadn't even flown back to New York with me. I didn't have words to make it up to her. But I had actions. That was the only thing she responded to anyway.

"Maybe you're right," I admitted.

Maybe I needed to win back my wife.

20

KATHERINE

"Girrrlll," Alexandre D'Oria trilled, "did you go down another dress size?"

Alexandre was the up-and-coming designer that I'd decided to work with for my Fashion Week dress. He was doing daring work that complemented my style. When I'd approached him, he'd fallen all over himself to say yes. My dress could make his career this Fashion Week, especially since he wasn't doing runway in New York, just exhibiting.

"I couldn't have," I said, running my hands down my narrow hips in the trifold mirror.

English stood nearby in black cigarette pants, a black tank, and a blazer. She shook her head. "Seriously, how do you do it? I'm going to need the name of that trainer. You'd think that I'd be losing a shit-ton because of the divorce, but *no!*"

"You're happy with Court. That's what happens," I told her.

"Well, we're going to have to take this in," Alexandre said. "If you go down another dress size, we might be in trouble. But, girl, you look so fab."

"Thanks," I said with a grin for both of them.

"You're next, baby girl," Alexandre said, waving his hand at English. "Strip, and I'll have Dominique get you into your dress."

"I can't believe you're doing this for me," English said as she removed her blazer.

"Of course," I said. "We must celebrate your official divorce."

English laughed and shook her head. Her divorce would be finalized the weekend before the annual Fashion Week gala. We'd all decided to throw her a huge party, but I'd also offered to get everyone into the Fashion Week gala as a second surprise with Alexandre designing a dress for English. Now that all of my girls were coming, I couldn't wait. This was going to be infinitely better than last year.

A phone buzzed on one of the tables.

English stepped over and picked it up. "It's yours, Katherine," she said. "Camden."

I shook my head. "Let it go to voicemail."

English frowned and then clicked the button for it to be silent. "Are you two still fighting?"

"No. The fighting is done," I told her. "Now, we're just not speaking. It's better that way."

"I hate that you two got into it on New Year's. I thought it was going so well. You guys were happy."

I shrugged. "It was just a lie. We'd made that truce and pretended to be happy. By the end of the week, the truth came out. We can't be around each other without screaming at one another unless we're faking it."

"That's sad."

"It is what it is. We're not a fairy tale. We're just... us."

"Yeah, but... don't you want to find love?"

I looked her up and down. The girl who had found the

man of her dreams, only for him to cheat on her. Then found love again with the biggest train wreck on the Upper East. Of course she believed in fairy-tale love. She'd lived it... *twice*.

I had none of that. I couldn't even imagine what it would look like.

"No," I told her. "Love is full of pain and disappointment and loss. I'll stick with what I know."

English looked like she wanted to say something else, but the phone started ringing again. She glanced at it. "Camden again."

I pursed my lips. "Just turn it off."

English frowned and then nodded.

"You're good, Katherine," Alexandre said. "English, you're up."

Alexandre helped me out of my dress, and I strode off of the pedestal in nothing but my bra, thong, and heels. I'd come here in all black, but I planned to leave in something else entirely. I had my first volunteer shift for ChildrensOne, and I knew what I would wear.

I zipped up a pink dress and changed out my cherry-red lipstick for a pale pink. I kept on my black pumps and black jacket, but somehow, the combination made me look... softer. Younger even. Like maybe I wasn't the villain today and I was the princess instead. Of course, the only time I'd been a princess for anyone other than my daddy, I'd been an ice princess.

"You look cute," English said. "Where are you off to?"

"I'm working with that charity. Going to get some time in at the hospital and do some party planning."

"Oh! You are doing a party then? I love it. I can't wait."

"Yes, I figure... if it's what I'm good at, might as well put it to good use."

English grinned. "Definitely."

After saying my good-byes to English and Alexandre, I took the Percy Mercedes back uptown.

My meeting with Deborah had gone off without a hitch by the time we were finished. I had a rough draft of the party and a timeline for how to get it all in order. I'd agreed to work on it all at home now that we had a schedule.

I swallowed back my mounting fear again as I walked across the street and upstairs to the cancer ward. I knew that hospitals shouldn't bother me like this. I was in control here. I was a fucking adult. Why did it *do* this to me? I shook out my hands and tried to channel some of my inner Jem. She was stuck in here and still had so much light inside of her. I just needed to find my light.

My heels carried me down the familiar hall. I passed Patricia's room, which was dark and silent. Then I continued toward where I'd seen Jem skip off to. After looking through a few doors into empty rooms, I came upon a nurses' station.

"Hi, I'm looking for Jem's room," I said confidently.

"And you are?" the black man asked, looking down at his computer.

"I'm here from Deborah's office over at ChildrensOne. I'm volunteering."

"Oh, great!" he said, his smile suddenly lighting up. "We love having the volunteers in for the kids. Let me show you to Jem's room. I need to check on her vitals anyway."

"Thanks. I appreciate it."

The nurse directed me down the hallway and to a room near the end of the hall. He knocked twice. "Jem, how are you doing?"

"Come on in, *Frank*," she said cheerfully.

He shook his head. "My name is Jerry. She calls every nurse on the whole wing by a made-up name."

I tried to suppress my smile but didn't manage it. "She must keep you on your toes."

"You have no idea."

He pushed the door open and bustled inside. "How are we feeling today, Princess Jem?"

"Queen Jem today, Frank," she said, tilting her chin up and trying to look as regal as possible. She really managed it, even with the series of cords running into her little veins and the half-moon circles under her eyes.

"Hey, Jem," I said as I followed him inside.

Her eyes lit up. "Frank! You didn't tell me that you brought Villain Katherine with you."

Jerry looked over at me and raised an eyebrow. "Is your name really Katherine?"

"It is." I turned back to Jem as I removed my black coat. "But I'm not a villain today."

Jem's mouth dropped open. "You're wearing a princess dress." She twirled her finger in place. "Do a spin!"

I laughed at her command but twirled on the spot as if I'd been meant for it. It had been a long time since I'd been in ballet, but the turn came back to me effortlessly.

Jem looked breathless with delight. "I need one. Frank, get me a matching princess dress."

"Right away, Your Majesty," he said, bowing at the waist. He fiddled with a few more things. "All right, I'm going to leave you with your visitor for a few minutes, but after that, you need to rest. You always get exhausted after a chemo session. I don't want the excitement to wear you down even more."

"Aye, aye, captain," she said, offering him a mock salute.

Jerry nodded at me. "I'll be back in ten."

"Sounds good. Thanks."

Jerry disappeared down the hallway, and I took a seat in the chair opposite Jem's bed. She leaned back in her bed and released a huff of air.

"I wish you'd come at a different time, Princess Katherine," Jem said.

"Well, why don't you let me know a good time, and I can come again?"

"You mean it?"

"Sure. I'm going to volunteer here regularly now."

Jem looked at me with naked disbelief in her eyes. As if people had said that one too many times. Even this angel of a child had cynicism. "Okay. Well, Thursdays are bad. But on Wednesdays, I get to do art. Can you draw?"

"Not at all," I told her. "But I can dance."

"I love to dance," Jem told me. "Dance and draw and run around and slides and singing and getting my nails painted and playing dress-up and having tea."

"I like all of those things."

"Oh, good. You'd be a villain again if you didn't like fun."

I cracked a smile. "Another reasonable reference."

I wanted to ask more questions. I wanted to ask why she was here and how long she'd been sick. I wanted to ask about her parents and how often they showed up and why they weren't here now, right after she had treatment. I wanted to find out how this precious child had so much life, considering her circumstances.

I could see that her playing pretend was her way of coping. I knew a little too much about that. But without meaning to, I cared for this kid. I saw my old self in her. I wanted to know more.

"Hey, Jem," I whispered. "Why are you here?"

She smiled softly at me, stifling a yawn. "Cancer ward."

"Right. But..."

Jem waved her hand faintly. "It's called ALL—acute lymphoblastic leukemia." The big words sounded ridiculous, coming out of her small mouth. "My white blood cells are eating my body like a dragon breathing fire at the princess."

I tried to hide my horror. I knew what leukemia was. I'd heard about it. And I'd known that she had to be here for something bad, but it still hurt to hear.

"Well, it's good that you're a dragon-slaying princess then, isn't it?"

Jem's eyes lit up. "You get me."

She sank back into her bed. Another yawn hit her, and she tried to keep her eyes open.

"How about I come again next week? I bet I can bring in a surprise," I told her.

"I'd like that," she said through a yawn. "I'll wait for you. Don't be late."

I stood as Jerry stepped back in, letting me know that our ten minutes were up. Jem was nearly asleep. I swallowed and then exited with Jerry.

"Are you okay?" he asked when we left. "You look a little shaken up."

"She... she told me a little about her diagnosis —leukemia."

He nodded. "It's always hard to hear, but it's actually the most common type of cancer in children." He gestured for me to walk with him. We fell into step. "We're hopeful in her case."

"How does she stay so... happy?"

"That's just Jem. She's a ray of sunshine. Never let the diagnosis bring her down. She's always been confident that she'll beat this."

"That's incredible."

"She really is. I wish I could say the same about her parents."

I raised my eyebrows. "I noticed that they weren't here either time I've been here."

He wrinkled his nose. "I doubt you'll ever meet them. It's good that you're coming around more to see her. She could use a friend."

My stomach twisted at that. I didn't like the idea that her family had abandoned her to this hospital. As mine had abandoned me. Even if my stay had only been for six excruciating weeks. This was something else altogether. How could they do it when their daughter was so amazing?

"I have to get back to my shift, but I hope you come back."

"I will," I told him confidently. Fear of hospitals or not, I wanted to see her.

I hurried down the hallway, another idea about what to do for Jem...and maybe the whole ward buzzing through my mind. I passed a group of women who also looked like they were here for volunteer hours and continued down the hall. I was almost to the exit when I heard my name.

"Katherine, is that you?" one of the women asked.

I turned around and was surprised to see a face that I recognized. Though... just barely. Last time I'd seen her, she had been under a hundred pounds, and her hair had been falling out. She'd been eating through a feeding tube for a while as the hospital tried to ween her off of purging everything she ate. We'd been in the same facility and then a closed therapy group in the city for a year after that.

"Melinda?" I asked in surprise.

"It is you!" Melinda leaned forward and pulled me into a hug.

She was no longer stick thin. She was now a shapely woman with sloping curves and a round face. Her hair fell to her shoulders and was as thick and curly as could be. She could have been a different person.

I held her at arm's length. "How are you doing?"

"Excellent. Really excellent. I'm working with the church now. I've found my calling."

"That's great," I told her.

"Yeah. I had a few rough years after we stopped our therapy sessions," she confided. "I got married, but... it didn't work out."

"I'm sorry to hear that."

"Yeah." She glanced down at the ground. "Maybe you'll understand. It's still hard to talk about at church."

"Your divorce?" I asked.

She shook her head. "They've been understanding about that. But... you know, the infertility."

My ears started ringing. I felt like someone had smashed cymbals against my head. "The... what?"

"Well, that's why you're here, right?" Melinda asked, biting her bottom lip. "This is the volunteer hour for the group I founded. It's for women who are going through the same struggles I went through. I want them to know that they're still strong, powerful women even though they can't bring a child into this world. We have so many anorexia cases."

Cotton balls clogged my throat. I couldn't speak. I couldn't think.

"Katherine?" she asked gently. "You can talk to me. We'd love to have you join us."

"No," I said roughly. "No, sorry, that's... that's not why I'm here. I'm working with ChildrensOne to plan an event to raise money for the cancer ward."

"Oh!" Melinda said, putting her hand to her heart. "I am *so* sorry. Look at me, letting my passion for my cause get ahead of myself. Well, thank God Almighty for that. I worry every day for all the girls that we knew during our dark days."

I nodded, feeling like I was going to throw up.

Infertile.

She'd used the word *infertile*.

I had known it was a possibility for people who had gone through anorexia. But I'd never considered it for *myself*. Not once.

I needed to get out of here. I needed to get far away. Somewhere safe, where I could hyperventilate in privacy.

"It's so good to see you again, Melinda, but I'm actually late for a meeting," I lied.

She said something in return, but I hustled out of there as fast as I could. It wasn't until I was in the comfort of my own car that I curled into a ball and tried to keep breathing.

21

KATHERINE

The logical thing to do would have been to take a deep breath and let it all out. Then release the panic quickly settling into my body and try to move on. Maybe even think about why this frightened me so much.

But I rushed right past logic into undeniable, impossible, desperate fear. Panic-inducing, hyperventilating, choking dread. And I couldn't think and I couldn't speak and I couldn't feel. Not anything other than anxiety. There was nothing else, except that one question.

Am I infertile?

Tremors ran through my body. I didn't know. I didn't know the answer to that question. I hadn't been as bad as Melinda, but we'd all been in the same hospital. We'd gone to therapy together for a year after that. She knew all the pains I'd had at the time. There was a reason I'd sharply cut anyone from that time out of my life. I didn't want a constant reminder of what I'd done to myself and how hard I'd given up on everything.

The only people I still talked to who knew what had happened was my crew. They'd stuck with me through the worst of it and promptly never brought it up again after I demanded they stop babying me.

But now? Now, I felt like I was in free fall.

I hastily canceled my training session. There was no way I was going to be able to compartmentalize this before I saw Rodrigo. I didn't even know when I'd be able to put myself back together.

The Mercedes dropped me off at my building, and I took the elevator to my penthouse. I marched right over to the wet bar and poured myself a stiff drink. I slurped it down and then poured another. I felt slightly more fortified after the first and took the second over to the couch.

I pulled my MacBook into my lap and did the sensible thing—I Googled my symptoms.

After only a quick perusal, it was clear.

I was going to die a long, painful death.

As with most of the medical information on the internet, it went straight to the direst conclusion. Even as I knew that reading all of this wasn't going to make me feel any better, I couldn't seem to stop. I devoured the medical advice, read every story out there about women who were currently anorexic and unable to conceive, and women who had been ten years healthy and still unable to conceive. Then I tipped forward into a deep dive, reading everything I could about what it would be like to be pregnant after having an eating disorder and how all the anxiety could come back when the body started to gain weight. Worse yet, the mind knew it was irrational to have these fears of gaining weight when the women believed they should only be concentrating on the health of the baby. But if I'd learned anything, anorexia was a hundred percent mental. It didn't matter if a woman wasn't *supposed* to think of her weight during pregnancy. It only mattered that she did.

By the end of it, I felt like a wrung-out towel.

My emotions were leaking out of me and onto the floor. My pain a constant knife through my stomach. My eyes blurry with unshed tears.

This couldn't be happening.

Anxiety at its peek, I stumbled into my bedroom, shucked all of my clothes onto the floor, and stared at myself in the mirror, pinching the small pockets of fat on my hips and waist and thighs. I wasn't like before. I *wasn't*.

There was nothing wrong with me. I was just working out. I was still eating. In fact, I was working with a nutritionist now. She'd helped me figure out exactly what foods to eat to power my body through my training. This was healthy. Everyone had said so.

With a sigh, I stepped on the scale like I did every single morning. I looked at the number and frowned. I got back off and then did it again. Same number. See, I wasn't going crazy. That was a healthy weight. I was still within the BMI. On the low side, but not in the underweight section. I'd been *way* in the underweight section when I had to be hospitalized. *Way* below.

This was... this was fine.

Fine.

My fingers fumbled for the shower, and I let it rain down on me, turning my skin pink. A hiccup escaped my lips, and I sank onto the tiled floor. I curled my legs into my chest, wrapping my arms around them.

Then I let go.

My chest heaved as I sobbed. All of my fear and anger and waves and waves of distress came out in that cry session. My eyes ached. I felt like I couldn't get enough air in. Still, I couldn't stop.

I didn't want to look at why this hurt me so much. I knew

K.A. LINDE

why, but looking at it would make it a reality. I just needed to stay here in this shower until it was gone. Until all of it was gone.

I didn't know how long I'd stayed in there. But at some point, I got out, put on an oversize T-shirt, and cried myself to sleep.

I woke to a hand touching my shoulder. Who the hell was here?

"Katherine, are you okay?" Lark asked.

I saw the concern on her face. I tried to reach back in my mind to find out why she was here. Had we had plans? My brain wouldn't go back far enough to figure it out.

"Hey," I whispered.

Lark settled onto the bed. "Your eyes are swollen and bloodshot. Have you been crying?"

I slowly sat up and brushed my hair back out of my face. "Yeah," I whispered. "What are you doing here?"

"We were supposed to do dinner, remember?" Lark asked, alarm on her face. "What happened? Did you and Camden get in another fight?"

"Oh, right, dinner. Sorry." Now that she'd mentioned it, it came back. "No, I haven't seen Camden since Puerto Rico."

"You're worrying me, Ren," Lark said gently.

"Because of this?"

"Yes, but before that. You're not eating enough. You're losing weight like it's your job. You aren't... happy. I mean, before, you always hid your happiness behind your bravado. But now, you're not even hiding. I don't like this. I don't want to find you passed out in your room when you'd said you'd meet me. It scares me."

186

"I don't mean to scare you," I told her. I looked down at my fresh manicure and back up. "I saw a friend of mine at the hospital when I was there for the charity."

"Oh no, were they sick?"

"No." Then I considered it. "Also, yes. She was a girl that I went to therapy with when I was hospitalized after high school. She started this group for... women who are infertile."

Lark listened intently. I kept waiting for her to make a judgment. For her to jump to the same conclusion as I had. But she said nothing. Just let me speak.

I took a deep breath. "She thought that was why I was there. Because a large percentage of women who had to be hospitalized for anorexia... can't have children."

"How heartbreaking," Lark whispered.

She didn't ask the question, but I saw it in her eyes.

"And I don't know if I can," I said softly.

She put her hand on mine. "Are you trying to have a baby?"

"No," I said automatically. Then I ran a hand down my face, completely devoid of makeup. Not an ounce of armor up against the questions I had to answer to my best friend. "But... maybe."

"Well, I don't know if you're infertile, but I think maybe you should talk to Camden about this."

"No!" I shook my head. "No way. I am not talking to Camden about this."

She sighed in exasperation. "Why not? If you're trying to have a kid, shouldn't he know about potential setbacks? You could go to the doctor together. You don't even know if it's the case. You're just worst-case-scenario-ing the situation. And even if you *are,* if this is what you want, there are treatments you could try before giving up."

"I can't tell him."

"Katherine…"

"It was part of the contract," I rushed out.

"Oh."

"Yeah. I… I got his money. He got me… and a baby. He wanted to start trying a while ago, and I kept putting it off. We were still arguing. I wasn't ready. And now—" I choked back a sob. "Now, what if I can't have one? Does that null the contract? Would he do that?"

Lark pulled me against her, wrapping her arms around my shoulders. "I don't know what he would do, but I do know that it's going to be okay. No matter what happens, it is going to be okay. You have me. You have crew. You do not have to go through any of this alone, Katherine."

Another tear fell down my cheek as I sat with my best friend. "Thank you."

"Of course. I'm always here for you. If you don't want to tell Camden, I can go to the doctor with you. There are fertility tests. I'm sure we can figure something out."

"I don't… I don't trust any doctors. Not enough for it to not get back to him."

Lark sighed. "Seriously?"

I bit my lip. "Think about what he's capable of, Lark. He had Thomas's gambling ring raided. He set the whole thing up. He got English's old boss arrested by releasing footage from within the hotel in LA. He's ruthless."

"He did all of that to protect the people he cares about though."

"Maybe." I shrugged. "But do you think that he wouldn't find out I went to the doctor? That he wouldn't find out what I went for? Even with all the legal restrictions?"

Lark rubbed my shoulder and then slowly shook her head. "I think Camden gets whatever he wants."

"Yes."

"Okay." Lark tapped her lip twice. "What about Whitley?"

"She's a plastic surgeon."

"Exactly. He'd never give a second look to you going to see her. But she went to medical school. She's brilliant. I'm sure she can get tests ordered for you. You can trust her."

My heart leaped at the thought. I had never considered that. Camden would never suspect a thing if I went to see Whitley. She was my friend. Plus, I'd had enough work done that going to see a plastic surgeon was more run-of-the-mill than a fertility doctor.

"Okay," I finally said, "I'll talk to her."

"Good. Do you want me to call to get you in?"

I nodded.

She stood and reached for her phone.

"Hey, Lark. Thanks for being here."

"How many times have you been there for me?" Lark said with a smile. "I'll always be there for you, too."

I might not have a real family anymore. But I'd found family regardless.

22

KATHERINE

Whitley didn't have an open appointment until the next day at four thirty. It was technically a twenty-minute consultation, but Whit had just told Lark to book it. She didn't even seem surprised. Apparently, she had been waiting for me to move over to her practice.

Of course, Lark hadn't told her why I was really going in. I was the one who was going to have to deliver that shock. My stomach was in knots about it. Even though it was the right thing to do. It was the only actionable thing we'd come up with anyway.

I was wearing my armor for this meeting. After a professional blowout and a full face of makeup, I'd changed into a cowl-neck cashmere sweater over black leggings and thigh-high black boots. I'd paired it with a gray peacoat with gold buttons and a snakeskin bag. If I was going to confess my sins, I wanted to look the part.

Whitley's office was on Park only a few blocks from the MET. Actually, it was surprisingly close to Penn's apartment. I was glad that he was working, so I wouldn't be tempted to go by and see him. He was probably the last person I should tell about any of this. He'd think I was insane to even want children with Camden Percy especially after how he'd behaved in Puerto Rico. But he didn't know the circumstances of our arrangement, and I didn't particularly want to inform him. In all this time, I hadn't told anyone but Lark.

My phone buzzed as I entered the building and headed to the set of elevators. I glanced down at the name and sighed. Camden. Again. He'd been calling steadily all week. Never leaving a voicemail. Never sending me a text. How was I supposed to judge whether or not to call him back when he didn't let me know why he kept bothering me?

Despite present circumstances, I was still mad at him for what he'd done in Puerto Rico. I didn't want to talk to him. I wondered how many days he'd call before he got fed up with me for not answering and came to find me. Maybe I'd talk to him if he did that.

I rode the elevator to the fifth floor and entered into a well-lit reception.

A woman in scrubs looked up at me with a smile. "Hello. Welcome to The Plastic Surgery Institute. How can I help you?"

"Hi. I'm Katherine Van Pelt. I have an appointment with Whitley."

"Ah, yes, you're her four thirty. Here, fill out this paperwork and sign the release. Dr. Bowen will be right with you."

Dr. Bowen, right. Not just my crazy friend Whit.

I took the paperwork from the receptionist and dutifully filled it out. Though I left plenty of it blank, considering why I was really here was a secret, even from the doctor.

My wait was short. In a couple of minutes, Whitley appeared in the doorway with a smile on her face. Her caramel-colored hair had strands of blonde through it now.

I swore this girl changed her hair color more than anyone else I'd ever met in my life.

"Hey, Whit," I said, coming to my feet.

"It's about time." Whit nodded her head to the back for me to follow her, which I did. "I've been waiting for this moment."

I laughed. "You're ridiculous."

"Always. Oh, want to hear my latest story?" Whitley asked, suggestively raising her eyebrows up and down.

"God, do I?"

"It's tame! Promise."

"Tame? Like the woman who picked you up for a threesome with her husband or like the guy who followed you around for a few weeks, leaving presents at your work and home?"

"Hey, I almost had to get a restraining order for that guy."

"These are your levels of crazy—stalker or threesome."

Whitley shrugged. "That seems reasonable. This isn't that though."

"Well, let's hear it," I said.

She stopped me at a station. She used a thermometer to get my temperature, checked my pulse, and then gestured to the scale. "Let's get your weight.". I gulped and stepped on the scale. She looked down at the number on the scale and frowned. She jotted the number down without comment. "Let's move into a room."

I followed her inside a consultation room and took a seat in the large black chair that dominated the center of the room. Whitley was making notes in an iPad. She looked back up at me.

"Okay, so..." Whitley said, biting her lip. "Robert and I are talking again."

"What?" I asked in surprise. That was the last thing I'd expected. "But you said in Puerto Rico that he liked you more than you liked him."

"Yeah. I mean... we talked it out when I got back. I think maybe I overreacted."

My eyes bulged. "You are the definition of overreaction, Whit. And trust me, this is coming from someone who constantly overreacts. But you don't say those things about a guy that you want to get back together with."

"I don't know. He treats me right. I'm not sure I gave him a real chance."

"But I thought you and Gavin..." I trailed off at the horror on her face.

"What makes you think that?" she stammered out.

"Uh, the fact that you two were all over each other on New Year's?"

"We're always like that. It's not... anything. He's just"— she shrugged "Gavin."

"Uh-huh," I said in disbelief. "And he's friends with Robert."

"So?"

"So, he'll back off if you start dating Robert again because he's a good guy."

"Gavin King?" she asked with a laugh. "A good guy?"

I could see it in her eyes in that moment. She and Gavin had definitely hooked up. It had spooked her. Now, she was trying to distance herself from what had happened. Classic Whitley.

"Okay, Whit. If you say so."

I let the matter drop when she turned back to her iPad.

"Anyway," she said, stepping back over to me, "what are we doing today? Botox? Filler? We could do under-eye filler. It makes everyone look like they're in their twenties. We also have light therapy for your face. Though I've seen you without makeup, and you're flawless."

"That's what happens when your mother insists on a skin-care routine before you turn twelve."

"Well, she's smart. Everyone should do that." Whitley's eyes flicked to my chest. "Your boob job is incredible, too. You have a killer rack. I'm a little pissed that I didn't do it."

"Thanks. They were a present to myself."

"If they make you happy—and they should... fuck, look at them—that's all that matters."

I actually was pretty proud of my boob job. It had cost a fortune but was worth every single penny. I fucking loved my fake boobs. I didn't care what anyone else said. Sometimes, people tried to infer that having fake breasts made me somehow less of a woman or slutty or something. I didn't understand the connection. All it meant was that I had silicone in my body and I'd have perky breasts... forever.

"So, where should we start?" Whitley asked eagerly.

"Actually, I kind of came for something else."

She raised her eyebrow. "Butt implants? You really could use a bigger ass."

I couldn't stop the laugh. "No. No, not butt implants. I like having a small ass, thank you. It's actually, um... a more serious matter."

"Lark didn't tell me what this was about."

"I asked her not to." I looked down at my hands. Fuck, I was not looking forward to explaining this. I'd had levity with Whitley to get me into this chair. Now, I had to tell her something almost no one else knew about me.

"You look scared shitless. Do I need to sit down?" Whitley asked, putting on her doctor voice for me. "Should we both sit over here?"

I shook my head. "No. I can tell you. I just... haven't told anyone this before who wasn't there at the time."

"Doctor-patient confidentiality. Anything you say to me here will never leave this room."

I swallowed and nodded. "Right. Okay. So, during high school, a lot of shit went down with my father when he was arrested, and then... well, my brother disappeared, and my mom became a zombie. I kind of took the brunt of it all, and to cope, I started trying to be perfect."

Whitley nodded encouragingly. I could already see the sympathy in her eyes, as if she knew where this was going.

"Long story short, I was hospitalized and told that I had anorexia. I was there for six weeks until they got me back on my feet. I attended group therapy for the next year and therapy for years after."

"That's good that you got help," she said. "Are you worried that you have it again? Your weight is... low. Lower than I thought it would be."

"I, um... no, I think I'm good. I'm working with a nutritionist and trying to stay on top of it."

Whitley frowned. "Maybe you should start therapy again, just in case."

"I'm worried I'm infertile," I blurted out.

"Okay," she said, completely serious.

This wasn't Whitley Bowen, the bisexual flirt who ran her love interests in circles. The pixie who did shots until she kicked her shoes off and danced her heart out. This wasn't story time. She was a doctor.

"I see. Tell me why you think this. You and Camden have been trying, I assume. How long have you been trying? How long have you been off birth control?"

"Um, no, I'm still on birth control."

She furrowed her brow. "I'm confused."

"We're not trying, but we're talking about it. I just... I saw a girl that I knew who had found out she was infertile, and it freaked me out. I wanted to... I don't know... do a test to see if I am."

"You're not even trying yet? Why do you think you would be then? When was your last menstrual cycle?"

"I don't know," I admitted. "I don't have one on the birth control I use."

"Did you lose you period for more than three months when you were underweight?"

I nodded, feeling sick. "For almost a year."

"Did it come back after you were a healthy weight again?"

"Yes. It was slow to come back, and then I got on birth control. But I just... want to get tested. I need to know," I insisted. "Lark said you could help."

"Katherine," Whitley said gently, "there are plenty of tests for this. Do you want my professional opinion or what I really think?"

"Um... both?"

"Professional opinion: go to a fertility doctor. I can recommend one. She's the best in the business and a friend. She's discreet."

"Okay."

Whitley sank into her hip and gave me a look that I recognized as, *Here it comes.* "What I really think is, you need to throw out your birth control, go home, and fuck your husband." I opened my mouth to object, but she kept going, "Fuck him *a lot.* Fuck him all the time. Download an ovulation app, if you haven't already, and figure out when you can conceive. Fuck all day on those days. Take off work and fuck day and night. The practice is the fun part. If you don't get pregnant in three months, come back and see me."

"Seriously?" I asked. "That's your advice?"

"Yes! There could be something wrong with you. But if you have no symptoms, except a history of anorexia and a friend with the condition, I think that you're scaring yourself with worst-case scenarios. Most people who heal from anorexia go on to have a perfectly healthy body with therapy and can conceive. I think you should give your body a chance before you tell it that it's broken." She put her hand on my shoulder. "Go home and fuck Camden. Let's do interventions when the need arises."

"I think he's probably going to be confused if I show up at his place and demand he fuck me."

Whitley laughed. "What person in their right mind would be confused by that? I sure as hell wouldn't."

"You're a good friend."

"Damn straight." She walked back over to the counter and pulled out a prescription pad. "Here, let me write you a note."

She scribbled on it and handed it over to me.

I read the prescription, *Have lots of sex. Doctor's orders.*

I shook my head. "Am I supposed to give this to him?"

"If he's confused, you can set him straight."

I'd come in, terrified to admit these things, and I was leaving with a prescription to have sex. Either Whitley was the craziest doctor in the world or the best one.

"You really think nothing is wrong?"

"I think everything that is *currently* wrong... is in your head, which is a terrifying place to be on a good day."

"Can't argue that."

Whitley crossed her arms and leaned back against the counter. "If something else *is* wrong, we can cross that bridge when we get there. I'll be here for it, too. Okay?"

"Thank you."

"Of course. If you ever need doctor's advice though," Whitley said, "you can just call. You don't have to make an appointment."

I laughed and stood from the chair, stuffing the note in my purse. "I'll keep that in mind."

"Hey, and if you want to fill me in on how it goes, I'm an excellent listener. I love sex details."

"Jesus Christ," I muttered under my breath. "I love you, you crazy bitch."

"Love you, too. Now, go get some ass!"

I snorted and left the office, somehow feeling better even though we hadn't done anything that I'd expected. But Whitley had put it all in perspective. She had figured out a way to talk to me that the plethora of information on the internet hadn't been able to convey.

Maybe there was something wrong with me, but I wouldn't know that until I tried. And if I was freaking out this much about not being able to have kids, did that mean I *wanted* kids? Did that mean I wanted them now?

Fuck, I really did need to talk to Camden. He'd been calling me all week, and I'd never answered. Which meant he wanted to talk to me, too. I knew he wouldn't apologize for how he'd acted in Puerto Rico, but maybe we could come to some common ground.

It'd be good to get it all out in the open instead of constantly hurting each other. Either way, he had a right to know what was going on with me. Even if I didn't want to tell him. And I really, *really* didn't want to tell him.

Still, I swallowed my pride and took the Mercedes back to Percy Tower. He should be home by now.

The car dropped me off, and I took the elevator upstairs. I couldn't stop fidgeting the whole way up. My stomach felt like it had bees buzzing around in it. I had no idea how he was going to react to this news especially because I had kept the hospitalization from him in the first place. He'd likely be pissed, but I was tired of running from my past. I had decided on Camden for the long haul. Maybe it was time to cash in on that promise.

The elevator dinged open on the top floor, and I stepped into the Percy residence. I only took a few steps before stopping in my tracks. Camden stood in the living room with his hands in his pockets. A woman stood across from him.

My stomach dropped straight through my body. Fiona was here. Camden's eyes lifted to mine, and for a second, I saw horror cross his expression. Then Fiona turned around to face me, and I saw why.

She was *pregnant.*

23

CAMDEN

Well, fuck.

Of all the bad times for Katherine to walk into my house. Now had to be the fucking *worst* time for her to choose. I could see on her beautiful face the realization that she must have come to when she saw Fiona's slightly rounded stomach. It was going to be like dropping an atomic bomb in my living room.

"What the fuck is going on?" Katherine demanded. She clutched her bag close to her chest, as if it would protect her from what she was seeing. Or maybe she just wanted better leverage to swing it.

"This isn't what it—" I began.

"Really?" she snapped. "This isn't what it looks like? Rich."

She rolled her eyes and then narrowed them on Fiona, who had, as of yet, said nothing. She stood there like a deer in headlights. She certainly hadn't been expecting to see my wife when she asked if she could come over. I hadn't seen Katherine in weeks. She had been avoiding me at all costs after what went down on that beach on her birthday.

"I can't even fucking believe this." Katherine shook her head as she glared at me. "That you would be careless enough to let this happen." Then to Fiona, she said, "That you would show your fucking face here."

"And why shouldn't I?" Fiona asked, finding her voice. Which was not a good thing. She should have kept her mouth shut and let me handle this.

"Because the man who knocked you up is married to *me*." She seethed, taking a dangerous step forward. "What exactly do you expect to happen? Besides humiliation."

"Katherine," I warned.

"Oh no, you can shut the fuck up right now." She pointed her finger at me. "I will deal with you later."

"You will deal with me now," I growled.

"Fine. *Fine*." Her eyes narrowed. "You act like I'm not trustworthy, get mad at me in Puerto Rico, say you can almost trust *me*. Then you do this shit? Camden, you are the epitome of hypocrisy. You act high and mighty when we're together, but on the side, you're fucking this half-wit."

"Hey!" Fiona called.

Katherine waved her away as inconsequential. "And you're not even smart enough to wrap it up? We're fucking arranged. So, sure, do whatever you want. But that didn't include embarrassing your fucking name and everyone associated with it. If you wanted to knock up your slutty side piece, then you shouldn't have married me."

"Are you quite through?" I asked in irritation.

"I have every right to scream my head off, Camden Percy. You did over a fucking birthday present, and now, you expect me to just roll over when your mistress shows up *pregnant*? I don't think so."

"God, you're such an insufferable bitch," Fiona crowed.

Katherine laughed in her face. "Why? For pointing out

the truth? It's amazing how often women are called bitches to shut them up. Call me a bitch, Fiona. I don't give a fuck. But I'm not sitting down and shutting up when you show up *pregnant*."

"Maybe you should just shut up," Fiona said. "I don't need to deal with this."

Katherine ignored her and looked at me again, putting the full weight of her wrath into the heat in her eyes. "I fucking *knew* you were together on Halloween. It's three months later, and look." She gestured to Fiona's stomach. "You *lied* to me."

"I'm not a liar," I told her with venom. "Fiona and I were not together on Halloween."

"Fine. The day before, the day after," she said. "Semantics. You knocked her up."

"Why would you even care?" Fiona asked. "You were the one who watched us walk out together and did nothing."

"I really don't want to hear anything out of your insipid mouth."

But that was what had happened. I had told Court that if Katherine cared, she would send Fiona away, out of her Halloween party. Instead, Katherine had done nothing. She'd turned her back on me when I went to see Fiona, and I'd gone to see her just to get a rise out of my wife. But I hadn't. Apparently, it took Fiona being pregnant to finally get a rise out of Katherine Van Pelt. Who knew?

"Why *do* you care?" I asked.

"What the fuck does that mean?" she snarled.

"I haven't seen you in weeks, and before Puerto Rico, we'd only been together for official engagements."

She ignored Fiona entirely as she took a step toward me. Her gaze was withering. "Imagine for a second, Camden dear, that I showed up at your apartment, pregnant by another man." She twirled her fingers. "Say Penn, for instance."

My hands clenched into fists at my sides. The thought sent me into a quick death spiral. It made me want to charge out of this room and beat Kensington until his face was a patchwork of blood and bruises. I couldn't even imagine stopping there. I'd kill him. I'd fucking kill him.

"Precisely," Katherine said as if she could read the thoughts so evident in my body language. "You'd freak the fuck out. Just like you did on New Year's! And I have every fucking right to tell you that I want you both dead for this."

And she meant it.

Her eyes had always been a window to her emotions. She kept them so guarded. Sometimes, I didn't even think that I could read her. But right now... right now, she meant death. Ruin. Obliteration. She'd leave me over this. Abolish our contract, walk away from me and my money and my obligations, and never, ever look back.

It was in my nature to say nothing. I had always prided myself on being the type of person who yielded results. My methods were unorthodox, but actions spoke louder than words. I didn't have to explain myself. Not to fucking anyone. I'd lived like this for so long that, somehow, even Katherine believed that I'd knocked up Fiona.

Because I'd let her believe it. I'd let her think Fiona and I were together this whole time. That I preferred her to my wife. That I was every inch the bastard she painted me as.

I wasn't a good person or the pinnacle of virtue, but I wasn't the person she thought I was either. And I was tired of seeing that in her eyes. After Court and I had talked about the Ireland deal, I'd realized that I needed to make this right with Katherine. I'd tried calling her all week. I hadn't been surprised that she was ignoring me. I'd been planning to track her down after this meeting with Fiona. But then... life had a funny way of throwing me under the bus.

I was done letting her believe the worst of me.

"We didn't sleep together on Halloween, before or after," I told her flatly. "And I didn't knock her up. One, I am not that careless. And two, I would never do that to you."

She paused at my words. The sincerity in them. "I don't believe you."

"Fiona," I snarled. She jumped at my voice. The command in it. "Tell her."

"Camden," she whispered.

"Now," I demanded. "Right now."

Fiona crossed her arms over her chest and stared at the floor. "Personally, I'd be fine with letting you think that we've been sleeping together all this time and that it's Camden's baby."

"But..." I ground out.

"But... it's not," she said in a huff. She lifted her gaze to mine. "Camden and I are just... friends."

"Bullshit," Katherine swore. "You've been sleeping together for years. You were sleeping together before we got together."

"We did," she said, withdrawing into herself. "Even up until... I don't know, August?" She looked to me for confirmation, but I didn't say or do anything. "We stopped when it was clear that he was only using me to get back at you."

Katherine's jaw dropped slightly at the words. She stared at Fiona as if she had sprouted a second head.

"So, now, we're just friends," Fiona said with bite in her voice. "Are you happy? You've taken everything from me. Just like you take everything from every other person you come in contact with. You're a disease."

"Fiona," I growled.

"She is!" Fiona spat. "She ruins everyone's life. Even yours, Camden. Especially yours. We had it good before you decided on this stupid arranged marriage."

"That's enough," I said in a voice that silenced her completely. "If my life were perfect before, then why did I choose Katherine?"

Katherine looked back and forth between us, as if she, too, wanted the answer to that question. I'd never been forthright with why I'd picked her. We'd come to an agreement quickly, but it hadn't been love between us. I still didn't know what was between us. I just knew that I'd wanted Katherine, and when the opportunity had arisen for me to claim her, I hadn't thought twice about the answer.

"I have no idea," Fiona said. "Baffles me to this day."

"Because she's the one that I want."

Tears pricked at Fiona's eyes, and she looked away from me. "I know," she whispered. "But I don't understand it."

Neither did I.

Neither did Katherine.

But it was the way it was.

I turned back to my wife. "I found out about Fiona's pregnancy right after Thanksgiving. She has been out of the public eye since then. Both because she wasn't sure if she wanted to keep the baby and because I assumed, as you did, that most people would think it was mine. And it is not."

"Is that why you answered her call on New Year's?" Katherine asked.

"Yes."

Fiona looked between us in anger. "Just tell her I was going to get an abortion, Camden. She can't think any less of me."

"She obviously didn't go through with it, but it was

supposed to happen on New Year's. That's why she called. To tell me she couldn't do it."

Katherine's eyes stayed on mine, as if she was trying to find the trick in my words. As if she couldn't believe everything that I was telling her. That it all felt too far-fetched.

How could I expect her to forgive me? I'd blown up on her on her birthday for talking to Penn. I'd let her believe that Fiona and I were together for months after I stopped seeing her. I'd wanted to hurt her, to elicit a reaction out of my ice-princess wife.

Now that I was giving her the whole truth, I didn't know if it was enough.

From her expression, it wasn't enough.

And I was going to lose her for good.

24

KATHERINE

"Let's say that I believe you," I said in a way that meant that I really, *really* didn't believe them. Because, right now, I had no idea what to believe. Fiona was pregnant, standing in Camden's apartment. What was I supposed to think? "If it's not your baby, whose is it?"

"That... is not my story to tell," Camden said with a glance to Fiona.

"Don't look at me," Fiona said. "She has no right to know anything. I didn't even want her to know that I was pregnant."

"She won't believe me unless you tell her."

Fiona shrugged. "That's not my problem, Cam. I don't owe her shit."

I cringed at the nickname she'd used. Camden was not the kind of person who had a nickname. He was only ever Camden. Not Cam. I hated that she'd called him that. That it felt so unlike him, and he hadn't even flinched.

"No, but you owe me," he said evenly.

She gritted her teeth. "She has a huge fucking mouth. She'll tell Harmony."

"She will not," he told her. "They don't get along as it is."

"Wait," I said in confusion. "Wait... I know who Harmony is dating."

Fiona's eyes went wide. "Shit."

"The father is Kurt Mitchell?"

"I did *not* say that," Fiona said, backing up a step.

"Jesus Christ, that guy fucks every girl on the Upper East Side, doesn't he?" I said with a shake of my head.

Harmony had claimed that Kurt was cleaned up and working for his father. I'd even joked and said bad boys were more fun. But I hadn't meant *this*.

"Yes," Camden replied, "he does."

Fiona glared at him. "Don't say a fucking word."

"What? That you should have known better?" he asked with cool malice in his voice. "That you should have expected a guy like Kurt Mitchell to fuck you and leave you?"

"Someone needs to tell Harmony that he's still a sleazeball," I interjected. "Obviously, he had no qualms fucking you while he was with Harm."

"I didn't *know* they were dating when we met," Fiona fumed.

"Oh, please, as if that would have stopped you," I spat. "You clearly have a type—unavailable men."

"Pot, meet kettle."

"Whatever."

She wasn't *wrong*. Not exactly, which made it all the worse. It wasn't that I'd had a thing for attached guys. It was that I'd always had a thing for Penn. Whether or not he was with someone didn't matter much to me. But... that wasn't reality anymore.

"The important thing here is that you believe that the baby isn't mine," Camden said. His eyes burned through me.

He seemed adamant about this, which was so unlike him. It almost made me believe him. "Who the father is and all the rest... doesn't really matter. Just that you believe me."

Fiona huffed.

"So... say the baby is Kurt's. Say you knew about this at Thanksgiving and she called you on New Year's because she couldn't go through with an abortion," I said, laying out the facts. "What the fuck is she doing here *now*?"

I gestured to Fiona, who stood nearby, protectively hugging her stomach, as if she thought I might lunge at her or something. They were both silent for a minute. I watched them exchange a long look. One I didn't particularly care for, but I could see they were having a conversation in that look. Deciding what to tell me.

"She's here for me to deal with it," he finally said.

I scrunched up my brows. "Huh?"

Fiona looked like she was going to explode. "Camden!"

"Just tell her, Fiona. I'm tired of this charade."

Fiona turned away from us both, as if his words hurt so much that she couldn't even look at him. "I don't have to do this. I'm leaving. Just... take care of it."

Then without another word, she disappeared, rushing toward the elevator. I didn't move or demand she stay. I was so confused. I didn't know whether or not to even believe anything that they'd said. I *wanted* to believe that they weren't together and that the baby wasn't his, but it felt too good to be true. I was willing to take them at their word.

"Kurt won't take responsibility," Camden told me. "He won't help, and he's calling her a liar. He called her a whore."

I shrugged. "What are you going to do about it?"

"What I do best. I handle shit, Katherine."

I couldn't argue that. Camden did handle shit. I'd seen

him do it on multiple occasions. Of course, I didn't know what that meant here. Was he going to threaten Kurt? Did he have some kind of blackmail on the guy? How far would he take this for Fiona? And why?

But I didn't ask any of those questions. Instead, I sank into a chair and put my head in my hands. "How did we get here, Camden?"

I waited for him to say some smart-ass response, but after a minute, he came and sat on the couch across from me. "Because we're both strong-willed and stubborn."

I choked on a laugh. "Understatement of the century."

"And we both have pasts that we haven't walked away from."

I looked up at him. Those were words I'd never thought I'd hear him say. Usually, when we talked about our pasts, he just got pissed off that I'd even had one. And I couldn't even stomach the thought of him with Fiona. Even when I was mad at him... even when I hated him, I still didn't *like* it.

"Why did we think we could make this work?" I whispered.

He didn't flinch from the question. "Because when we agreed, this was just an arrangement."

I raised my eyebrows. "And what is it now?"

"A marriage."

A breath escaped me. It was, wasn't it? Somehow, it wasn't what we'd agreed to anymore. We'd both crossed that line too many times. The line was blurry, brushed-over chalk.

"Would you like a drink?" Camden asked.

"No," I said, reaching between us and taking his hand. His eyes widened slightly. "I want us to talk."

He wavered for a minute, as if a drink would calm him, steady him. But he relented. "All right."

I released his hand and sat back. He looked down at where I'd released him. "I don't want us to argue. I just want the truth... from both of us. I'm tired of dodging and parrying here."

"Katherine Van Pelt tired of emotionally fencing?" he asked with a smirk. "Now, I've heard everything."

"Just with you," I amended. "Or at least... just for now."

"Ah, a truce?"

I shook my head. "I don't think that works. What happened in Puerto Rico only happened because we were ignoring the source of the problem."

"I thought you quite liked what had happened in Puerto Rico," he said, his voice laced with command that thrilled my body.

I cleared my throat. "Be that as it may... I still ended up alone in the sand."

"On your birthday."

"Yes."

"Without a New Year's kiss."

"Yes," I repeated, clenching my jaw.

"That should not have happened."

"Is that an apology?"

"It's a statement of fact. I was mad at the situation with Fiona, and then, when I saw you with Penn, I just lost it."

"I noticed that," I told him. "Can we go back to Fiona? You really haven't been together?"

"Not since the raid on the gambling hall."

My jaw dropped. "That was in August, Camden."

"I'm aware."

"But why?" I gasped out.

"I realized it was too easy to leave Fiona behind. My instinct was to protect you, which was what I did. Fiona was pissed at me for leaving her there that night. She had to find her own way. I decided that it was best to cut ties then."

"Why didn't you tell me? Why did you let me believe that you were together?"

"You never asked."

I narrowed my eyes at him. "Should I have to ask if my husband is seeing his mistress?"

"I am accustomed to letting people think whatever they want of me. It serves me in business for my adversaries to believe that I'm ruthless and above the law. Whether or not that is true is another matter. One that doesn't actually have any bearing on reality."

"But this isn't business," I said, my voice rising. I couldn't keep it down. I'd said that I didn't want to argue with him, and here I was. I tried to breathe and focus on the present. I bit my lip until it hurt before speaking again, "Don't you think it would have been different if you'd just told me?"

"I'm telling you now."

"It would have been easier to believe you weren't the father if you'd told me you hadn't been sleeping together months ago," I ground out.

"I had no idea that she would be foolish enough to get pregnant."

I tipped my head up in exasperation. This was going nowhere. I had to take him on faith. Either he was or wasn't the father to that baby in Fiona's stomach. Fiona had all but said that it was Kurt's baby. She'd seemed genuinely afraid underneath her bitchy veneer. If it were Camden's, wouldn't she have thrown it in my face? Wouldn't she have shown up well before this to let me know?

In some way, her coming here to get Camden's help actually... made sense. It was crazy to even consider, but Fiona and Camden were a bit like how I felt about me and Penn.

Penn was my person. I'd known him since I was young. He'd always been there for me. The person I'd thought I'd always end up with.

And while Fiona and Camden hadn't known each other that long, they'd been together before Camden and I had decided to try this thing out. She had taken the news that we were together about as well as I did when learning that Penn was with Natalie. Which was to say, terribly, *burning the world to cinders* terrible. When things went bad, I turned to Penn. When things went bad for Fiona, she turned to Camden.

How strange it was that a pregnancy was what made me realize the connection. Made me actually... understand Fiona. I didn't like understanding her, but it didn't stop the fact that I did.

"What are you thinking?" he asked.

"You're Fiona's Penn," I said softly, knowing the words would draw backlash.

He frowned and withdrew like I'd hit him. "I don't particularly like the comparison." He gritted his teeth. "Though I do see what you mean."

"If I were in Fiona's position, the first person I would have turned to was Penn."

Camden's hands balled into fists. "I like that comparison even less."

I held up a hand. "I'm just saying that Fiona turns to you when things are hard, like I used to do with Penn. I guess... I kind of understand why she was here, asking you to deal with Kurt."

"Are you saying that you believe I'm not the father?"

I slowly nodded. "I guess I am."

"Good." He stood and held his hand out to me. I let him lift me to my feet. "Now, my question." I raised an eyebrow.

"I've been trying to call you all week. You've ignored all my calls. Why did you decide to come here today?"

I swallowed. Oh, right. The real reason that I'd hurried over here after my doctor's appointment. Now that the time was here and we finally had so much out in the open, I clammed up. I didn't know if I was ready to tell him. Telling Whitley had been hard enough.

"I think I'll take that drink," I said with a half-smile.

He shot me that knowing look. "One drink, and then you will be as forthright as I was."

"Okay," I told him as he walked across the room to the wet bar.

I was not ready for this conversation, but I knew that it was time to put it all on the table.

25

KATHERINE

Camden returned with two glasses of scotch. The good stuff. I didn't normally drink scotch, but it felt appropriate for the moment. I took the drink out of his hand and took a small sip, letting the heat burn through me.

Here goes nothing.

"I went to the doctor today."

He had just settled into his seat and came half out of it again at my words. "What's wrong? Are you okay?"

"I'm fine." I gestured him back into his seat. He reluctantly sat, but his gaze still weighed on me heavily. "I think."

"You think?"

I took a deep breath. This was going to be fun. "I'm worried that I can't have a baby."

Camden stilled completely. "What?"

"I... I think earlier complications in my life might have made me infertile. So, I went to the doctor."

"What did they say?" he asked, his voice suddenly low and almost... afraid?

"Nothing." I laughed sardonically and ran a hand back through my hair. After another gulp of the scotch, I continued, "They told me to stop taking my birth control and to go home and have sex. That I was stressing myself out."

"That's bullshit. If you're afraid, they should test you," he demanded.

"Yes, well, I went to see Whitley."

"She's a plastic surgeon," he said in exasperation.

"I know, but she went to med school, and I trust her. I just needed an opinion. I can get a second. She said she'd recommend a fertility doctor if I wanted it."

He downed the rest of the scotch and then set it aside. His eyes were steely. "We haven't even started trying, Katherine. You made it seem that you didn't even want a baby... or that you weren't ready. What brought this on?"

I bit my lip and looked away. "I saw a friend yesterday who is infertile."

Camden touched my chin, dragging my face back to meet his dark eyes. "What does that have to do with you?"

"We were... in therapy together." I gulped. "After we were hospitalized for anorexia. She'd... she'd lost so much weight that even when she was better, she couldn't have kids. It broke up her marriage."

Camden hadn't even blinked at those words—*therapy, hospitalized, anorexia.* "And you think you will be the same?"

"Maybe," I whispered. "You seem very... calm about all of this."

"You think I didn't know that you were hospitalized?"

I wrenched back in shock. His hand dropped from my chin. All warmth fled me. "What?"

"Katherine, we were getting married."

"The records were expunged," I gasped out. "No one should be able to access them."

"I'm very thorough."

"No," I whispered. "There's no way. No one knows what

happened to me. No one but the crew and my parents. My mother made sure that all evidence disappeared."

He shrugged, unconcerned. "I had to make sure I knew the woman I was marrying."

I stood. My mind was reeling. On one hand, it was good that I didn't have to explain what had happened. But on the other, he had violated my privacy. What else had he looked at when he agreed to marry me? What else did he know that I'd wanted to keep from the world?

"You should have told me," I said. "Just because you read some hospital papers doesn't mean that you know what I went through."

"You were kept in a private ward for eating disorder patients for six weeks."

I clenched my hands into fists. "Yes, against my *will*."

"Ah," he said softly. "That's why you hate hospitals and have to be in control."

"I don't *always* have to be in control."

He raised an eyebrow, but I ignored his look.

"Those six weeks were a nightmare," I told him. "They say they saved my life. They don't say what they took from me."

I strode away from him, the anger still rushing through me. It ached that he'd known about my hospitalization from the start. He shouldn't have known, and yet he did. Was that why he asked about my food choices so often? He'd done it on the night of our anniversary. He'd looked at me strange in Puerto Rico.

He came up behind me, running his hands down my arms and drawing me against him. He pressed a kiss into my hair. I wanted to yank away from him, but... I didn't. He'd gone behind my back to get information about me. But he didn't appear to think any less of me. In fact, he was...

comforting me. I never would have guessed this of Camden Percy.

"Don't run from me," he said against my hair. "I've seen the worst of you, Katherine, and I'm still right here."

I closed my eyes. Those words held power. A power that had nothing to do with his dominating personality and everything to do with... safety. I was safe here with him in this moment. He'd seen my fall, and he'd caught me.

"I want you," he breathed a second later.

"You do?" I whispered into the empty apartment.

"Yes."

"What if I can't have a baby?" My deepest fear spoken aloud.

"I'll still want you," he confessed.

I swallowed. I couldn't believe this was happening. That Camden Percy was saying these words. That he cared about me. That we were here right now.

"Okay." I leaned back into his chest, letting him draw me flush against his body. "Okay."

His breath moved to my ear, where he placed a soft kiss. "But it won't come to that. We can figure it out together. There are so many options in front of us."

"You're right," I agreed.

His lips landed on the sensitive spot right below my ear. "I love when you say that."

"Ass," I muttered, even as I tilted my head to the side. He dragged my hair over my shoulder and trailed kisses down my neck. "Katherine," he said, tightening his grip.

"Hmm?"

"I want you to move back in."

I stilled under his careful ministrations. I hadn't lived here since it had all fallen apart between us. I stayed carefully sequestered at my own penthouse. Thankful that I'd never gotten rid of the place even though others thought it strange that we had two residences.

"I don't want you to stay in your place anymore," he continued. "I want you here, in my home, with me." He drew the strap of my dress down and kissed my shoulder. "In my bed."

I shivered at the words. "Camden..."

"Say yes, Katherine. Just say yes."

God, wasn't he offering me so much more than I'd ever thought I'd get from him? I'd thought I was marrying the devil. Well, I supposed that I had. But perhaps he was the devil I could live with. The devil I could even... come to love.

"Yes." The word released from my lips. "Yes."

He spun me around until I was facing him. I looked up into those dark, depthless eyes. My heart beat furiously in my chest. I felt like everything was shifting between us. That nothing would ever be the same.

"Do you have your birth control with you?" he asked.

"Uh, yeah," I said, surprised by the question.

"Go get it."

I narrowed my eyes at him, but he didn't even blink. I walked back to where I'd discarded my purse. I plucked out the small packet of birth control. The piece of paper that Whitley had given me sat on top of everything else. I wavered for a second and then grabbed that, too.

He took them both out of my hands. "What's this?"

"Prescription from Whitley," I said.

He flipped the paper over and read what Whitley had written. He cracked a smile and shook his head. "I think I will keep this prescription for rainy days," he said, stuffing it into his pocket.

"What are you doing with—" I began.

But he was already heading toward the kitchen where he

opened the drawer for the trash and casually tossed my pills inside. My mouth dropped open.

"Camden!" I gasped. "You can't just throw away my birth control pills."

"You don't need those." He strode back over to me and pulled me into a hard kiss. "The doctor said to get rid of your pills and have sex with your husband."

"Yeah, but..."

"Katherine, you want a baby," he said, looking deep into my eyes. "That's what this is all about. Let's stop pretending otherwise. I'm happy to follow the doctor's orders."

I blinked. "You are?"

"Yes. I am more than ready to fuck you."

"I thought you were waiting until I earned it," I reminded him.

"Oh, darling, you've earned it," he said, his voice raw and throaty.

I shivered at the words. Finally.

He crooked a finger at me. A half-smile on his perfect lips. "Come here."

He retreated a step at a time, and I uncertainly followed him into the rec room. The room was dark, lit only by recessed lights in the ceiling to illuminate the poker and pool tables.

He stopped me in front of the pool table and twirled his finger. I turned in place, taking direction without comment. He tugged off my jacket, then gradually pulled my shirt over my head. My boots and leggings followed until I was in nothing but La Perla panties.

"Do you remember the first thing you said to me when we started this?" he asked as he gathered up my long, dark hair into his hand. Then, he twisted it into a fist and pulled my head back, baring my neck.

"Yes," I chirped.

He placed a kiss on my neck. I whimpered against his touch. I did remember, but I didn't know why he was asking.

"What did you say?" he asked, completely in control but somehow gentler than I'd ever heard one of his commands.

"I said... you were an insufferable ass, and your money couldn't buy you everything."

"I decided in that moment that I wanted to break you." His voice was a sensuous brush against my skin. His hand slid down my stomach, enhancing that touch.

I huffed in a breath. Break me. He wanted to *break* me.

His hands slipped to the front of my panties, sliding just under the lacy material. I wanted to force his hand lower, but I knew he'd stop.

"I'm sure you think that I meant I wanted to break you—body, mind, and, spirit." He moved an inch lower, pressing just one digit to my waiting clit. My body was on fire. My mind trying to stay present. "Truth be told, I wanted all those things. But mainly, your will. That thing that writhed under your skin and came out with a vengeance anytime I talked to you."

He slicked his finger through my wetness and began to lazily circle my clit. I was caught between wanting to argue and wanting this so fucking bad. But I couldn't stop my mouth from retaliating.

"My will could never be broken," I ground out.

He didn't stop at the words. Just breathed a laugh against my neck and pushed his fingers down so he could tease the opening to my pussy. "Oh, I could have broken your will, but I realized that as it fractured, I didn't want that. I didn't want you to become a shell of yourself."

"What do you want?" I barely managed to get the words out as he slipped a finger inside of me.

"I want to shatter your mask," he whispered against my skin. "I want to break down all those walls you put up against the world. So, when you look at me, the only thing I see is the real Katherine Van Pelt and not the pretender who parades around the Upper East Side."

He released me, and I stumbled forward against the pool table. I gasped slightly at the loss of him, coupled with his words. How had he done this to me? My walls were down. Any I'd had left disintegrated at our conversation. I'd spent so long building them that I hadn't known if I could even take them down.

"You've succeeded," I breathed, turning slowly to look at him. "It's just me."

He cupped my cheek, firm but tender. "Good."

Camden released me long enough to undress, and I watched his glorious body materialize. The gorgeous contours of his chest, the tempting V at his waist, the powerful structure of his legs, the muscular arms that so often held me in command. Everything I wanted. Just not what I'd known. Not with all my walls. Not as we had been. Finally, he stepped out of his boxers, revealing his cock to me.

I stepped forward, eager for him.

"Touch me," he said before I could get myself in trouble.

I took his cock in my hand and ran it down the smooth, strong length. At my touch, his cock was hard and pulsing. He was as ready for me as I was for him.

Camden immediately grew impatient. He hefted me up and set me down on the pool table—at the perfect height for his taking.

"I've wanted this for so long," he told me.

I saw sincerity in his eyes. He actually wanted this. Not just sex, but... me. Camden Percy wanted me. Just me.

His hand slipped between us, parting my lips and making sure I was ready. I groaned and leaned back on my elbows.

"You're going to let me take care of you from now on," he told me.

I nodded. With his hand between my thighs, his cock poised to take me, there was no other response.

Then he positioned himself at my entrance, and it felt momentous. He was in control, but this... this wasn't like before. This was something new. No condom between us. No birth control. While I knew none of it worked instantaneously, I felt the difference between us. This was a choice, and we were choosing it.

"Please," I begged him.

Something feral lit in his expression. I'd begged. He gripped me harder as if the words had made him want me more. What had I given up by refusing to beg him?

And I found out.

He entered me in one swift movement. His cock burying deep, deep, deeper until I thought I was going to collapse from the sheer force of him. He stayed there a second, as if breathing me in. The feel of me wrapped all around him. His eyes met mine, cool and hungry.

Then he began a bruising pace. He was in control. He would always be in control here. And I wanted him to be. I wanted this.

"More," I gasped.

He hauled my ass against the wood so that I was all but hanging off the edge of the table, giving him better leverage as he thrust into me over and over again. I lay back against the green felt. My body rocked every time he plunged into me. Then he gripped my hands, pinning them to the table. I was immobile, at his whim, and a fire burned through my core.

This was fucking and so, so much more than fucking. I couldn't look away from his face as everything came into sharp clarity. I could feel him draw close. And I knew what I was going to scream into the empty room.

"Oh fuck, Camden! Yes, I'm so close. Please, please, more. Just please, don't stop."

And for a second, I thought he would stop just to hear me beg him to continue. But he was too close. He'd waited this long for me. The next time would be devoted to my sexual torment. Another time, I'd get welts across my bottom and thighs for my perfect insubordination. Perhaps he'd even choke me to remind me who was in charge. I was ready for it all. Right now though, I felt like I was going to black out as the pleasure hit me head-on.

I came, crying out his name over and over again until it became a whimper. He continued to pummel inside of me as my walls contracted around his cock. My orgasm shuddered to a close, but he still pushed me and pushed me. Harder and faster still. Then, his eyes rolled into the back of his head, and he roared as he shot straight inside of me. He was magnificent. A triumph.

He leaned forward over me as he came out of the throes of his orgasm. He rested his head against my stomach, releasing my hands. "Fuck," he groaned.

"Yes," I agreed, running my fingers through his dark hair.

"I've wanted to do that for so long." He placed a kiss on my stomach.

"Was it worth the wait?"

There was fire in his eyes as he looked up at me. "Always, love. Always."

PART IV

ALWAYS

26

CAMDEN

Katherine moved back in the next day. She slept in my bed. Well, truthfully, we'd slept very little those first few nights. But just having her there... it felt like a step in the right direction. I had told her I wanted her, and I'd meant it. I hadn't known how much until I had her all the time.

"What are you daydreaming about, you sap?" Court asked as he stepped into the rec room on Thursday evening.

I glanced up at him and raised an eyebrow "Watch it, Kensington."

He just laughed at me and flopped into one of the poker chairs. Katherine had promised to be scarce during our monthly poker game. She'd headed out in skintight leggings and a sports bra a half hour ago. I'd nearly kept her inside and fucked her all evening instead of doing this. But I hosted every month. As much as I wanted to keep her, I couldn't cancel the game.

"This about Katherine moving back in?"

I hadn't told him that. Which meant that Katherine must

have told the girls. Which meant all the guys would know when they showed up.

"English told you, I presume?"

He scoffed. "Give me some credit."

"Hardly."

"All right, yeah, English told me. But hey, I'm happy for you, man. You've wanted this for a long time. You both were too fucking stubborn to actually acknowledge that you liked each other."

"Is that what you think?" I asked in the bored, detached voice I used for Court's musings.

"Don't do that shit," he said, pointing his finger at me. "I know you."

"We're working it out."

Court nodded enthusiastically. "Good."

The elevator dinged then, announcing the rest of the party. Sam and Gavin strode into the penthouse. Gavin gave a quick salute, and Sam just nodded his head. They took two of the remaining chairs.

"Waiting on one more," I said.

"Nah," Gavin said, glancing toward the wet bar. "Robert's not showing tonight. He's with Whitley."

I raised an eyebrow at him. "He didn't tell me that."

Gavin shrugged. "It's Whit." He looked over at Court. "Hey, Kensington, you playing bartender?"

"Yeah, yeah," he grumbled and got out of his chair.

"So, Whitley got back together with Robert," Sam said thoughtfully. "How do you feel about that?"

Gavin looked at him in confusion. "What do my feelings have to do with anything?"

Sam gave him a perfectly measured look that said, *Confess all your sins.*

I nearly laughed at it. He was so good at getting people to talk. Just one look, and he ensnared them.

"I don't know why you're looking at me like that," Gavin said.

Court dropped a drink in front of him. "Probably because you two were all over each other in Puerto Rico."

"Yeah, so? That was, like, a month ago, and we're both always all over someone."

I methodically shuffled the cards, waiting for one of the guys to get it out of him. I already had my suspicions, but usually, I didn't have to say much to get to the truth of the matter.

"Uh-huh," Court said.

"What?" Gavin grumbled.

Sam gave him an incredulous look. "You've been mooning over Whitley for at least the last six months. I thought you'd have made your move while we were gone."

"Me?" he gasped. "Mooning over someone? Have you met me?"

"Yeah," Sam said.

Finally, I set the cards aside and leaned forward. "You two had sex while we were on vacation."

"I didn't say that," Gavin said, looking between us all as if he were caught in a trap. Then he sagged. "But... yeah."

Sam chuckled. "Knew it."

"Did you already know?" Court asked me.

I shrugged. "When have you ever seen Gavin babble this much? Let alone deny his conquests?"

"I'm not... denying shit," Gavin growled. "But Robert's my buddy. I wouldn't have done anything if I'd known they were going to get back together. We were both single at the time. Now, they're together. So, I was trying to keep it on the down-low. I don't want him to think I'm moving in on his girl."

"That's awful gallant of you," Court drawled.

"Just deal the cards," Gavin muttered.

I set to dealing for the table as they continued to bicker. I suspected that Gavin was lying. I'd seen the way that he'd been looking at Whitley for months. And it hadn't been until we were all on vacation that Whitley started looking at him like that, too. He hadn't just stumbled into her bed for a one-night stand. He'd premeditated that shit. And now, he was backing down because he didn't want to hurt his friend. It was... nice of him, but it didn't sound like Gavin King. What was it about Whitley that kept the compulsive flirt at bay? And when it would all irrevocably boil over?

We let him be and returned to the cards. As usual, Sam swept the table over and over again. I swore that he could count cards. I'd never caught him at it, but it didn't make sense that he kept hustling us. It was like when I went to Hank's. I could crush everyone in that place with how good I was at pool, and it defied logic that I would win time and time again. That was Sam at poker. I didn't know why I kept inviting him. Except that he was one of the guys now. Not that any of us liked losing to him every week.

"Hey," Gavin said near the end of the night, "I heard another piece of juicy gossip." He looked up at me and then down at his cards.

I knew what he was going to say before it was out of his mouth. I braced myself.

"I heard Fiona's pregnant."

Everyone's gaze snapped to mine. I kept my face perfectly blank. At least I'd prepared for neutrality or else I might have scowled.

"Why are you all looking at me?" I asked.

"Camden," Sam began.

But Court cut him off, "You asshole, you didn't tell me!"

"So," Gavin asked, leaning in, "is it yours?"

"No way Katherine would have moved back in if it were his," Court snapped.

"You're not that stupid," Sam said.

At least someone believed that. Christ.

"I was already aware," I said, laying down my cards.

Sam revealed his cards, too. Beat me again. Motherfucker. He cleared out the pot, and I resumed shuffling.

"And?" Court prodded. "If it's not yours, whose is it?"

"Don't you dipshits pay attention?" Gavin asked.

Court raised an eyebrow. I actually hadn't been paying much attention. My days and nights had been filled with nothing but Katherine.

"Harmony and Kurt broke up," Gavin explained.

Sam shrugged. "So?"

He didn't understand the dynamics happening here, but Court did. "Wait, are you saying Kurt knocked up Fiona?"

"That's what's going around. That someone strong-armed him into helping Fiona." Gavin's gaze stayed on mine, but I refused to confirm or deny a thing. "Wonder who has enough power to get Kurt Mitchell to take responsibility for anything."

"Huh," Sam muttered.

"Well, shit," Court breathed.

I dealt the cards. Nothing else needed to be said. They all knew what I'd done. What I always did when confronted with a problem. I solved it. And Kurt Mitchell had been an easy mark. It had barely taken any pressure to get him to sing to my tune.

"You're a scary motherfucker sometimes, Camden," Gavin said.

I smiled. And we continued to play.

By the time I called last hand, I'd managed to keep about half of what I'd put in. Sam had most everything else. He looked satisfied. Bastard could earn enough every game to keep him happily living on the Upper East Side without his billionaire girlfriend. I really needed to figure out how he fucking did it every time.

Sam cleared his throat. "Before we all go, I wanted to say one more thing."

We all looked at him expectantly, but instead of speaking, he removed a small blue box from his suit coat. He opened it and placed it on the table. Inside was a glittering diamond ring the size of a dime. Fuck.

"I accept," Gavin said with a laugh.

"You're proposing?" Court said with wide eyes.

I stood and held my hand out. Sam took it warily at first and then enthusiastically. "Congratulations, man."

"Thanks. I thought it was about time to right all those wrongs. She's the only one I've ever wanted, and I'm not ever going to let her get away again," Sam told us.

Gavin called for congratulatory shots, and he and Court hustled to the wet bar to round up some tequila shots. They brought them back over and settled them around the table. We lifted them in the air.

"To bagging Larkin St. Vincent," Gavin said with a cheer.

We all just shook our heads at him.

"To Sam and Lark," Court said.

"To a happy union," I added with a tip of my head at Sam.

Then we downed the shots and dropped them back on the table. We laughed and sat back into our seats. This was good. Another one of my friends getting married to the woman of his dreams. Just as it should be.

A woman cleared her throat behind us. As Katherine's sweaty body came into focus, Sam snatched up the ring and stuffed it out of view. My eyes crawled her lithe form as the clothes clung to her body. My cock jerked painfully at the sight of her.

"Hey, boys," she trilled.

All four of us stared at her. Even the ones presently attached and soon-to-be engaged. My wife was a sight.

"Katherine," I said.

"Always a pleasure, Ren," Court said.

She narrowed her eyes at him but didn't comment on the nickname his brother used for her.

"I was just... going up for a shower," she said. Her tongue flicked out to lick her bottom lip. "I didn't mean to interrupt."

She winked at me and then disappeared upstairs.

Gavin cleared his throat. "Well, fuck."

"Yeah," Court agreed. "I think that's our cue."

I rose to my feet, my gaze tracking her as she disappeared upstairs. "I do think that's the end of our game. You'll see yourselves out."

Gavin snickered. Court smacked him on the back of his head. Sam just laughed. I left the three stooges to figure it out. I couldn't stay here another moment with my aching cock and my naked wife upstairs.

I took the stairs two at a time and strode into my mammoth-sized bathroom. I could hear the shower was running. A trail of workout clothes revealed the way to me. And there she was, stripped naked and soaking wet. Her eyes closed. Her dark hair a fountain down her back. Her ass on full display.

I shucked off all of my clothing and then stepped in after

her. She turned around to face me with a smirk on her full lips.

"You tease," I warned.

"Me?" she asked innocently. "I was sweaty. I needed a shower. Rodrigo worked me *real* hard today. I'm going to be sore for days."

My hands came to her sides, pushing her through the spray and against the tiled wall. "I don't like another man's name in your mouth."

She smiled wider. "He's just my trainer."

"I'll make you sore for days."

"Please," she murmured.

I grasped her shoulder, turned her around, and bent her at the waist. Her hands clasped the bench. I spread her cheeks wide, palming them in my hands. She moaned as I slicked my thumb down her crack from one hole to another, slicking myself through her wetness. She squirmed, aching for me to take her.

So, I did, thrusting deep into her pussy. My thumb pressed against the pucker of her asshole, and she tightened like a snake, trying to constrict the life out of me. I pressed deeper, a full digit, and she did nothing but groan and tighten further.

"My filthy wife," I said, keeping up a pace against her. "You're going to come for me just from one digit."

"Yes," she whimpered.

It only took a few thrusts before she cried out and came all over me. I tried to keep it together, but the way she was bucking and writhing did me in. I came long and hard deep inside of her. My fingers bruising her hips. My cock doing the same to her pussy.

When I withdrew, she collapsed onto the floor. Her eyes glazed and happy. I gently lifted her to her feet and began soaping her body, cleaning away all the filth I loved so much from her.

"Camden," she murmured as I finished and gestured for her to get under the water. I made a questioning noise. "Will you come with me to the children's hospital tomorrow?"

"What for?"

"I'm throwing a party, and there's... there's someone I'd like you to meet there."

I knew that she'd been going to the children's hospital regularly, but I hadn't asked any questions. I'd let her have her time. Figured she would tell me when she was ready.

I turned her to face me. "It's important to you?" She nodded. "Then I'll be there."

27

KATHERINE

I stood before an assembly for my first official event for ChildrensOne. Nerves bit into me, even as I saw a sea of familiar faces. So many of my friends had volunteered to come help, bringing with them makeup artists, hairdressers with collections of wigs, and nail artists. Someone had even gotten a children's designer to donate a whole rack of sparkly dresses and fanciful dress-up clothes. I couldn't believe we'd gotten this all together so fast. It really was the power of our collective connections. Now, I could bring a full-fledged makeover party to kids on the cancer ward.

Jem had no idea what she was in for.

"Welcome, everyone, to the first ever ChildrensOne Dress-Up Party," I said with a smile. "I've already separated you all out into teams. Let's try and get to as many children as we can in the two hours that we have. We want to make every child feel like a prince or princess."

Deborah fluttered at my sight with excitement. Her eyes were wide. "Thank you all so much for coming. You have no idea what this will mean to the kids. Not all of them will be able to get out of their beds, but as long as the door is open, you can go room to room to help out. There will be refreshments provided by ChildrensOne as well."

"Let's get in there," I said as I turned with Deborah to escort the group to the cancer ward.

Lark and English had been able to take off work to help out, and they entered the first set of elevators with me.

"This is so amazing," Lark told me.

"It really is, Katherine. I can't believe you did all of this," English said.

"She's a dream to work with," Deborah said affectionately. "We're so lucky to have her."

A blush crept into my cheeks. "Thank you. I'm not really doing it for me though. I want the kids to have something in their life other than the hospital."

We exited the elevator onto the bustling cancer ward. My eyes lit up. I'd been coming to the ward for two weeks, and I'd hardly seen anyone else but my old friend Melinda and a random pair of parents. I'd never seen it *alive*.

More than half of the kids were out in the halls or farther down in the waiting room we had converted for our purposes. Balloons hung throughout the halls. Smiles were on everyone's faces. And there were parents. So, so many parents. We'd had the hospital staff send out requests for parents to be here for this day. I was delighted that they'd agreed to come. We'd converted this sad wing into something filled with joy.

I sent my friends onward to meet the kids, and Deborah went to say hello to the parents that she knew. All the volunteers were being filtered through the elevator, so I stood sentinel, giving them directions. Once everyone was where they needed to be, I'd go find Jem. I couldn't wait to see her transformation.

The last group came upstairs, and I watched for a few

minutes as the crowded hall got louder and louder. Hearts filled with happiness and real smiles on their faces. I knew many of the kids on the hall now. Jem had introduced me to a number of them on my last couple of visits. All these kids were so sick ...too sick at such a young age. It wasn't fair, and I hated it. At least I could bring a modicum of fun to their lives.

The elevator opened behind me one more time, and I turned to see who else was coming to the event. I knew Camden had promised to show up, but he wouldn't be here until the end.

Harmony stood in the elevator. "Hey, Katherine," she muttered.

I frowned at her appearance. The usually perfectly put-together model looked like she had been through the wringer. Her platinum hair was up in a messy, high ponytail. Her eyes were puffy and red-rimmed. She didn't have on a lick of makeup. I was shocked that she was even here.

"Harmony."

"Go ahead. Make some quip about my appearance," she said, gesturing to her workout leggings and long-sleeved shirt.

I pulled her aside. "Are you doing okay?"

She warily narrowed her eyes. "What do you want?"

"Harmony, remember when we went up together against Candice?"

"Yeah?"

"Pretend we're doing that again."

Harmony deflated. "Kurt and I broke up."

My stomach twisted. I'd heard through the gossip groups that they'd broken up. No one had confirmed why, and only I could make a guess at what had happened. I hadn't asked Camden what he'd done to Kurt or if he even had. But Harmony didn't look this rough for no reason.

"I'm so sorry," I told her. "What happened?"

She shook her head. "He was sleeping around with other people."

"Fuck."

"Yeah, he knocked some bitch up. Wouldn't even tell me who."

I winced. "What a dick. You can do way better than him."

"I guess. I mean"—she shook herself out of her stupor—"I know that I can. I thought we had something real. You know?"

I nodded. I did know. She had been optimistic at Christmas. I'd even wanted it to work out for her.

"Maybe you should head home. You don't have to do this today."

"No, no, I want to help. I know I look... rough." She rubbed at her eyes. "Let me put on some makeup. It'll be good to see the kids. Make me feel less shitty."

"You're sure?"

"Yeah." She ran a hand back through her hair. "And, hey, uh, thanks for being so nice to me."

"You know... I think our whole petty squabble was pretty stupid," I admitted. "What were we even still arguing about?"

Harmony laughed softly. "Yeah. All that shit happened in high school. I guess the Upper East Side teaches us to hold on to grudges."

"It really does," I agreed.

"Well, I'm glad it's over."

She squeezed my hand and then disappeared into the nearest restroom.

A weight seemed to have lifted off of my shoulders. Harmony and I had been at each other's throats for so long. I hadn't even known how heavy the grudge was. Not that I was ready to give up every argument I'd ever had with anyone, but the thing with Harmony was ancient history. She was my sister-in-law now. Wouldn't it be better to be on good terms with her?

A small smile crept onto my lips, and then I headed into the fray to help the kids.

After two hours of playing dress-up, dancing, and taking pictures, most of the kids were back in their beds. The festivities had worn them out. Parents came by to thank me before leaving. Only a few stragglers stayed behind.

Jem was seated on a couch in the waiting area we'd converted for the dress-up event. I could tell that she was exhausted, but she refused to take off her princess dress. She'd chucked the wig within minutes, claiming she liked her bald head or scarf way better. And that princesses could have no hair anyway. That one day, she was going to be in her own princess movie without any hair to show everyone how beautiful and strong bald heads were.

I honestly believed her. Jem was going to take over the world. Rip those stupid beauty standards to shreds.

I wished that her parents had come for the party. I'd wanted to tell them how amazing their little girl was, but they'd never shown. Jem pretended like she didn't care, but underneath, I could tell that it bothered her.

"It's about time, Jem," I told her, nodding toward her room.

"Can I keep the dress, please?" she asked, her eyes wide.

I laughed. I could afford it. Why not? "Sure."

"Yippee!" she cheered. "I'm going to be a princess forever."

Footsteps sounded down the hallway, and we both looked up to find English walking toward us with Court and Camden. Lark had left ten minutes ago on a mayoral emergency.

"Look what I found," English said, nodding her head at the boys.

Jem's eyes widened. "Whoa. You didn't tell me you were friends with Cinderella."

English laughed. She'd worn a blue dress for the occasion, and with her bright blonde hair, she really did look a little like Cinderella. She curtsied to Jem. "I've seemed to have lost a glass slipper. Have you seen it?"

Jem giggled. "I can help you look!"

"I think I saw it on the stairs," Court murmured, pressing a kiss to English's temple. He was dressed down in navy slacks with his sleeves rolled up to his elbows. He'd ditched the jacket entirely.

"But you already found your Prince Charming."

I snorted. "Court Kennington as Prince Charming. Now, I've heard everything."

Jem looked to Camden, dressed to intimidate today. He'd come straight from work, and he wore an all-black suit with a black shirt and tie, too.

Then she turned her sharp eyes to me. "Is that *your* boyfriend?"

Camden actually cracked a smile.

"Yep. That one is mine," I told her. "I brought him here to meet you."

Jem tapped her lip thoughtfully. "He suits you. Villain Katherine and her Dark Prince."

English and Court laughed together.

"She has you both pegged," Court said.

"Well, that Dark Prince is buying your princess dress, missy," I said, leaning forward and tickling her.

She giggled. "Okay, okay. Stop." Her eyes fluttered up to Camden's. "Thank you for my princess dress."

He didn't miss a beat. "You're most welcome. It looks perfect on you. Does it twirl?"

Her eyes lit up. "It does!"

Then she stood and rotated in circles, so her dress flew out in all directions. English pulled away from Court to turn with Jem. And soon, I was on my feet, spinning in circles with them. My dress didn't flare out, but it didn't even matter. I tipped my head back, a real, raw smile on my face, and laughed with them.

I got dizzy and stumbled. Camden caught me with one arm and Jem with the other. Jem was breathing heavily.

"I think that's probably enough for today, Jem," I said, looking at her face growing paler.

She sighed. "I hate this part."

Camden bent down and whispered in her ear. I couldn't hear a word that he said, but her entire face brightened, and she enthusiastically nodded her head. A second later, he scooped her tiny body up into his arms.

She dramatically put her hand to her forehead. "I nearly swooned."

I couldn't stop laughing as I showed Camden which room was Jem's and watched him carefully deposit her back in her bed. A nurse followed close behind, preparing to check all of her vitals after we were gone.

As I watched Camden fuss over Jem, a light lit in my chest. Something I had never considered before, especially since I knew Camden's father, but... Camden would make a good dad one day. Just seeing him with Jem, it made my heart want to burst out of my chest.

He fussed with her hair, and she giggled.

"See you around, Dark Prince. Come with Katherine again."

"I'll do that," he said with an exaggerated bow in her direction. Then he left her in the care of the nurse and headed back out into the hall with me.

"You're... really great with her."

"She makes it easy," he admitted. His gaze snapped to mine. "This is why you wanted me to come. To meet Jem."

I nodded. "She's sunshine. The first day I came here, I had a panic attack. You know my fear of hospitals and being forced back into them. I couldn't even breathe. I thought it would help me to try to overcome it, but it overwhelmed me instead. Then Jem was there, and... it all receded."

He brushed a strand of my hair out of my face. "I'm glad that she was there when you were in distress. She seems like a very special girl."

"She is."

"I've never seen you like this before," he said seriously and then slowly laced our fingers together. "So... carefree."

I glanced down at where our hands were joined. I wasn't sure that I'd ever held hands with Camden before. Butterflies took flight in my stomach.

"I'm not sure I've been like this since... before my father was arrested. He made me feel like this once." I let out a slow breath. "Every year my father would give me a charm for my bracelet on my birthday. It was our thing. He added to it every year.

Camden assessed me. "That was the charm that Penn gave you for your birthday."

I nodded. "Yes. Penn kept up the tradition after my father was sent away."

"I see," he said softly. "I see why that would be important to you."

I stared down at the passing tiles. "It was."

"You seem to have made a huge difference here."

"Oh, I don't know if I'd say a huge difference. But I think our party went off without a hitch. We're having a fundraising event at the beginning of March so that we can do things like this more often. I know it's another party and that you said that I only did charity to benefit me, but it's really not like that."

He pulled me to a stop and tipped my chin up to look at him. "Whatever I said when I was angry, I was wrong. What you're doing here is incredible. You're incredible."

"Really? I was worried you'd think that I was throwing this party to make myself look good... or something."

"Have you posted a single picture about this party on your social media accounts?"

I frowned and pulled out my phone. I just realized that I hadn't looked at it in hours. Hours and hours. I hadn't taken a single picture the whole time. We'd had a photographer set up for the kids. I'd been in a few of those, but nothing on my phone. Nothing for myself.

"I... forgot actually," I said, momentarily stunned.

He pressed a kiss to my forehead. "Exactly. You're doing good work. Work that you're passionate about. I'm glad that I got to see it."

My heart constricted at the words. I might be falling in love with my husband.

28

CAMDEN

"What the hell are you wearing?" Katherine asked as I headed down the stairs to the living room.

I stopped at the bottom and took in her outfit. A skirt so micro short that her ass nearly hung out of the bottom and a slinky gold halter top that was completely open in the back, except for a tiny string holding it up. She wore six-inch stilettos and enough makeup to completely transform her face. Even her hair had been done up in sexy supermodel curls. She looked like a knockout.

"What am I wearing? What are *you* wearing?"

"I'm in my divorce party outfit," she said, gesturing to her skirt. "All of us girls are dressing up super slutty and getting wasted since English's divorce was official last night."

I strode over to my wife and pulled her against me. "You're practically naked."

"So?"

I tugged on the string that held her shirt up. She gasped, but I'd already slid underneath it and cupped her breasts. Her gasp turned into a moan.

"Camden," she muttered, "I... I have to go soon."

"I can be quick," I told her.

Her heart hammered in her chest. I could feel the pulse pick up under my touch. But then she stepped back with a gulp. Her pupils dilated as she retied the string.

"Next time," she assured me.

I sighed. I had known that she would turn me down. She was supposed to take the limo to pick up the girls any minute. But I liked seeing the reaction I could get out of her. So easy. So wanton. Fuck.

"Now... tell me about this outfit," she said. Her gaze traveled down my body, lingering for a second too long on my erection.

"It's just an outfit."

"You're wearing *jeans*. I didn't even think you owned jeans."

"Everyone owns jeans, Katherine."

"I've never seen you wear them."

I shrugged and adjusted myself. My cock was still growing at the sight of her. I was envisioning bending her over the arm of the sofa and fucking her, and I couldn't get the thought out of my mind.

"This is a T-shirt," she added.

"Yes. You've seen me dress down before."

She shook her head. "But that was in Puerto Rico and the Maldives or, like, at night. Not when you're going out. Where are you going anyway?"

"Just going to go get a drink since you're going to be out in that fucking outfit all night. If I stay here, I'll jack off, thinking about you."

She flushed, and a teasing smile lit her cherry-red lips. "Oh, yeah?"

"Do you like the idea of me touching myself when I think about you?"

I bridged that gap again and slid one hand up her inner thigh. The skirt was so short that I met the edge of her lace panties almost immediately. She shivered at my touch.

"Maybe I do."

"We still have time for me to fuck you."

A small huff left her lips, and then she reluctantly stepped back. "I'm already late. Fuck."

"Later then," I told her. She nodded. Her eyes were glazed with desire. "Where will you all be?"

"We're going to bar hop. I think we'll start at Sparks and end at Club 360."

I pointed upward. "You're ending at the club on top of Percy Tower?"

She shrugged. "I thought it would be easiest for me. Plus, it really lights up at around two in the morning."

"Find me after," I told her.

"Oh, I will," she said, placing one kiss to my lips and then darting for the elevator.

I adjusted my jeans again. I really didn't wear them very often. Only when I was going to Hank's, but I wasn't ready to tell her about Hank's. Soon but not quite yet.

I headed downstairs and took the Mercedes out of the Upper East Side. It was forty-five minutes before I made it to Hank's. The traffic was horrid as everyone drove through the city on Saturday evening. Normally, I only came to the bar on weekdays. I remembered why.

The bar was packed. Twice as many people than the last time I was here. It was likely because it was a Saturday night but also because the weather was unusually mild for an evening at the end of January. As if some of the ice had thawed. Though I suspected it was only a matter of time before the chill returned. Our winters rarely disappointed.

I saw Ricky and Big Al playing a team game against two

women I'd never seen before. They appeared to be losing. That was something. Maybe I'd offer to play one of the women after I got myself a drink. A new challenge was always welcome.

"Camden," Monica said with a wide smile on her face. "Long time. Haven't seen you since Christmas."

"It's good to be back."

"You look to be in better sorts than the last time I had to carry your drunken ass to your place."

I grinned as she slid a glass of scotch across the bar. "As much as I appreciate you helping me back to my place, I don't think I'll need that tonight."

"Excellent. A woman can only do so much." She poured two tequila shots without comment. "You have some pep in your step. What's going on in the world of Camden Percy?"

I took the shot, and we held it aloft before downing it. Someone called for Monica's attention. I waved her off to fill some more drink orders. She came back about fifteen minutes later and refilled my scotch.

"So... tell Mama Monica what's going on."

"Things are good," I confided. "They're really good."

"I love to hear that," she said as she poured a pitcher of beer. "Is this about your wife?"

I nodded. "Yes, she moved back in."

"That's great, Camden," she said, pushing the pitcher down to a group of guys and pocketing the tip. "Was it the truce? Did you take my advice?"

"Yes, and no."

I had no idea why it was so easy to talk to Monica. But she was probably the only person I'd met who actually seemed to care. She had no stake in the outcome. Who the hell was she going to tell my problems to? I'd known her two years, and she'd never once blabbed my problems to the press. I came as close to trusting her as anyone.

"We tried the truce, but it ended up backfiring. Got a lot worse from there. But we talked, and I think we're back on even footing."

"Love to see one of my boys in love," Monica said, batting her eyelashes at me.

My lips turned down at the comment. In love. It was hard to even think that word. Love meant criticism. Love meant responsibility. Love meant pain. Love had never meant Katherine Van Pelt with all of her fire and all of her fierce determination. It had never meant...happiness.

"I've... never actually said that to anyone before," I said in such a small voice that I wasn't sure she'd even heard me.

She was busy putting together a round of shots for six women who didn't even look to be of legal drinking age.

But when she finished, she whirled back to me. A frown was on her lips. "That's awful, Camden. Your family never said it?"

I shook my head with a stiff laugh. "You don't know my dad. He's not exactly the affectionate type."

She sank her hip into the bar. "I know his type."

"Yeah? A right bastard?"

She chuckled as she grabbed the tip from the girls, who had turned their attention to me sitting there, alone. One of the girls giggled and nudged her friend forward.

Monica put her hand out. "Sorry, ladies. Wouldn't try your luck with this one."

The girl's eyes rounded, and her cheeks flushed with embarrassment.

"Here," I said, putting down a fifty. I nodded at the girls. "Shots on me."

"Oh, wow, thanks!" she said with another giggle and returned to her friends.

"You know that's going to bring upon unwanted attention," Monica admonished.

"After you shooed them away?" I asked. "I softened the blow."

"Well, fine then," she said as she disappeared to take another order.

I slid my glass across the bar and lounged back, observing the crowd playing pool. I was intrigued by the women playing Ricky. It appeared they'd beaten him. Ricky was an all right player, too. I'd have to get in on that.

Monica appeared then with a beer with an orange slice on the rim. "Can you take this to Big Al when you go over there to beat those women?"

"How did you know?"

She snorted. "I've been watching you for two years, son. I think I know who your next victim is."

"Fair enough. I'll take another scotch, too."

"Sure thing." She poured the drink but held on to it as she looked up at me. Her eyes were full of concern, where there was normally only humor. "You know... if you love this girl, you let her know. You hear me? Waiting doesn't help anyone. Take it from someone who knows."

Then she passed me the drink and disappeared again. I considered her words. They were heartfelt. I could feel it to my bones. I knew that she was right.

Maybe I should tell Katherine how I really felt. Maybe the time for waiting was over.

29

KATHERINE

My girls looked like straight fire. I hadn't seen so much skin in one place since Puerto Rico. English was in a teeny-tiny little black dress with mile-high heeled booties. She wore a sash that read *Divorced AF* and a shiny tiara. The rest of us were in gold outfits to complement her black. Together, we looked like every boy's wet dream.

By the end of the night, when we'd finally dragged our drunk asses from Sparks to Factory and then from there to Club 360, we were a hot mess. English's tiara had been lost. Her sash was askew. We were stumbling through the crowds, laughing and having the time of our lives.

I pushed through the crowd at the top of the world and ordered shots from the bartender. We had a booth at the back, but we hadn't been in it for more than a minute since we got here, all of us preferring the high energy on the dance floor. Or possibly it was the alcohol talking.

Still, shots appeared before me a minute later. I had no idea what I'd ordered, but the liquid was clear. Probably a good sign.

The girls each grabbed one from the bar and held it aloft.

"To English!" Lark cried.

"To freedom!" Whitley added over top of it.

Then we tossed the shots back and dropped them back on the bar.

"I'm so fucking happy for you," I told English. "You and Court and your little kitten."

"Trouble is the most adorable thing in the world," English confirmed, swaying on her feet. We had pretty high tolerances, but tonight was above and beyond.

Whitley giggled and tipped her head back. "There are so many fucking hot women here tonight."

"How fucked up are you?" Lark asked with a laugh.

"Drunk enough to take one into the bathroom," Whitley said with a giggle. Then she leaned forward and put her finger to her mouth. "Shh... don't tell Robert."

I snorted. "You wouldn't do that to Robert."

She winked at me. "You're right. I'm not that kind of girl."

"But if you were single..."

She sighed as her eyes scanned the crowd. "If only I were single."

"Like when you slept with Gavin," English chimed in, slurring her words together until it sounded like *slepwifGavn*.

"I am *not* wasted enough for this conversation," Whitley said, teetering in her heels.

"Here you go." Lark plopped a drink into her hand. She passed out the others she'd ordered. "Now, you can tell us about it."

"How do you even know?"

"Besides the fact that you were all over each other?" English asked.

"The guys told us," I let Whitley know.

Her jaw dropped slightly. "How do *they* know?"

"Poker night. Gavin told them," Lark confirmed. "Sam told me when he got home."

"Bastard!" Whitley chimed in.

"So, how was it?" I prodded.

Whitley flushed even more than she already had been, standing sloshed on a rooftop in Manhattan. "He was good."

"Good?" I asked incredulously. "Whitley, the slayer of men and women alike. Whitley, the storyteller. You have to give us more than good."

She rolled her eyes. "He was *good*. I don't know what you want me to say. I shouldn't even be talking about it. I'm dating his friend."

"We haven't seen Sir Robert in a while," English said sloppily.

"Sir Robert?" I asked, looking at Lark.

She shrugged and mouthed the word, *Wasted*, to me.

"He's trying not to be clingy. He'll be at the Fashion Week gala with me though."

"Uh-huh," I muttered.

"What?" Whitley asked. "You got something to say, Van Pelt?"

"Robert's fine. I like him. He's a nice guy. But I always thought you'd want something a little more..." I trailed off.

"More what?" Whitley asked.

"Flashy," Lark finished.

"Robert is flashy."

Lark and I exchanged another look.

Whitley huffed. "Whatever, y'all," she said, her Southern accent coming out thick in her inebriated state.

"What about you and Camden?" Lark butted in.

"What about us?"

"Are we going to have a baby Percy soon?"

English's eyes went round as saucers. "Are you pregnant?" She snatched the drink straight out of my hand.

I couldn't stop my laugh. "I'm not pregnant, English! Would I be drinking if I were?"

"Oh, right," she said, offering the drink to me.

I shook my head and let her keep it.

"We're... we're talking about it."

I told them how we'd started trying as we all swayed to the motion of the club. The night was almost over, and I was surprised that I'd made it this long without this conversation.

"Yay!" Lark cried.

English danced in a circle. "You're going to have a baby."

"I talked to Whitley, and she helped me see that I had been having panic attacks for nothing."

Whitley breathed a sigh of relief. "Not talking about it has been killing me. Did you take my advice and go home and fuck him?"

I laughed. "I did. I still have the prescription you wrote."

Whitley told the other girls in on what she'd prescribed, and they all went up in an uproar.

"And you want this, right?" Lark said. "You and Camden?"

I nodded, a real smile coming to my face. "I think... we're finally in the right place. So, we'll see what happens."

Lark cleared her throat and tipped her head toward the entrance. "Looks like someone didn't get the message about girls' night."

I whipped around and found none other than Camden Percy standing at the front. He'd changed out of the jeans he wore earlier, and he was looking through the crowd as if waiting to find me. A shiver ran down my spine in anticipation.

But then I bit my lip. "Should I tell him to go?"

English rolled her eyes. "Go fuck that husband of yours." She pushed me toward him.

"You're all sure?"

"Go!" Lark and Whitley said together.

"I love you, bitches," I cried.

Then I stumbled through the crowd until I came to a halt just outside of the line of people. Camden's eyes snapped to mine. I was sure that I looked like an intoxicated fool, but just the sight of him set a trail of fire down my spine.

"Hey," I said, stepping toward him. "Thought you were going out for a drink."

"I closed down the bar, darling," he said, wrapping an arm around my waist. "Then I came to find you."

"I thought I was supposed to find you."

"I'm impatient." He pulled me in for a hard kiss.

"Then let's go."

He gestured for me to precede him. My heel caught on absolutely nothing, and I almost went tumbling face-first into the doorway. Camden was there right away, catching me and keeping me from falling.

"You're obliterated," he said with humor in his voice.

"I don't know the last time I was this drunk," I said as he helped me to the elevator. Once inside, I leaned back against it. My head was spinning. "Maybe not since... ever."

Now that I was out of the pounding of the club, I felt weak and dizzy and *totally fucked up*. I'd thought it was only Whitley and English who were that drunk. Lark and I were practically professionals. But here and now, I couldn't even think straight.

"How much did you have to eat before this?" Camden asked.

I shook my head. I didn't remember. Had I eaten dinner? Or lunch? I'd definitely had something to eat. A lettuce wrap of some sort. "Um..."

The elevator dinged open to our penthouse. *Our* penthouse.

"Come on. Let me make you some food. You're going to be hungover as shit tomorrow."

"I'm not hungry," I told him as my stomach grumbled slightly.

He arched an eyebrow and waited.

"Fine," I muttered and followed him into the kitchen.

He sat me down at the kitchen bar and rummaged through the refrigerator. He plopped down a large glass of water. "Drink that."

Then he went back to work. My eyes could barely process what I was seeing as I sipped on the water he'd given me. Camden Percy was... cooking.

I blinked and blinked again. But, no, he was still there, cooking me eggs on the stovetop. I'd never seen him cook before. I hadn't thought that he even knew how. He usually went out for food or had a chef come in to cook dinners.

"You're cooking," I said.

"I do have some rudimentary life skills."

I laughed. "I've never seen you cook."

"It doesn't happen very often."

"Jeans and cooking, all in one day. Be careful, Camden, or someone might think that you're normal."

His eyes slid to me. "No one would ever think that."

And he was right. How could they? Not when he was

back in his Tom Ford suit with dark eyes that knew all and a sternness born of deep emotional trauma in his formative years. Camden Percy was power and dominance.

And he was cooking me scrambled eggs. A duality.

He set a plate with eggs and toast in front of me and then one for himself. Then he took the chair next to mine and sat down.

"You're going to eat with me?" I asked, incredulous.

"I'm a bit drunk myself," he admitted.

Not that I could see it on him. Not even a little.

"Eat," he commanded.

And so... I ate.

Even the toast. I didn't usually bother with refined carbs, but I clearly needed some sustenance to soak up all the alcohol in my system. By the end of the meal, I was feeling almost human again.

"Thank you," I said softly.

"You're welcome. It's good to see you eating bread again."

He collected the empty plates, washed them off, and put them in the dishwasher. Then he leaned against the counter to stare up at me.

"You're not sick again, are you?" he asked softly, gently.

I stilled under his look. Then I slowly shook my head. "No."

"Are you sure?"

"Yes, I'm sure."

He sighed. "Okay. I just... you keep losing weight. And don't get me wrong, you look fucking gorgeous, but I don't want to neglect your past problems."

"It's not like before," I assured him. "I promise."

"You'd tell me if it was?"

I bit my lip and then nodded.

"Okay."

Then he stepped around and held his hand out to me. I took it and unsteadily stood on my heels. He shook his head at me before removing each of my heels, one at a time. He scooped me up in his arms and carried me up the flight of stairs as if I weighed nothing at all, and set me down on my side of the bed. *My* side. Then he untied the bow at the back of my shirt and dropped the halter to the ground. He found the zipper on my skirt and let it follow.

My core heated at his movements, even as I fought the alcohol in my system. But he didn't push me to have sex. He didn't even have the heat in his eyes that I was used to. He just tugged the covers back and eased me under them.

"Camden?"

"Shh," he said, pressing a kiss to my lips. "Let me take care of you."

He pulled the covers over my shoulders. Then he slipped into the bed from the other side, cradling me against him.

"I thought you'd want to have sex," I whispered into the silence of the darkened room.

"I do." He pressed a kiss to my shoulder. "But my job is to take care of you first and myself second."

"It is?"

"Yes," he assured me. "Now, get some rest. If you're lucky, I'll fuck you in the morning."

I shivered at the words and sank back against him, releasing the final bits of tension in my body. It felt great, having him pressed up against me, his body cocooning me as I drifted off.

"Katherine," he breathed, placing another kiss at my shoulder.

"Mmm?"

"I love you. You know I love you, right?"

I turned over to look into those bottomless, dark eyes. And there it was... that look that I hadn't been able to explain for so long. It was... love. He loved me.

My heart expanded. And I nodded. "I love you, too."

He drew me in close to him. "I love to hear you say that."

"I love you," I repeated. "You know what?"

He shook his head. "What, love?"

"This was my birthday wish."

His smile was wide at the revelation. Then he kissed my full lips, and everything in the world felt inexplicably right.

30

KATHERINE

"Seriously, you cannot lose another pound between now and the gala on Saturday," Alexandre complained.

"I didn't!" I insisted. "My weight went up this week."

And it had—by three pounds. I was sure that it was muscle, but it could have been the alcohol and bread. Or any number of things, stress included.

"Well, we have to take this in again. And if you lose anything else, you're SOL, baby girl."

"It's fine," I said through gritted teeth. "I'm not doing anything differently. And I can't exercise this week because it's Fashion Week."

"Yeah, yeah," he grumbled. "Let's get you out of this."

He helped me out of the dress, which I had *no* idea how it was going to be brought in again, but I'd leave that to the designer. I only had twenty minutes to get across town to the Cunningham Couture runway. I had a front row ticket and intended to be seen by everyone present.

I quickly changed back into the charcoal high-waisted skirt and tight white blouse I'd chosen for the event with black tights and heeled booties. My black leather jacket went on last and then dashed out to the Mercedes to make it to my event. With barely a minute to spare, I waltzed into the event as if I owned the place and had done it all on purpose. To my surprise, Harmony was already seated with an empty chair next to her. *My* empty chair. Well, that was a change from last year.

"Hey, Harm," I said, setting my Hermès bag down and taking the only empty seat.

"Oh, hey, Katherine," she said with a half-smile before her eyes darted back to the front.

"I thought you'd be backstage since you're working for your mother and all."

"I should be," she said tightly. "We're not showing any of my designs, and Mother thought it'd be better for me to be seen in the crowd. That it would look better."

She probably wasn't wrong. Though I could see the anxiety warring on Harmony's face.

"Well, you can't change it. So, don't let the cameras see you worrying about it. You'll have your day."

Harmony shot me a skeptical look. "Was that a back-handed compliment?"

"There was nothing backhanded about it," I said, settling back into my seat. "That was sincere."

Harmony assessed me. "You've... changed."

"Have I?"

"No," she said finally. "Maybe not. Maybe you're the same Katherine after all."

I stared back at her without a fraction of a question in my expression. I knew her well enough to know she'd explain.

"You've always only ever cared about your own. You and Camden are both that way. Loyal to a fault. But only to your own people. No matter how small that circle is." Harmony tilted her head. "I think maybe... the circle has just grown, and somehow, I've ended up inside of it."

She was right. My circle had always been small and very tight-knit. I liked it that way. But things had changed. Penn getting married had changed much. Falling in love with Camden had changed everything else. My crew wasn't the same, and my husband was somehow my... protector.

"Old grudges don't seem to matter much anymore," I said.

"I never thought you'd get over him."

"Who?" I whispered even though I knew.

"Penn."

I swallowed and shrugged. "Didn't have much of a choice, did I?"

Harmony arched an eyebrow. "Who knew Camden would be so good for you?"

"Probably not even me," I admitted.

And then the lights went down, and Elizabeth Cunningham stepped on the stage to announce her new runway line. Harmony lit up with excitement, and it all happened so fast. One minute was the whirlwind of anticipation. The next was the final run-through, and the lights were coming on. The crowd soared to their feet, applauding Elizabeth's genius. She had a knack for color and style and design that few other designers truly possessed. It was a marvel to watch on display.

"She did great," I said, catching Harmony's arm.

"She really did." She drew me into a hug. "Come back with me."

I nodded and grabbed my purse before following her toward Elizabeth and the string of media. I'd already posted a picture of my outfit and checked in for the event, but it wouldn't hurt to get some more material. I'd been slacking lately on my social accounts with all the time I'd been spending at the hospital and planning the charity function for ChildrensOne. I didn't want any of my followers to wonder where I was and what I was doing.

Elizabeth put her arm around Harmony to take pictures for the cameras. Then she gestured me over. I walked over like I was supposed to be there, but I was genuinely shocked.

"Need both of my daughters for the pictures," Elizabeth said.

I smiled for the cameras, but I couldn't believe those words had come out of her mouth. We'd been civil for years... but her *daughter*? She had never treated me like that. Had Harmony told her what I'd done and how I'd been there for her? Or was Elizabeth just playing it up for the cameras?

Elizabeth winked at me when we were done. "Look at you. You're so trim right now. You could be up on that stage."

I laughed. "There's no way. I haven't walked a runway in, like, five years."

"Well, with this perfect figure, we should put in the advertising again. I have this new line, and you'd fit into it perfectly."

"Count me in," I said with a shrug.

Why not? She likely wasn't serious anyway.

"I will." She looked like she was going to turn back to the others who wanted her attention, but then she pointed her finger at me. "Get me the name of that trainer you're working with. I'd like to speak with him."

I nodded. "Of course. I can do that."

"Keep it up, Katherine."

She smiled one more time and then disappeared. I let the rest of the crowd wander off without me, only stopping to talk to a few faces that I recognized or who wanted a solo picture.

I didn't have another runway for a few hours. I'd been planning to walk to a few of the boutique pop-ups and possibly sneak in an interview if I had time. I was so giddy for it that I could cry. Fashion Week was like Disney World for us in the industry.

But as I stepped out into the daylight again, I found Camden waiting for me. His eyes strayed from his cell phone up to me, and he smiled. Not a full-watt thing, but one that was private. Just for me.

"Hey, I thought you'd be at work," I told him.

He drew me in and placed a kiss on my cherry-red lips. "I wanted to take you to lunch."

I nodded. "That sounds nice."

He slid an arm around my waist as we walked out of the park toward a little café that I knew he loved.

"Don't you have your secret society meeting or whatever?"

"No, that's on Mondays."

"Ah, so it *is* a secret society."

He shook his head. "Not exactly. Just where we all get together to talk business."

I wrinkled my nose. "You do that everywhere."

"An exclusive place to do that."

"Semantics. Sounds like a secret society to me."

"It's truly very dull," he assured me. "Are you ready for the gala this weekend?"

"Yep. I had my final fitting this morning. I'm excited for you to see it."

His eyes lit up with desire. "I'm ready to take it off of you."

I bit my lip. "That would be good, too."

"You know, I had a thought for this gala."

"Oh, yeah?"

"Maybe... we could go together."

My feet stalled, and I looked up at him in surprise. "Together? Like, you want to show up with me and walk the red carpet?"

"I do."

I couldn't believe it. Camden and I had been married over a year. We'd "dated" long before that, and I couldn't remember a time that we'd shown up to an event together. We always showed up separately and then co-mingled in the room when it was necessary. But... things were different now. This time... we were in love. This was how it always should have been.

"I'd like that," I admitted, "very much."

"Consider it done then," he said as he looked down at his phone again. We'd just reached the restaurant, and he froze in place. "Would you get us a table? I have to take a quick call."

My eyebrows rose. "Everything all right?"

"We'll find out."

Then he turned and walked off. I frowned in confusion and wondered what that was all about. But I stepped inside to the busy café and gave them the Percy name. I was seated in minutes despite the crowd outside. Benefits of being long-time customers, and... well, the Percy name opened doors.

I perused the menu, debating between a salad and a sandwich. I didn't really *need* the bread. But I had been trying to be better ever since Camden asked me last weekend if I was sick again. I didn't *feel* sick. Though I hadn't felt sick when I was hospitalized. I'd stopped shedding weight, and Rodrigo thought that I was finally starting to build up muscle mass, which was something I'd never been able to achieve. Maybe a sandwich would be fine.

Then I looked around the room and saw all the waiflike models and fashion people in the café. Every one of them was eating one of the dozen salads on the menu. It was our job to stay thin... and Elizabeth had suggested I could walk for her. It'd been years since I even considered it.

I worried at my lip indecisively when the waiter came over with waters. He looked frazzled. This place wasn't normally this busy.

"I'll take a half caprese sandwich and a side Caesar salad." Best of both worlds. "Camden will have his usual."

His eyes lit up. "Oh, Percy. Yes, excellent." He scooped up the menus. "I will get everything covered."

I sat back in my seat and checked my messages and responded to followers until Camden returned. He dropped into his seat, looking furious.

"What's wrong?" I asked, setting my phone aside.

"Remember the Ireland deal that I had that fell through?"

"Of course."

"And my father said that they didn't want to work with me?"

"Right. Which sounded like bullshit."

He sighed heavily and dragged a hand down his face. "Turns out, it was bullshit. I decided to send a follow-up email to them. Just a standard *thanks for working with us, let us know if you change your mind, I'd be happy to discuss options with you*. That sort of thing."

"And they just responded?"

He nodded. "They didn't want to work with *my father*," he ground out. "And the bastard lied and turned it around on me, to make it look like I'd lost the deal instead of him."

"God, he's such an asshole," I snapped.

"That he is."

"So... the deal is still on?"

"They want to come into New York next week to finalize negotiations... without my father present. But then, yeah, it looks like we'll have a Percy Tower in Dublin, and I'll close the deal."

"Camden, that's incredible," I gushed.

But he didn't look pleased. He was a mix of pissed off and resigned. "Tell that to my father."

"He'll understand."

Camden shook his head. "He won't, but I'll have to find a way to tell him."

"Maybe... just surprise him."

"That would go over well," he said sarcastically.

I reached across the table and took his hand. "You're a better man than your father. And certainly better than he gives you credit for."

"Thank you." He leaned forward and pressed a kiss to my hand.

I pulled back as our food arrived. My stomach growled slightly. I hadn't had that big of a breakfast, and all the running around had made me hungry.

"You got a sandwich," Camden said softly.

"Well, a half-sandwich," I said, picking it up and taking a small bite.

He smiled to himself and then dug into his Italian sandwich without another word. And I knew that this was a win. For me and for us.

31

KATHERINE

The Percy limo pulled up in front of the towering Greco-revival facade of Cipriani Wall Street. For dozens and dozens of events, I'd shown up in this limousine with a parade of my friends in tow—all in coordinating outfits and happily drunk by the time we arrived.

Today was different.

Today, Camden Percy stepped out of the limo first. He reached back, offering me his hand, and I took it. Then I stepped out onto the red carpet with my husband at my side. It felt monumental in that moment. Something that would feel so ordinary to most couples, but we weren't most couples. We weren't really like anyone else. An arranged marriage was strange enough. Though it had worked for us. Until now... when it didn't work anymore because this was more than just an arrangement. It was more than me marrying him for his money. This was me putting my heart back out on the line.

The train of my red silk Alexandre D'Oria gown trailed behind me as my husband walked me down the red carpet in a tuxedo. He looked calm, confident, and dominating. My perfect match.

Who would have guessed?

We stopped for a series of pictures and then entered the vast ballroom, which was classically decorated for the event. We were directed toward our table for dinner. I recognized the other names at our table. All of our friends in one place. I knew that Lark had taken the St. Vincent limo for the rest of the party once I let her know that Camden and I were coming together. So, they shouldn't be too long behind us.

I looked to the table directly to our right and stopped in my tracks. "Candice?" I asked in shock.

"Katherine!" Candice cried, rushing over to me and trying to bring me in for a hug. But her stomach was so enormous that she could barely even get her arms around my shoulders.

"I thought you were on a yacht in the Caribbean," Camden said dryly.

As far as I knew, he'd personally shipped her and Lars off on the Percy jet to get her out of his hair.

"I was! But I'm so close to my due date, and I thought it'd be nice to come back to New York for delivery. Then I got the invitation for the gala. Lars thought it was *crazy*, but we live for crazy around here." Candice's eyes lit up. "How are you two lovebirds? Fucking like rabbits?"

I shook my head at her. She was just so outrageous. But... the venom I'd had toward her at Christmas when I was in such a deep, dark place and Camden and I were fighting like mad, well, it wasn't there anymore. I'd spent so long finding Candice's eccentricity a burden at best and a complete disgrace every other time. But maybe... she wasn't so bad.

"I'm glad you could make it back. When are you due again?"

Candice grasped my hand and put it on her stomach. "Do you feel him kick?"

"Him?" I asked hesitantly. "It's a boy?"

She shrugged. "I think so. Lars is convinced it's a little Candice, but we don't want to know. We want nature to take its own course. It's going to be a surprise!"

And then I felt it. The baby *did* move. It kicked its little foot against the wall of her stomach.

"Wow. He is a strong thing," I told her.

"He's going to be a real swimmer, just like his dad," she said with a bawdy wink. "Can't wait for him to get out of there because I am dying to be properly fucked. Know what I mean?"

Camden sighed, but I actually laughed and nodded. "I think I do."

"Also, I would kill for a drink right about now."

"Speaking of," I said, raising an eyebrow at Camden.

He just shook his head at his sister. "I'll get us something."

He disappeared then, leaving me alone with Candice, who regaled me with stories about her pregnancy on the yacht. It sounded like such a Candice adventure.

A throat cleared behind us, and I turned to find none other than Penn Kensington standing before me in a tuxedo. The bastard looked like fucking James Bond in that suit. It was uncanny. And though he admittedly looked very handsome, I didn't have that same pang that normally came with coming face-to-face with my first love. Instead, I just was happy to see him... even with Natalie on his arm.

"Hey, Ren," he said with a smile. "Thought I'd catch you before..."

He didn't have to say what he meant. I was sure he'd only come over because Camden was gone.

Instead, I stepped forward with a smile. "It's good to see you."

My eyes darted to Natalie. She looked like such a different person than she had been a year ago at this same event. She'd had the world on her shoulders as she'd been set on ruining my empire. Now, we were both just occupants of this strange, strange world.

"It's good to see you, too, Nat."

She raised an eyebrow. "Really?"

I laughed and shrugged. "Crew for life, right?"

"I suppose so," she said tentatively.

Then she gave me such a Natalie smile. The real one, the defiant one that had made me like her the first time I met her. So much had changed between us since that day. It was nice to know she was still there underneath it all.

"I hope you two have a fun night," I told them honestly.

Penn shot me a skeptical look, but it was doused by the appearance of my husband. Penn didn't back down. Though I could see he wanted to get out of the line of fire.

"Kensington," Camden said, passing me a glass of champagne.

"Percy," Penn said stiffly.

Then to the surprise of everyone assembled, my husband stuck his hand out. Penn looked at it as if it were a bomb. Like he was trying to find out what part of this was going to backfire.

But slowly, he eased his hand into Camden's. They shook once. Nothing fancy. No words necessary. There was still mutual disdain. Just not as much as there had been in the past. This was a world in which they wouldn't kill each other. Maybe, just maybe, we could survive this.

Penn nodded his head at me, and Natalie gave me a knowing look before they both traipsed back off into the crowd.

By then the rest of our table had arrived. Court and English, Lark and Sam, Whitley and Robert, and Gavin with his date... Harmony Cunningham. I gaped when I saw her on his arm.

"Harm!" I gasped. "You and Gavin?"

She shrugged one shoulder and glanced back at him. "It's not serious. We were both going stag, and he offered for me to go with him instead."

"That was nice of him."

Too nice of him. Gavin wasn't normally the magnanimous type. He usually chose the hottest... sometimes the easiest date for the evening or found someone to hook up with when he was there. If he was here with Harmony, there was a reason. Did it have something to do with Whitley being here with Robert?

My focus shifted to the pair. Robert stood rooted to the spot, watching Whitley flit around from person to person like she was wont to do. But even more so than normal. Whitley was particularly performative when she got nervous. I wondered what Robert saw when he saw her skipping about like that. Did he know her like I did? Robert watched people in the same way that I did. I was surprised that he put up with her, but I could tell he deeply cared. I just... wasn't sure Whitley felt the same way.

We all settled into our seats for dinner. I hadn't eaten much that day to prepare for getting in this dress, but now that I was in it, I could hardly eat more than a few bites. I was envious of my friends in less constricting attire. Why did beauty have to come as such costs? I would have happily finished off my meal and eaten some of Camden's, but the stupid silk did not breathe.

Fuck, it was constricting. It wasn't a corset, but it was not meant to stretch at all. Alexandre had warned me of that, but I hadn't considered what it would be like to sit and stand and dance in it for hours. I took shallow breaths to compensate and concentrated on my friends instead.

It was only a few hours. I'd survive.

After dinner, we sat through the presentation for the individuals and businesses with considerable contributions to the HIV/AIDS foundation for this year's charity measure. Then the dance floor opened, and we all poured onto it, desperate for the release.

My dress was still tight. Next time I saw Alexandre, I was going to have to tell him to consider that people needed to breathe in these goddamn things.

"I'm so glad I came tonight," Harmony said with a laugh to me and Robert.

I hadn't realized that they were friends, but she seemed relaxed around him.

"Me too," Robert said. "That shit with Mitchell..." He trailed off as Harmony's face went pale.

"What?" I asked, looking over my shoulder.

Then I saw what had drawn her attention. Robert seemed to have produced Kurt out of thin air.

And on his arm was none other than Fiona.

"Oh fuck," I ground out.

I didn't know why I'd thought that Fiona would scamper off and disappear after Camden got Kurt to own up to his mistake. She'd never disappeared before when I wanted her to.

"I can handle this," I told Harmony, going into full-on bulldog mode.

Harmony caught my arm. "Don't. I just... I want to forget about it."

I opened my mouth to object. That wasn't in my nature. Harmony was in my circle now. Which meant I protected what was mine. I already despised Fiona—pregnancy or not. She didn't need to rub it in Harmony's face.

But before I could say anything, Harmony turned and fled. I sighed and turned to go after her, but Robert stopped me.

"Hey, just keep an eye on Whit, will you?" he asked.

"Sure, but I can talk to her."

He smiled with that characteristic charm. "Don't worry about it. Harmony and I have been friends since we were kids. Let me talk to her."

"You're sure?"

"Yeah, she'll be fine. Let Whitley know I'll be back."

"Sure," I agreed, and then he traipsed off, following in Harmony's wake.

What a fucking clusterfuck of a night.

Things were actually going amazingly well for me and Camden, but everyone else seemed to be falling apart. Peace always seemed like just another truce. Maybe I was just waiting for the other shoe to drop... and it was dropping for everyone else.

I let Whitley know what Robert had said as she dragged me into a dance with English and Lark. I had to spend half of the time concentrating on my breathing just to get through this. Camden zipped in and out, bringing me fresh drinks and kissing me between making small talk with other friends.

But then I realized it'd been forty-five minutes, and I hadn't seen him. That was a long time for him to keep his hands off of me. He'd been just on the boundary of our group all night. My eyes scanned the crowd. Where had he gone?

"Hey, have you seen Camden?" I asked Court.

He frowned and then darted his gaze around. "No, I haven't."

"That's weird."

I pulled away from my girls. My heart was in my throat. Was he... with Fiona? It didn't make sense. She was here with Kurt. He and I were on strong footing. Why did my mind always go to the worst-case scenario? My breathing became erratic as I searched him out in the crowd. I didn't know why I was freaking out, but I couldn't keep it in check. A long, long lifetime of fears coiled in my belly. I hated having these fears, but I knew only time would make them better.

I was still looking for him when I felt a hand on my elbow.

"Katherine!"

I looked up at Penn in surprise. "Hey, have you seen Camden?"

"That's why I came to find you."

I braced for the worst. "What happened?"

"His sister just went into labor."

I stumbled back in surprise. "Wait... what?"

"Candice went into labor. I saw her with some medical staff. Camden sent me to find you."

"He sent *you*?" I asked in shock.

"Yeah. Come on. I think, they're heading to the hospital."

I took one step after him, trying to draw air into my lungs, but everything felt unsteady. I hadn't had enough to eat. I couldn't breathe. Something settled on my shoulders, and before I knew what was happening, blackness tipped into my vision. And everything else was lost.

32

CAMDEN

"Look, you can take the limo," I told Lars as I bent over my pregnant sister.

Her water had broken minutes earlier, and now, she was standing in a puddle of goo. The bottom half of her silk dress destroyed.

I turned to the EMT. "What's the closest hospital?"

"New York-Presbyterian," the woman said at once. "We have an ambulance nearby. We can take her ourselves."

"Is it that serious?"

The woman considered it and then shook her head. "Only if you want a rush job. If you don't care how long it takes, then your limo should do the trick. This is a first birth. I would say, at the minimum, she has another twelve hours of labor ahead of her."

Candice moaned. "Get me the fuck out of here. I don't care where I go."

"Honey, we don't have a birth plan for this hospital," Lars interjected.

And my sister looked at him as if she were going to filet him alive. "Lars, get me to a fucking hospital."

"Yes, honey," Lars said automatically. "I'll call the doula on the way."

Good man. That was the right answer.

"We can help you out to the limo," the EMT said.

I didn't hear Candice's response. I'd turned to see where the hell Katherine was. I didn't know if she'd want to go with Candice or if she'd want to wait until the baby was born and then we could meet her at the hospital. But I didn't see her. And I'd sent fucking Penn Kensington of all people to locate her. Where the fuck was he?

Then I saw someone else running toward me—Natalie Bishop.

"Camden," she said breathlessly as she teetered to a stop in her heels. "Katherine just... passed out."

Everything froze inside of me at those words.

"What happened?" I asked with lethal calm.

"I don't know. Penn went to get her for you, and when they headed over here, she fainted."

I straightened as everything came into sharp focus.

I knew it.

I fucking knew it.

Katherine was sick. People didn't recover from anorexia. It was a mental illness. They learned to live with it. And she had learned to live with it, but it had gotten worse. I'd asked her about it to see if she knew how much worse she'd gotten. I'd been planning to find a way to get her into therapy after this weekend, but I was fucking late.

And now, she exhibited one of the biggest signs. Dizziness and fainting were what I'd been looking out for. She was sick again. The anorexia had never left. Not really. But it was worse than it had been before we were together.

This ended now. I'd just gotten her. I couldn't lose her.

"Take the limo," I told Lars dismissively and came to

Natalie's side. "Show me where they are." I pointed at the EMTs. "Come with us."

Natalie nodded and headed back the way that she had come. The EMTs followed quickly behind me. A girl fainting appeared to be higher priority than my sister going into labor. Good.

We didn't go far before I saw Kensington on the floor with my wife pillowed in his lap. Something hitched in my chest. A molten magma that was ready to spew up out of me and destroy everything in its path. But of course, I couldn't direct that at Penn right now. Because the real problem was my wife... lying there, unconscious.

"What happened?" I demanded as we all rushed over.

Penn looked up at me with wide eyes and shook his head. "I have no idea. I came to get her for you, and she just fell. I barely caught her in time."

"I brought medical staff," I told him as I sank down next to Katherine.

Penn moved out of the way as the the EMTs got in close and began checking her vitals. "She's breathing."

"Blood pressure is low," the second one said and then rattled off the numbers.

I blinked. That *was* low. Really low.

They went back and forth as they checked her over.

Then Katherine's eyes fluttered open. "Wha—" she began.

"Katherine, can you hear me?" I asked, dropping down to her side.

"Camden?" she whispered. Her brown eyes searched me out. She looked incoherent.

"Are you okay? What happened?"

"Dress," she whispered. "Dress is too tight." She blinked

and looked up at the medical staff in confusion. "Where am I?"

"You're still at the Fashion Week gala."

The EMT stepped in. "Ma'am, your blood pressure is dangerously low, and you appear to have fainted. How are you feeling now?"

"Fine," she said, but her speech came out disjointed. She pushed herself up onto her elbows, but the team tried to stop her. "I'm fine. I just... I think the dress is too tight. I think maybe I... I don't know. What's going on?"

"Katherine, lie back," I instructed. "You're sick. You fainted. Tell them the truth."

She looked back at me in confusion and shook her head. "What do you mean?"

The EMT looked at me expectantly.

"I'm her husband. She has anorexia. She needs to be taken to the hospital right away for recovery."

"Camden," she whispered in horror. "I don't... I'm fine. It's the dress. I swear."

"She has a history of the condition. She's been hospitalized in the past," I said to the EMTs. "You can see all the signs."

"I'm not going to a hospital," she said sluggishly. "Camden, you know... you know how I feel."

Then she tried to shove away from the EMTs and sit upright. But her breath hitched, and suddenly, her eyes rolled back into her head. She fainted a second time. If I hadn't been there, she would have smacked her head on the carpet.

I did know how she felt about hospitals. She hated them. She would hate me for making her go there, but I'd do it anyway to save her.

The EMTs nodded at each other. "Let's get her into an ambulance."

And then everything was a rush. It all happened in such a blur that all I knew was, one minute, we had been in the gala, and the next, I was in an ambulance, zipping uptown to the hospital, while my wife was being hooked up to an IV and her dress was being cut off of her frail body.

PART V

HISTORY

33

KATHERINE

I awoke in a hospital bed. Machines beeped all around me. An IV ran into my vein. I was in a scratchy hospital gown. I was also freezing. My head felt fuzzy, and I couldn't remember how I'd gotten here.

Just that I'd been rushing after Camden because of Candice's pregnancy and then... oh. Oh, right. Camden had ordered me to go to a hospital. Camden had sent me here. Camden had gone against my wishes. He'd *known* my darkest fear, and still, he hadn't listened to a word I'd said. He'd just rushed forward, taking charge, as if my feelings about the matter were inconsequential.

My husband was seated in a hospital chair to the side of my bed.

"You're awake," he said gently.

"How long was I out?"

"Not that long. You... came to in the ambulance and started thrashing around and screaming." He kept his face blank, neutral, but I could see through him. I knew he dreaded what I was going to say. "They had to give you a sedative."

I closed my eyes again. A sedative. Well, didn't *that* just feel familiar?

"Katherine..."

I held up my hand to keep him silent. I needed another minute to process all of this. Maybe if I processed it, I could hold back the panic attack clawing at my throat. The feeling of overwhelming, oppressive bullshit that raked fingers down my back. The one that said I was here again, I was never going to get out, and this was my new life.

And I'd just felt like I was getting better. Seeing Jem in the hospital and being around her sunshine had made it bearable to even be in a hospital setting. But this? *This?*

Camden had *done* this to me. This was... horrific.

This was my worst nightmare all over again.

My breathing turned erratic. I balled my hands into fists. I was going to hyperventilate. I couldn't get enough oxygen in. That was how this had all started. That damn dress had been too tight. It had been so goddamn tight that I couldn't breathe. Then I'd fainted, and everyone had thought the worst. Camden had assumed I was sick again. He'd fucking *told* everyone about my past illness with anorexia. Who'd heard? Who knew now what I'd tried to keep secret for a decade?

"Katherine, can you hear me?" Camden squeezed my hand. "Are you okay? Should I call a doctor?"

I wrenched my hand away from him. "I don't need anything from you."

He didn't move. Not a single flinch. As if he'd been bracing himself for however long he'd been sitting there. Anticipating my anger.

"Why am I here?" I demanded.

"Because you have anorexia, and the doctors wanted to

keep you overnight for monitoring," he said flatly. No life in his voice. Just cool calculation. Camden Percy to the max.

"I am *not* anorexic anymore! My dress was too tight. I'd gained weight, and I wasn't supposed to move a pound. It was like pulling the strings on a corset. I couldn't breathe. That's all that happened."

"Katherine, you and I both know that isn't true."

"Well, if you say so, then it isn't, right, Camden? You are the be-all end-all."

"That's not what I'm saying. You have been getting worse for months. You've lost too much weight. You're hardly eating. You're obsessed with your body image. You count calories and work out multiple times a day for hours on end." He flattened his hand on the bed. "You have anorexia."

"No, I don't," I spat back at him. Fury rising up in me. "You think, because I was hospitalized before, that you know something about my previous condition, but you don't! You know nothing. You weren't there. You didn't see what I was like. I was skin and bones. I didn't even have muscle. I was sick all the time. I was frail and could barely eat more than a few bites."

Camden clenched his jaw. "You're frail now. You barely eat more than a few bites *now*," he growled. "And you don't even see it."

I closed my eyes. He had no idea what he was talking about. "I've lost weight, and I've been exercising but not like before. I knew I was spiraling around Puerto Rico. Lark asked me about it, but I was careful after that. I didn't want to be back in a hospital bed. Then you and I... well, we were together, and everything was looking up. I knew I wasn't sick. I was just living in the moment with you. Then I wear a too-tight dress one time, and you assume that I'm as bad as before."

"I'm not assuming anything," Camden said. "The last thing I want is to see you here, Katherine."

"You're the one who put me here! And you know how I feel about it."

"I know," he said, his voice still hard. "I knew that you'd hate me for doing it, and I did it anyway. Because you were sick, and you *lied* to me."

"I didn't lie to you!"

"Yes, you did. I asked you the night of English's party if you were sick, if things were back to how they had been, and you said no."

"Because they weren't back to that." I took a deep breath and blew it out. "I'm being so careful, Camden. I'm actually happy again. Our relationship is great. I actually *want* to eat. Of course I care what I look like, that's part of my job, but I'm trying to starve myself."

He shook his head. "And you still don't see it."

But I did. I saw exactly what he'd said. It was just skewed. He expected me to have anorexia, so he saw it in every aspect of my life. I had been exhibiting signs of previous behavior, but I'd been able to pull myself out of that. I didn't need to be in a hospital. I wasn't a threat to myself. I wasn't a shell of a person anymore. If anything, I was so, so much better than I'd ever been. He just couldn't see it, refused to see it.

"You should go," I said softly, turning my face away from him.

"I'm not leaving you."

I clenched my fists and tried not to cry. "I don't want you here."

"You're sick, and I should—"

"You should what?" I snapped. "Haven't you done enough? You command me to go to the hospital because you're my husband. As if that gives you some authority over my body. Then you demand to stay, watching me suffer through my fears. No, you should go."

"I don't want you to be alone."

"Tough shit. You ignored my wishes. I told you that I feared ever coming back and that I never ever wanted to do this. And you... you betrayed me." Tears welled in my eyes despite me wanting to push them down. "You betrayed everything."

He straightened at that. Going stiff and looking remarkably like his father. "All right. Stay here and wallow then."

I balked at his tone. "Don't try to turn this around on me, Camden Percy."

"No, of course not, Katherine. It would be much better for me to slowly watch you kill yourself at home."

"God, did you not listen to a word I said? I was better. We were better. *This*," I said, gesturing to the room, "is only necessary to your ego. You have to be in control. You have to be the one to *save me*. But you don't realize that you had already been doing it."

"Then it wasn't enough," he said flatly.

"Well, if you weren't enough at home," I growled, "you certainly won't be enough here."

He flinched slightly at that. As if I'd struck true.

"Okay." He backed away from me. "If that's what you want."

"It is."

He stepped around my bed and headed for the door. He stopped with his hand on it and looked back at me as if he were going to say something. I could see it in his eyes, how earnest he was in that moment, but then he buried it deep down. The way both of us had always been taught to deal with our problems.

"I'm going to check on my sister. If you need anything, you can text. I'll be upstairs."

Then he departed without another word.

The wind rushed out of my sails. Everything ached—my body, my head, my heart. I hadn't wanted to send him away. And yet, I couldn't draw him back. I couldn't forgive the trust that he'd shattered so callously.

I knew... some part of me knew that he'd only done what he thought was best, that he was afraid, and he wanted to prevent a repeat. But there were other ways. There were so many other ways than forcing me into a hospital again against my will. He had known how much I would completely freak out and be unable to survive in here.

Six weeks. I'd spent six weeks locked inside and away from the rest of the world. I wouldn't do it again. They couldn't make me. Not even my husband could force me to do it. I wasn't sick. Not like that. Not anymore.

I could get through this at home like a... normal person. Couldn't I?

I balled my hands up and pushed them hard against my eyes. I didn't want to cry. I didn't want to feel any of this. Not my panic attack held at bay by anger. Or the fear that I might still... maybe... possibly be sick. And what that could mean for my future. And still, I felt like I shouldn't have sent Camden away at all.

Because, now, I was alone.

I was facing this all alone again.

But wasn't that the story of my life? I didn't have a savior. My father wasn't a white knight. My brother wasn't ever coming home. Penn had chosen someone else. And now, Camden's betrayal cut like a knife. In the end, I only had myself.

I'd dug my own grave.

Time and time again.

I would survive this, as I always did. Because every time I opened my heart up... someone came through with a bulldozer to crash into it.

Maybe it would be better to seal my heart off for good and save myself the heartache. If this was always the outcome, why did I even bother?

34

CAMDEN

I'd known she'd be angry.

I hadn't known she'd be *that* angry.

I deserved it. Every word that she had thrown at me. I had done precisely what she had told me not to. It had been out of fear... blind terror, if I was being honest. The sight of her lying on the floor, unconscious, would never leave my mind.

Not that it mattered to her. What mattered was that I had stepped over a line. An unforgivable line in her eyes.

She'd told me the one thing she feared. That she was only beginning to get over because of Jem, and what had I done? At the first sign of a problem, I'd packed her away into an ambulance and sent her to the hospital without a second thought, just like her mother.

She was right to hate me. I couldn't help her. I wasn't enough. Nor had I ever been enough.

Now, she was gone. Long gone.

I couldn't see a way to bridge what I had destroyed. Especially since she still wouldn't recognize that she had a problem. I knew that was a sign of anorexia. No one wanted to believe they were sick, especially with a mental illness. She wanted to think that it had something to do with her job or that she was just working out to try to stay healthy for her socialite status. But she just didn't see it.

And she had *lied* to me.

No... it hadn't even been to me. She was lying to herself. She was so deep in this shit that she couldn't even see.

I didn't know how bad it was. She was right that I hadn't been there to see her hospitalized right out of high school. But I knew that it was bad enough for me to worry, for Lark to worry, for her to faint at the gala. I wished there had been another way. A way where she wouldn't hate me. But that solution hadn't been present when I fucking lost it at the gala.

And I'd rather her hate me and be alive and get help than her to still be lying on the ground, pretending nothing was wrong. Pretending it was the fucking dress and not the fact that she hadn't eaten anything for days.

I stomped upstairs and found Candice's room. I knocked and then entered. Candice was lying in the bed, hooked up to an IV so very similar to Katherine's. Lars looked pale and uncomfortable.

"How's it going?" I asked.

"Excellent now," Candice said. "I have drugs. We're setting up for an epidural."

"You don't look so good, Lars."

Candice just laughed. "He doesn't like that we're going against the birth plan. But I am all about spontaneity. Modern medicine is here for a reason, Lars, darling!" She smiled up at me. "Where's Katherine? Is she doing all right?"

"She is... downstairs."

Even though I'd declared to everyone present at the gala

that Katherine had anorexia, it felt different to do so here. I'd been in the midst of an emergency. I'd just taken charge, as I so often did. But I'd seen how much it upset her. I didn't want to destroy her privacy.

"She's not feeling well."

"Well, I'll be here all night. So, she can come see me later when she's better." Then, Candice moaned. "Ugh, contraction. Hold on."

Lars was there, holding her hand as she squeezed through it.

"Phew," she said. "That wasn't fun."

"I'll leave you guys to this. I can be here later if need be. I'm going to get a drink."

"Oh my god," Candice sighed. "I'll finely get a fucking drink tomorrow. Camden, you'd better be ready with the best gin and tonics in the city."

I chuckled dryly. "Will do."

I headed out of the hospital and stared up at the sky of scattered stars overhead. They were hard to see in the city. The pollution and smog obscured most of them, but I could still barely make them out. I wanted to be light-years away from here. So very far away from all of my problems.

My chest tightened with pain and also a hollowness that I knew all too well. I needed my inhaler. I'd been so good without it since Katherine and I made up. Fuck, my lungs felt so tight. Everything hurt.

I buzzed the limo, and it pulled up almost right away. I piled into the backseat and dove toward the box where I'd left the lifesaving device. I found it and took two quick puffs off of it.

Fuck, fuck, fuck.

I didn't even feel better.

I lay out longways inside the limousine and stared up at

the top of the car as if I could see through it to the sky beyond. Everything hurt. Was it supposed to hurt this much? Was losing her really worth it all?

Fuck, I couldn't do it. I couldn't go on without her. I didn't even fucking want to.

I might be a bastard in the boardroom, but I didn't want to lose my wife. I felt adrift with the knowledge that I'd die before letting her go. Actually, literally die. I felt like I could at any moment.

"Where to, sir?" my driver asked.

I closed my eyes and tried to decide what to do. It would probably be smartest to call Court, get wasted at his place, and wake up the next morning, ready to deal with all of this. Somehow, I couldn't bring my problems to Court's doorstep. He'd be offended that I ever thought that, but he and English were *so* happy. I couldn't even fathom being around anyone that happy right now.

No, I couldn't stay in the city. I couldn't stay so close to Katherine and yet so far away.

"Hank's," I finally said to the driver.

The car drove off, shepherding me away from the hospital. Katherine had told me to leave. All but forced me out. And yet, I didn't want to do it.

Stupid.

It was all so fucking stupid.

Was I determined to be just like my father?

Unable to fix anything. Only make problems worse. And then abandon the problem when it got to be too much. Was I just trying to control her the way that my father had always controlled me?

The thought left me feeling sick. I was not my father. I'd spent my life learning to emulate him, to guard myself against his attacks. And also figuring out how to slowly eradicate any part of him that had touched me.

Apparently, I hadn't done a good enough job.

And in the end, I was just like the old man.

In nearly every way.

***

The limo pulled up in front of Hank's. By then I'd gone through several small bottles of liquor that I'd found in the minibar of the limo. I wasn't even close to drunk yet, but I was well on my way. Maybe I could convince Monica to slip me a bottle, so I could forget the shitshow that had happened tonight.

I stumbled out of the limo and told my driver to go home. I'd crash at my apartment nearby. He could come get me in the morning, or I'd catch a cab. Right now, I didn't even fucking care.

Hank's was slammed. The bar was packed wall to wall with patrons enjoying the finer points of the steady establishment. Ricky called out to me, but I didn't even stop to see where he was in his game. I just needed a drink. Several drinks.

There were two bartenders at Hank's tonight, and I slouched into a stool in Monica's section. It took her a few minutes of pouring drinks to even see me sitting there.

"Camden," she said in surprise. "Wasn't expecting you in here tonight."

"Me either," I grumbled.

She reached for the scotch and slid a drink to me.

"Keep 'em coming."

"Will do. Tequila tonight?"

I shook my head and downed the drink. "Nothing to celebrate."

She frowned and passed beers to two guys nearby. "What's up with you tonight? Thought things were going well for you. Did you tell your girl you loved her?"

"Sure did," I said, reaching for the drink as she poured me another knuckle's worth.

"Didn't go as planned?"

"It did. But... it's complicated."

"Let me get a few more drinks covered for the tables, and you can tell Mama Monica all about it."

I waved her off, burying myself in the drink instead. I could have played a game or two if there were any tables open, but there weren't. It probably was for the better. With how morose I felt, getting competitive wasn't a good idea. I might blow up on someone. Take out my anger on an unsuspecting victim. At the end of the day, I was still Camden Percy. I couldn't do that for my image.

Monica came back fifteen minutes later and refilled my drink again. She'd pulled in a third bartender, who had been hanging out in the back. Everything seemed to be running much smoother with the help.

"Now, tell me what's going on," she said with a wink.

"My wife is... sick," I told her reluctantly.

"That's not good. Is she going to be okay?"

"I think so. She fainted, and now she's in the hospital. But she's terrified of being there after she had to stay in one when she was younger."

"That's unfortunate."

"It is. Well, I got mad at her for lying to me about her illness. So, I just kind of... made her go to the hospital. Even though she didn't want to. Now, she feels betrayed that I did that without consulting her. That I had to be in charge and in control, no matter what." I blew out a breath. "That I'm just like my father."

"But you were doing it to help her?"

I shrugged. "Yes. I was terrified that she was going to hurt herself."

"Sometimes, people don't know when they need help. You can't blame yourself for doing the right thing."

"I don't know. Was it the right thing?"

"You don't normally second-guess yourself," she observed as she added ingredients to a shaker for a pair of shots.

"No, I don't. But then again, neither does my father, and he's a jackass. So, maybe stopping and thinking might have been good for once."

Monica leaned forward. "Do you love Katherine?"

"Yes."

"Would you go back and change what happened?"

I hesitated. "No."

"Then this sounds like it has nothing to do with that situation. You did the right thing by Katherine even if she doesn't like it. You two can both be in the right in an argument. That's allowed when things are complicated."

"That's true," I said, downing another gulp.

Monica looked to the ground and then back up at me. "Finish up that drink, kid. Let's go for a walk."

I raised an eyebrow. I was pretty drunk. Walking didn't seem like a good idea. But the look she shot me brooked no response. So, I finished the drink and stood unsteadily. I blinked a few times to force back the feeling of intoxication.

"Hey, I'm going on break," Monica said to the other bartenders and then slipped under the bar to meet me.

She gestured for me to take the side entrance out the back. There was a couple making out against a brick wall and another cluster of guys smoking nearby. Monica dragged me away from them until we reached a beaten-in, old bench.

I was still in my tux.

It took me a minute to realize that I'd shown up to Hank's in my tuxedo. What the hell had I been thinking? No wonder everyone was looking at me funny. Even Monica. I'd untied the knot at my throat and undone the first button at the hospital, but that didn't seem to matter. I'd shown up here as Camden Percy from the Upper East Side. Not the pool shark that they were used to. I was me either way, but this... this outfit changed things.

Fuck. I hadn't meant to do that. I was so fucking out of it.

I slumped onto the bench next to Monica.

"You're a bit of a wreck tonight," she said.

"Tell me about it. What are we doing out here?"

"You looked like you needed some fresh air."

I shrugged. "Sure."

"And I have to tell you something."

She actually looked... frightened. I straightened slightly. I'd never seen anything but the hardened, badass Monica behind the bar. She seemed so... small out here, on this bench.

"Tell me what?"

"I want you to promise me that you'll let me explain."

I raised my eyebrows. "Okay."

"Promise, Camden. Say the words."

I stilled even further at that. "I promise."

It felt like a curse out of my mouth. I stared into her eyes and wondered what in the hell she was going to tell me. And why she looked like she was going to cry.

She took a deep breath. "I'm your mom."

35

CAMDEN

"Camden," Monica said gently, "I know it's a shock."

A bomb had gone off.

My ears were deaf.

There was a ringing as I stared through the debris.

"Please say something," she whispered.

"You're not my mother," was the only thing that I could get out.

She frowned. "I know this is hard to take in, and I'm sorry for that. I wanted to tell you. I wanted to tell you so many times."

"I don't believe you."

She looked hurt, but she still had that stubbornness about her. "About two years ago, you went to the police chief and asked him to help you find your mother," she said. "That's why you became friends in the first place. It's why you came here with him."

"No one else knows that," I hissed.

"I know. You had to go to José directly—with blackmail against him, I might add—so that he wouldn't take it to your father."

I stood and shook my head. "How the hell do you know this?"

"You promised," she cried as I turned away from her. "You fucking promised."

My teeth ground together. This was too much. Way too much. This night was a disaster. And this... this couldn't be happening. It wasn't possible.

But I had promised. As much as I wanted to walk away and never, ever look back, I turned, and I waited.

"I don't know what you had on José. It doesn't matter anyway, but he did what you asked. He came looking for me."

"My mother's name is Helena Percy," I spat at her. "She was born Helena McAdams on Long Island, New York. She didn't... she wouldn't..."

"I know," Monica said flatly. "I know what I was. Securely middle class, wide-eyed, innocent, beautiful, and everything a domineering, excessively wealthy man wanted to own. And I loved your father for many years. I really did."

"Stop," I said, wanting to block out the words.

"Carlyle was doting and kind. He showed me a world that I never could have imagined, and then a miracle happened—you."

"This isn't real," I said, denying reality. "You know nothing."

"But the baser tendencies that I ignored so I could love Carlyle came out with a vengeance after you were born. I tried to flee to escape him. I tried to take you with me, but you know who he is. What he's capable of. He hamstrung me through the divorce, took everything, including full custody of you. He told me if he ever saw me near *his* son again... he'd kill me."

"No," I croaked.

But I knew it for truth. There was something in my chest that said that she wasn't making this up. This was the father I'd grown up with. I could see him doing this precise thing. If he couldn't have the woman he claimed to love, then *no one* could. Not even me.

"I'm sorry," she said, a tear running down her face. "I was so young. I didn't know how to fight for you. He wouldn't let me. So, I ran. I changed my name. I escaped his shadow, and I tried to move on."

"But your husband and son..."

"They were your father and you." She choked. "I never married again. No other children. I dated, but..." She shook it off as if she couldn't ever explain how much she had been hurt by my father.

How we both had been destroyed by him.

"If all that's true, why didn't you tell me who you were?" I turned back to look at her. This woman I'd trusted, who I'd turned to for advice. She'd felt like... family. Like a new family. But I'd never known what... who she truly was.

"I wanted to tell you," she said, swiping at the tears running down her face. "When José found me, he came to the bar. He knew my past with Carlyle. He wanted to keep me safe. We agreed that he'd bring you here, to Hank's, where I worked. That we'd meet, and at the end of the day, I would decide when to tell you."

"He told me it was a dead end," I said angrily. "He told me that Helena Percy no longer existed."

"Which is true. Helena Percy no longer exists," she said, holding her palms out to me. "I'm just Monica now. I'm not what I once was. And... I'm glad. I'm stronger." She stood to meet me, and I saw that strength on display. "But I should have told you before today."

"Why didn't you then?" I snarled.

Something broke inside me. Some part of me unraveled, and all the cool calm that I'd managed to keep in check for so many years just went up in smoke.

"Why didn't you tell me who you were, Monica? I came here at least once a month for *two years*. I stood at your bar. I played pool. We joked and laughed and gambled. You gave me advice. I dropped my problems on your doorstep. You laughed about my issues with my father. All while hiding behind the fact that you had been *married* to the man! That you'd left me! That he'd apparently forced you out of my life!" I couldn't hold back as I raged against the woman before me. "How could you look at me—knowing I was your son, knowing what I was going through—and say *nothing*?"

Monica didn't back down. She didn't even flinch at my outburst.

Instead, she stepped forward, and she put her arms around me. I struggled against her for a second, but she held steady. She didn't let me go. Now, after all this time, when I wanted to be left alone, she wouldn't let me go.

"I'm sorry," she said firmly. "I'm so sorry."

I cracked again and slowly put my arms around her, too.

"I should have been there. I should have told you. You're right. You're so right."

"Why?"

"At first, I was afraid that you'd reject me," she said, pulling back to look up into my eyes. "I thought you'd see the woman I'd become... and walk out. Or that you'd believe whatever your father had said or that you'd become him in my absence. I didn't want you to run away. I wanted to get to know you. And I'm so glad that I did." She brushed my cheek with her fingers. "You're nothing like him, Camden. You are your own man. Despite all he has done to hurt you, you've never let him break you."

"I wanted you there."

"I wanted to be there," she admitted. "After I got to you, I admit to selfishness. We had a relationship. Albeit not the one that I'd wanted. But it was more than I had ever dreamed of having. I worried if I revealed myself, then Carlyle would find out, and he would try to silence me again. Then I worried that... I would ruin our friendship. It was selfish, all of it, and I'm so sorry."

I wanted to break away from her. I wanted to curse at her. I wanted to escape and never look at this moment again. But she'd gone through enough. We both had. At the end of the day, didn't we deserve this after all we'd endured with my father?

So, I pulled her in for a hug and just held her. I held her without a word. Just the two of us for the first time in forever.

When we finally pulled apart, she brushed another stray tear with a laugh. "This is the most I've cried in years."

"Thank you...for finally telling me."

"Oh, Camden, I should have done it ages ago. Things were so complicated. I knew that my reasons for not telling you were right, but you not knowing was wrong. I... I just had to tell you today. I couldn't let you sit there and think that you were like your father. Not when you were protecting Katherine at all costs. Even when she didn't want your protection, you were still there. That is the opposite of your father."

I ran a hand back through my hair. "I can't believe he did all of that to you... and at the same time, I can totally see him controlling you to the point that he made you want to leave."

She glanced down and back up again. "Well, that... that wasn't all of it."

The way she'd said it made something burn up inside of me. It was fear. "What did he do?"

"He... he was abusive," she said finally. "At first, he'd grab me and shake me, but it got worse. It wasn't as if I could get a restraining order or anything. He owned the whole city. No one would have believed me. No one would have convicted him."

"That son of a bitch," I snarled. "I'll kill him."

Monica reached out and grasped my arm. "Please, don't do anything rash. It's long since over. I just want a relationship with you."

"You don't know the half of what he's done in his life. This is just... the icing on the cake. The point where I'm fed up with his absolute bullshit. He's done nothing but push me down my entire life. A bully trying to keep others in line. Well, I won't stand by and let him do this any longer."

"Camden, I know that you think you know your father, but if you go after him like this, he will try to ruin you," she said desperately. "It's in his nature."

"Well, he won't succeed," I told her. "He might have raised me, but I'm twice the man he'll ever be. And I know how to finally stop him."

"Camden, please," Monica cried. "Please... just stay here tonight. I don't want to lose you, and I don't trust him. Please."

She grasped my arm in her hands, and I looked back to see my mother begging me, pleading with me. My *mother*. The woman I'd spent so long looking for. The woman I'd blamed for abandoning me, only to find out it wasn't true. And she wanted me here. She wanted me to stay.

So, I nodded. And I stayed. My father would get his due. I would damn well make sure of it.

36

KATHERINE

"I brought you clothes," Lark said early the next morning as she entered my hospital room.

I was still waiting for a doctor to discharge me. They were swamped, and the nurse had kept putting me off. I didn't particularly like it, but it didn't seem like there was much that I could do. So, I'd been sitting around in this horrid hospital gown until Lark showed up with a change of clothes.

"Thanks," I said, taking the bag from her.

"I cannot believe they cut you out of an Alexandre D'Oria original."

"Tell me about it. I haven't told him yet. He's probably going to cry."

"I feel like crying," she said as she sank into a seat.

I eased out of the bed and slid into the soft leggings and long-sleeved shirt she'd brought me. I'd told her how freezing I'd been all night. When I sank back into the bed, I saw she was wearing the Lark concerned face. I should have expected it earlier. I was amazed she'd even managed to hold it off for that long.

"I really don't want to hear it."

"And I really don't care," she snapped back.

I winced at her tone. Lark didn't often get mad. But when she did, she reverted back into her old self, in which she exploded. I prepared myself for that.

"You know the entire crew wanted to come here, but I told them that you wouldn't want all the fanfare."

"I appreciate that," I told her.

"But I should have let everyone show up," she said as she began to pace. "I should have let you see how many people care about you. How many people worry for you. How many people you could *hurt* by doing this shit again, Katherine."

"I'm not sick."

"And you're still denying it!" she yelled at me.

"I *was* sick," I amended. "I was sick, and I didn't realize it. Even when you asked me about it in Puerto Rico. I was sick then, but... I didn't know it."

I'd had all night to think about it, and I'd come to the conclusion that I hadn't seen what was going on in my life. That I'd been too wrapped up in my own misery to realize it. Yes, I was exercising more. Yes, I was seeing a nutritionist. I was still depressed and worrying about my body image to a point that was beyond reality.

But I was getting better. No matter what Camden had said about my fainting. I'd been pulling myself out of it with his help.

"You think you're magically better?" Lark asked.

"No. I think that I was on the mend, and now, I'm *here*. Everyone is freaking out for no reason."

Lark shook her head. "You're unbelievable. You always think you're one step ahead of everyone. Even one step ahead of yourself. Well, could you put on the brakes and look at the situation at hand?" Her lips quivered. "We're worried about you, Katherine. We're scared. I'm scared. You need help." She stepped forward, taking my hand. "Please listen to me when I say that I want you to get help. And I'm going to be here and annoying you about it until you do."

The first thing I wanted to do was argue. I wanted to yell at Lark to mind her own goddamn business. But when I looked up at my friend, I couldn't do it.

I saw only love in her eyes. She'd stood by me through thick and thin. We'd known each other too long for bullshit in this moment. She was worried about me. She had reason to worry.

"Okay," I finally said.

"Okay?" she asked.

"Yeah, okay. I'll start going to therapy again. I'll see what my psychiatrist says."

"Really?"

"I don't want everyone to worry about me. I don't want to be the person I was when this was bad."

"I didn't think it'd be this easy," Lark admitted.

"It's not easy. I'm still mad. I don't want to be here. I don't think that I'm bad enough to be here. There could have been another way."

"What other way?" Lark asked. "You weren't listening to us. If you hadn't ended up in the hospital, would you have ever come around to going to therapy again?"

No. That answer was on the tip of my tongue.

I knew that I hadn't wanted to go back to therapy. Even seeing the fear in Lark's eyes, I hadn't wanted to consider it. Until I'd ended up here, I hadn't even stopped to look at it. It had taken a night in solitude to make me see the reality of what had been happening.

I didn't think that I looked too skinny. In fact, I still felt like there were places that I needed improvement. But wasn't that normal? Didn't society tell us to keep working on our body? That we could always be healthier? Hadn't people complimented me on my newer, smaller figure? Wasn't that what everyone said they wanted? I'd been given all of these opportunities because my body was smaller.

It was a total mind-set change to realize... maybe my body size didn't even matter. It certainly didn't mean that I was healthier. I'd seen girls who were waif thin, who were deathly ill, that society still complimented.

I hated the whole thing. Everything that told me that being smaller, taking up *less* space, made me *more, better, worthy*. I was Katherine Van Pelt. My personality took up the entire room. And somehow, my body had to take up no space?

Why was that what brought value to my life? Why did others make it the highest priority? And... was there ever going to be a way to stop it?

"I hate feeling like this," I said softly to Lark. "I don't know what to do. People praise me for looking like this."

"And since when does Katherine Van Pelt care what other people think?"

"Always," I whispered.

Lark sank against the bed. "Listen, I've known you for a long time. I know that this socialite business hangs on your appearance. You've always been beautiful and thin, and you think that matters, but it doesn't matter. What matters is what you do with it. Like with the work you're doing at the hospital for the children. For Jem. That's what matters more than any body image out there."

"Jem," I whispered. "She's such a ray of sunshine even though she's sick."

"Society would say she's not the standard of beauty. But the girl didn't even wear a wig! She wants everyone to see her bald head or her head scarf because that is beautiful to her. We cannot define our worth based on what is dictated to us by the media."

"I know. I know." I shook my head. "I know that intuitively. But at the same time..."

"At the same time, society has decided what beauty is. And women have to fit into that mold." I nodded at her words. Lark shrugged. "Fuck it."

I laughed. "What?"

"Just fuck it, Katherine. You don't have to live up to anyone's standards but your own. And I know it's not that easy to dismiss everything we've learned. I know there's a long road ahead of you. But I've been doing research on anti-diet culture, and I bet it would really help to find a therapist with that mind-set. Your body size doesn't make you any happier. If anything, the skinnier you get, the more miserable you are."

I bit my lip. She was right. I'd lost weight when I was unhappy. And then I'd kept losing it because it seemed to make more things right.

"What even is anti-diet culture?" I asked warily.

"It's the belief that diets don't actually work. Most people lose the weight and then gain it right back, plus some. And that it's damaging to have an unhealthy relationship with food, to offer good or bad qualities to food, to count calories or macros, to weigh yourself, to limit what kinds of food you can eat, to be heavily restrictive, even to take before and after pictures, as that focuses on the skinnier body being the better body. It's just learning to live and love yourself again without qualification."

"That sounds... impossible."

Lark shrugged. "It feels like that at first. But I've tried to give up all my preconceived notions about it. I eat a burger when I want it. I eat a salad when I want it. I thank them both for nourishing my body. At the end of the day, I want to be happy and healthy and not constantly worrying about what I put in my body."

"Well, I guess I could try it."

"Along with therapy," Lark said quickly.

"Yes. I mean... it took over a year last time in therapy for me to be human again. I can't imagine not looking at food that way. But... I'll talk to someone about it."

"Good. That's the first step."

Lark opened her mouth to say something else, but then a knock at the door stalled her. A second later, the door opened and revealed, to my shock, my mother.

"Hello, Katherine." She tipped her head at Lark. "Lark."

"Mother."

"Mrs. Van Pelt," Lark said, jumping to her feet.

She glanced over at me once with wide eyes. So, she hadn't been the one to tell her.

"Do you mind if I have a minute alone with my daughter?" my mother asked.

"No, of course not." Lark snatched up her purse and darted to the door. "I'll be back later. Text me if you're let out early."

"Will do."

And then she was gone. The door closed behind her. It was just me and my mother.

"How did you find out?"

"The real question is, why didn't you tell me?"

I shrugged. "I wasn't sure that you'd care."

My mother dropped her bag off in the chair and came to stand next to me. She looked as imposing as ever in a Chanel pantsuit. Her hair styled and makeup perfect. Everything I'd learned about how a woman was supposed to act came from her. And I felt so small and insignificant under her gaze.

Then her hand came to rest on mine, and I saw something else there.

"Of *course* I care, Katherine," my mother said, emotion thick in her voice.

I remained silent. A deer ready to bolt at a single provocation. I'd never heard that sound in my mother's voice, and I didn't know what to expect.

"I was the first person to put you in the hospital," she continued. "I was the one who had found you. I don't know if you even remember. I'd come home from a luncheon, and I found you on the living room floor. You were barely breathing. I panicked. I had no idea what to do. I called 911 and rushed you to the hospital. I'd just lost my husband and my son." She choked on the words. "I couldn't lose you, too. I *wouldn't* lose you. So, when the doctors said anorexia, I made you stay in that hospital. I didn't think twice. I knew you might hate me for it, but if I kept you alive, then that was all that mattered. Because I didn't know whether or not you'd live."

Tears welled into my eyes. My mother had never told me this story. I'd known the outcome, of course. I'd known that I'd been furious at her. That I'd blamed her for so long. For being callous. But... had it actually been the opposite?

"You cared about me *so* much that you sent me to the hospital?" I whispered.

"Of course. It was done out of love. Even if you never saw it that way. I was terrified to lose you."

I swallowed. Oh god. "I never... I never knew."

"That's my fault as well," she said, dragging a seat closer to me and sitting down. She looked so impossibly... frail in that moment. My mother, the giant... looked frail. As if life had hit her so much harder than she'd ever let on to me. "I wanted to do right by you. But in trying to do right, all I did was push you away. And... I think that's what Camden tried to do last night."

I sighed. "So, Camden messaged you?"

"He did, and I'm glad that he did. He's looking out for you, even when you don't want him to."

"I do wish that looking out for me didn't always end up with me in a hospital."

"Katherine," she said, drawing my attention back to her, "he loves you. He cares for you. And he's not going to ruin your life like your father."

I winced at the words. "How do I know that?"

She gave me a perfect Celeste Van Pelt *bitch, please* face. "Because you do."

And she was right. I was mad at Camden for what he'd done. But if he was half as worried as my mother had just admitted to being, as Lark had admitted to being, maybe... just maybe, he'd done the right thing. I didn't want to be here. I didn't think I needed to be here.

But he had.

There hadn't been another option either.

He loved me, and in his own way, he had been taking care of me. I didn't want to end up like my parents. I didn't want a loveless marriage where I was doomed to be unhappy. I just wanted... Camden.

"I think I probably need to talk to him."

My mother tapped my hand twice, and a real smile split her features. "I think you do, too."

37

CAMDEN

I'd stayed with Monica—my mother—all night. We'd talked and shared stories and had a lot of alcohol. By the time morning came, I was ready to deal with my father and his decades of lies. I was ready for it to be over.

She didn't approve.

I could see it in her expression. I could see the fear still buried down in there. It didn't matter that she had left him over thirty years ago. My father still elicited a fearful response from her. She didn't want to see this all go up in smoke. But she only knew half of the man that I had become. She'd seen the Camden Percy who came to the bar. The one who needed an escape. Who knew that he could be nothing but himself, even in unassuming clothing. But she didn't know the man in the boardroom. The man who had made something of himself.

My father had done his best to keep me down. I'd long thought that it was something to do with me. Something to do with my mother. But now, I knew the truth. He was just a worthless, piece-of-shit human, and he would tear down anything in his path.

I'd spent my life silently saving my friends. Enacting revenge on the people who had hurt them. It was time to do the same for myself and for my mother. Time to take matters into my own hands.

On my way back into the city, a group text came in from Lars, letting all of us know that Candice was about to have the baby. Elizabeth responded immediately, saying that she and my father were on their way. I didn't respond. Just tucked the phone away and changed the direction of the limo.

The hospital it was.

I arrived thirty minutes later and headed up to Labor and Delivery. Part of me wanted to check in on Katherine first. But knowing her, she'd need more time to process what had happened. I would have liked to have her at my side through this though.

My father and Elizabeth were in the waiting area when I arrived. Elizabeth stared out a window. I could see the anxiety in her body language. My father was seated, reading *The New York Times*. Not a single care. I was surprised he was even here for this.

"Oh, Camden," Elizabeth said, rushing toward me and enveloping me in a hug. "I'm so glad you could make it. Have you heard from Harmony? Or Katherine? I thought they'd both be here already."

I shook my head. "Katherine isn't feeling well. I'm going to check on her after this. No word from Harmony."

She sighed heavily. "Well, I guess I shouldn't be surprised. But at least you're here."

"What took you so long?" my father asked, folding the paper and looking up at me.

"I wasn't in the city last night."

My father raised his eyebrows. "It was the Fashion Week gala last night."

"I am well aware," I said through gritted teeth.

"Leave him be, Carlyle," Elizabeth said, returning to her window.

"Allow me to parent my son," Carlyle snapped. It was more forceful than I'd heard him be with Elizabeth.

A hole in the careful facade of their relationship he'd put up. I hadn't seen them argue. Not that it meant they didn't argue. But usually, my father was careful with who he showed his faults to. This was his fourth wife after all. He likely had a system down.

Elizabeth didn't say anything. She clenched her jaw and looked away. Apparently, she was going to let it slide. Big surprise.

"Parenting? That's rich," I spat back.

"I have done nothing but give you every opportunity to succeed. You're helping to run my company. You're living on the penthouse of my hotel." He stood to his considerable height. There were a few feet between us, but we might as well have been nose to nose. "A little gratitude goes a long way."

"Gratitude," I said with a shake of my head. "How could I feel gratitude to someone like you?"

He raised his eyebrows. "What the hell does that mean?"

"You're really going to make me spell it out, aren't you?"

"Clearly, I have no idea to which you are referring."

"How about we start with the Ireland deal?"

"The deal that you managed to lose for the company?" my father asked. "Doesn't seem like the place you'd want to start to gain my goodwill."

"Oh, I'm well past wanting anything from you. You *lied* to me. *You* lost the Ireland deal and then blamed the entire thing on me to save face. You lost the company millions and wouldn't even own up to it."

"I have no idea where you're getting this."

"From the person who ended the deal," I told him. "The deal that I saved by following up with him. He's coming into the city next week to close it. You're welcome."

My father's face contorted into one of rage. I'd gone behind his back. This was a matter of pride.

"I think the board might be happy to hear about that, don't you?"

"Are you threatening me?" he snarled.

"Yes."

My father cleared the distance between us. "How dare you go behind my back for this deal. You're even more worthless than I thought. The board is going to hear *none* of what you said. None of it."

"Oh, really?"

"Yes, because, effective immediately... you're fired."

I laughed. I couldn't help it. I laughed in his face.

His cheeks turned a bright red. Not from embarrassment. Though he should be embarrassed. But it was that Percy fury. He was offended that I'd laughed at him.

"What are you laughing at?"

"I'm not fired," I told him. "I already emailed the board about what happened. Actually, I'd be shocked if *you* weren't let go."

"I can't be let go from my own company."

"Beg to differ."

My father grabbed the collar of my tuxedo. I was still in the damn thing. Rumpled and smelling of cigarette smoke, but still dressed to impress. He nearly tore the damn thing off.

"Carlyle!" Elizabeth said. "Let him go!"

But we just stared at each other. I saw my father for what he really was—a coward. He didn't stand up to his foes. He ran. He didn't make others feel bigger by the force of his personality. All he cared about was making everyone else smaller. And I wouldn't back down. Not from him.

He finally released me, pushing me backward. "You're bluffing."

"Ah, you know so little about me." I angled my head down and stared him squarely in the eye. "I always follow through on my promises."

"You've never had the spine."

"That's where you're wrong. For a long time, I let you walk all over me," I told him confidently. "I let you have your tantrums and your bullshit negotiations. I let you blame me and push me. I thought you were trying to make me a better man."

"And I see, that was hopeless," he said, trying to cut me down.

"Then I found out what you did to my mother."

My father stilled completely. Preternatural stillness. Death. "What did you just say?"

My anger was a supernova, ready to consume everything in its path. He stood no chance. None against me.

"You'll pay for what you did to her."

"Your mother abandoned you," he snarled.

"That's the lie you have to keep telling yourself? You beat her!" I crowed. "You left her no choice but to flee your presence. When she tried to take me, you used all your influence and money to keep her from getting custody of me. Just to punish her."

"You have no idea what you're talking about." He lost his conviction. His face went pale.

"I would have let you get away with it. But not her," I snarled. "Not her."

"Your mother was a low-class *whore*. She was running around on me. You're not even my son!"

I clenched my fists at my sides to keep from punching out his teeth. "She said that you'd say that. That you'd accused her of that when she ran away. But we both know it's not true."

"How did you find her?" he demanded. "Where the hell is she?"

"Far, far away from you."

My father snapped. He grasped me by my lapels again. There was more than anger in his eyes. He was totally mad. I'd never seen him like this. Even when he'd been horrible when I was younger, he'd always had this calculated control to him. But now, he was just that bully that I'd painted him as.

"Carlyle," Elizabeth cried. I could hear the pain in her voice. She was witnessing his deterioration, too. And I was sorry for that. I could tell she cared for him, but I didn't put it past him not to do the same to her.

"Violence is all you know," I told him evenly. "You divorced and abandoned your first wife. The second ended up dead. The third was annulled, but there were bruises on her. I remember them now. Did you kill Candice's mom? Is that why she isn't here? Was my mom the lucky one who got away?"

"Camden, stop!" Elizabeth cried.

And then my father lost it completely.

I watched in slow motion as he pulled his fist back. I didn't think he'd actually do it. Even as it was happening, I didn't believe he'd hit me.

K.A. LINDE

Not until his fist connected with my jaw and I was thrown backward, my head snapping sideways.

My hand came up to my busted lip and touched the blood now running down my chin. I looked back at my father. I saw nothing living inside him. Just the monster I'd always known was there.

"You'll pay for that," I told him. "That's a promise."

38

KATHERINE

I screamed.

There was no thought to it. Just fear.

Carlyle had punched Camden. Oh god! I couldn't even imagine what had provoked that. What had made him do it. I had known he was horrible, but I'd never thought that he'd *hit* Camden. Not in a million years. And from Elizabeth's horrified expression, neither had she.

Lark gasped in shock. "Oh my god."

"The police." I told Lark before rushing forward to pull them apart.

My scream must have drawn a crowd. Suddenly, there were nurses coming out of doorways, ready for whatever new horror awaited.

"The police," I shouted as I passed one. "Get the police. This man just assaulted my husband."

I didn't wait around to find out if she listened. I had to get there now. I didn't know if Camden was going to retaliate. I didn't know if it was going to turn into a full-out brawl. And it couldn't.

I knew his father. I knew how manipulative he was to

Camden. If Camden threw that punch—and I was sure he *wanted* to throw it—then his father would use it to his advantage. No matter how mad at Camden I was for what had happened in my life, I didn't want his father to hurt him again.

"Stop! Carlyle, stop," Elizabeth cried out, wrenching on her husband's arm.

But the two were immovable.

Then I was there. I pushed myself between the two men. "What are you doing? Are you out of your mind?"

But Carlyle didn't look at me. His gaze was fixed on Camden. He grabbed me as if he were going to throw me out of the way to get to his son. I wrenched away from him and toward Camden

"Tell her," Camden taunted behind me. "Tell her why you assaulted your son."

"You are no son of mine," Carlyle snarled.

I retreated in disgust. What the hell was he talking about?

But I didn't even have time to ask that question, because the hospital police had arrived. They barreled down the hallway, right for us.

"He's the one," I said, pointing at Carlyle.

His eyes widened slightly in shock. That I'd actually called the police. That they'd actually arrived. Maybe he was finally realizing his mistake. He should have realized it long before he threw that punch.

"Sir, you're going to need to come with us," the first officer said, reaching her hand toward him.

"Don't touch me," Carlyle said, wrenching his arm out of her grasp. "Do you know who I am?"

"Sir," the woman said calmly, "we're going to have to ask you to leave."

Carlyle glared at the police officer. He looked like he wanted to throw a barrage of curses her way. Instead, he straightened his suit. "My daughter is giving birth right now."

"I understand, sir," she said. "But you were reported, assaulting this man."

"It was... an accident," he lied through his teeth.

"It was assault," Camden growled.

The woman nodded at Camden. "Would you like to press charges?"

"No, he would not!" Carlyle spat.

"Yes," Camden said flatly, "I would like to press charges."

Carlyle's eyes narrowed. "You wouldn't. You know how that would look to the company. You know what it would do to *you*."

"Sir, please come with us," the woman said, grabbing his arm now and directing him toward the exit.

"You taught me to never back down from a fight," Camden said, lethally calm. "If no one else can stop you, I will."

Carlyle shook off the police officer and started toward the exit. He looked like he wanted to yell back a cartoonish, *You'll never get away with this*. But instead, he raised his chin and strode out confidently. As if he had nothing to fear from his son. He was so very wrong in that regard.

When he was out of our sight, Camden's hand finally moved to my waist. "Hey, what are you doing out of bed?"

I turned in his grip. "Me? Why the hell did your father hit you? Why did he claim you aren't legitimate?"

"It's a long story. Maybe you should sit down," he said gently.

"I don't need to sit, Camden. I'm fine."

I heard sniffling behind us and looked to find Elizabeth

had collapsed into a chair nearby, crying. Lark sank into the seat next to Elizabeth, and absently patted her back. Lark looked at us in distress. I sighed. I wanted to deal with Camden first, but Elizabeth seemed to need us both now.

I took the seat opposite Lark. "Hey, are you okay?"

She looked over at me with raw emotion in her eyes. "I just watched my husband assault his son and then get arrested. No, I'm not okay."

"Right. Of course. Is there anything I can do?"

"No."

"We're here for you either way," Lark said gently.

"We are," Camden said.

"I've... been there," I admitted reluctantly. "Not exactly the same. But I was there the day my father was hauled away, and I know the trauma of watching someone you love turn out to be a liar."

"I don't know what could have possibly prompted him to do this. He's such a kind, caring man," she said. Her eyes lifted to Camden's, who stood by silently. "Was what you said true? Did he... hit his other wives?"

Camden solemnly nodded. I braced against that revelation. Carlyle Percy was an abuser. Fuck that man.

"I don't know what to say," Elizabeth said.

"You don't have to say anything," I assured her. "You don't have to do anything today either."

"There's plenty of time to figure out where we all go from here," Lark told her.

Elizabeth brushed the tears from her cheeks. "No, I won't be the woman who claims he's never done it to me. Because, one day, he will." She looked at Camden wistfully. "One day, he will, won't he?"

I wanted him to lie for her benefit. She was already hurting so much. But Camden wouldn't.

He just nodded.

She swallowed hard and then seemed to steel herself. "Well, that's unfortunate."

And I saw her make her decision. She didn't tell us that she was going to divorce Carlyle over this, but I saw the resolve in her expression. She'd been single, living her best life as a designer for long enough to know she didn't need a man to be happy. And that she couldn't live with a man who acted like this. Eventually, he'd come for her. Elizabeth Cunningham wasn't a victim.

We were all clustered around Elizabeth that we didn't even see Lars appear until he said, "It's a girl!"

We straightened ourselves the best that we could and followed Lars to the room they'd been transferred into. Lark waited outside as we all entered. Candice held a tiny bundle in her arms. She looked so young and so happy in that moment. As if her entire world had been flipped on its axis.

"She's precious," I told her.

"Isn't she?" Candice said. "We named her Carrie... after my mother."

"That's beautiful, dear," Elizabeth said.

"A good tribute," Camden agreed.

"Carrie Sparrow," Candice added. "So that she can have wings."

I laughed softly. That was so Candice. But somehow, it was perfect. Fitting.

We all needed wings right now.

———

Candice and Lars were simply exhausted. We couldn't stay long but promised to come back later to see Carrie more. She was the cutest, squishiest little ball of joy that I'd ever seen. A part of me actually hoped that Candice stopped traipsing around the universe long enough for me to get to know my niece.

As soon as we left, Elizabeth rushed out of the hospital. I didn't know what her plans were, but I was sure she'd figure it out on her own. Lark squeezed my shoulder once we were outside the hospital and gave me a hug.

"I see you're in good hands," she said.

Camden nodded at her. "Thank you."

"Anytime."

She squeezed me one more time. "I love you."

"I love you, too," I told her before she left.

Camden bundled me up into the limo and took me home. We had a lot to discuss, and I was exhausted. I'd barely slept a wink the night before in the hospital. Too much anxiety. Now, it was all catching up with me.

I couldn't sleep yet though. I needed answers.

"So, tell me what happened," I told Camden once we were inside the penthouse.

He gestured for me to follow him upstairs. "I want to get out of this tux first."

"Why didn't you change last night?"

"It's part of the story." He stripped out of his tuxedo and left it in a heap on the floor. Then he pulled on jogging pants and a T-shirt. The whole thing seemed to completely transform him.

He sat on the edge of the bed and told me everything. About Hank's and his mother and her confession. About her fear of telling him who she was and losing him again. How he'd confronted his father and his claim that he wasn't his son. All of it up until the punch.

Halfway through, I'd dropped into a chair and stared at him in shock. "That's... crazy, Camden."

"I know. I've been looking for her for years, and she's been there all along."

"And your father..."

"He's a bastard," Camden swore. "A right bastard."

"Are you actually going to press charges?"

"I'll do whatever it takes," he said honestly.

"Good."

He assessed me then. "You're not frightened that I'd do that?"

"Frightened? Me?" I laughed. "You know who you married. Let's take him down together."

"God, I love you," he said, sweeping me to my feet and planting a kiss on my lips. He pressed his forehead against mine and sighed. "Katherine, I'm sorry."

I froze at those words. "You... you don't apologize."

"I know."

"Why now?"

"Because I was wrong, and you need to hear it. I'm sorry for taking you to the hospital the way that I did. I shouldn't have done it."

"Oh, Camden," I said, bringing my hand up to his jaw.

"I almost lost you. I did it, knowing I might, but I just couldn't imagine life without you anymore. I'm so sorry I hurt you."

"It's okay," I told him, drawing him in for another kiss. "It's going to be okay. I still hate that I was in the hospital at all, but I realize now it was your only option."

He nodded. "It was. Or it felt like it was."

"My mother came to see me in the hospital. She actually... expressed emotions and told me about the first time I went. I realized her fears were the same as yours. I hate that I put you in a position to even have to worry about me like that. And I've agreed to go back to therapy."

"I'm so glad, Katherine," he told me. "And shocked by your mother."

I laughed softly. "Me and you both."

"I want to see you healthy. I don't want to lose you."

"You'll never lose me," I told him confidently.

And I meant it.

He gently tugged my ponytail out, and my hair spilled down around my shoulders. Our eyes connected. I knew that we had a long way to go from here. That neither of us was completely healed from the ordeal of this weekend. But this was a promise of moving forward. That we'd do this together from now on.

His lips met mine. His tongue delved into my mouth. Tasting me, touching me, claiming me. I wanted this from him. I wanted to relinquish control to the man who I knew would catch me when I fell. Even when I didn't want him to.

We peeled our clothes off, taking our time to savor the feel of each other's skin. We were the villains of everyone else's story. We were the hardened, darkened core that did whatever we had to in order to survive. To come out on top. But here, together, we were something else. Something more.

Together, we could move mountains.

Camden's fingers slid between my thighs. I gasped as he slicked through my wetness and circled around my clit. My body trembled. He eased me back on the bed and then crawled forward after me. I crooked my finger at him. He took both of my wrists and pinned them over my head. I laughed. No control for me. And I didn't need it.

Then he pressed his cock against my opening. I moaned at the feel of him there and tried to push him deeper into me. He retreated, and I opened my eyes to give him a pleading look.

"Ask me for it, love," he said.

It was a command that I'd never agreed to before.

"Fuck me, Camden," I breathed out.

He moved forward an inch. "Say please."

"Please," I gasped. "Please, oh please, Camden. I need you inside of me."

He moved another inch forward. "Do you think you've earned it?"

I bit my lip and nodded my head. "I have."

He started moving slowly in and out. Just the tip. Just enough to drive me completely mad.

"I think you've been bad and need to be punished."

I swallowed. "Punish me then."

He groaned at my words and then plunged inside of me. "This one is for us," he told me into my ear. "The next one, I'm going to spank that ass until it's raw."

I moaned. "Yes."

"Would you like that?"

"God, yes."

"You want me to make it so that you can't sit for a few days, darling?"

I gasped as he bottomed out in my pussy so hard that I saw stars. "Please."

He tipped my chin up and pressed kisses down my neck. He nipped at my exposed skin. I thought I was going to come right then and there.

"Camden, please," I whispered. "More."

"You're close, love?"

I nodded, staring up at him as he towered over me.

"Don't close your eyes. I want to watch you come."

He picked up his pace, and we crashed over the edge together. I fought to keep my eyes open as I called out his name. He finished, collapsing on top of me.

My chest heaved at the effort of it all.

Then he released my wrists and tenderly kissed my lips. "You're perfect for me."

My heart fluttered at the words. "Who knew we'd find our match in this arrangement?"

He brought my hand up to his lips and began to kiss each knuckle. "You are my match. In every way."

As I lay there, secure in our relationship, I felt myself drifting off. The force of the weekend pulling me under. Camden pulled me tight against him. Safe and secure, as I hadn't been in a long, *long* time.

39

KATHERINE

I hadn't believed that much could change in a week, but I was wrong.

I'd started therapy for my anorexia. The new therapist took no shit. Already, I could see where I'd gone wrong this past year to end up where I was. I had a long road ahead of me, but I had the support to get through it.

Camden hadn't ended up pressing charges against his father even though he really really wanted to. Once the board got wind of what had happened at the hospital along with Carlyle's negligence with the Ireland deal, they'd let his father go, effective immediately. Not that he'd gone quietly. Camden had stood there and watched as he'd railed against him to the board until they'd had to have Carlyle physically removed from the building and a restraining order put in place. It was the least he deserved after how he'd treated Camden all these years.

Then once his father was gone, they had named Camden the new CEO of the entire Percy company. In fact, the board had been looking for a reason to do this exact thing for years.

After our sexcapade, I'd gone with Camden to meet his mother, who ended up being cool as shit. I was pretty excited to take all of our friends to Hank's tonight. It wasn't our regular scene, not by a long shot, but we all wanted something different.

Camden and I had one more errand to run before we grabbed the limo and took our friends to the pool hall.

"You're sure about this?" I asked Camden for the third time that day.

We stepped out of the elevator and onto the floor for the cancer ward.

"Of course I'm sure. She'll love it."

"You're right." I nodded confidently and strode forward.

We passed the nurses' station.

I waved at Jerry. "Hi, Frank."

He laughed. "Villain Katherine, come to see your princess?"

"Of course."

"She's in a good mood today."

"When isn't she?" I asked with my own laugh.

And then we were at Jem's door. I saw why, today of all days, she was in a good mood. Her parents were here.

We knocked once, and I peeked my head in. "Hi. I didn't mean to interrupt. We can come back if need be?"

"Katherine!" Jem cried. "Come in. Come in. Meet my parents!"

I stepped inside with Camden behind me, and Jem practically swooned.

"You brought my Dark Prince!"

I grinned at her. "I did. He insisted on seeing you."

"Excellent! Did you bring me presents?"

"Jem," her mom admonished gently.

"Hello, I'm Katherine. I volunteer with ChildrensOne," I

said, holding my hand out. I shook her mom's hand and then her dad's.

They both looked weary, as if life had taken a heavy toll on them. With their daughter on the cancer ward, I could see how that was the case.

"It's nice to meet you," her mom said. "I'm Liza, and this is my husband, Paul."

"Pleasure," Paul said. "We've heard a lot about you. Princess dresses and parties?"

"Yes, I help run the fundraising division of the charity and try to bring smiles to the kids," I explained. "Though Jem seems to bring everyone she knows a smile."

"She does," her mom said. She affectionately ran a hand across Jem's hand. "I wish we could see her more often."

"Mom and Dad are heroes, Katherine," Jem explained. "Dad keeps Columbia looking spotless, and Mom knows how to get a stain out of anything. Even blood!"

Color came to Liza's cheeks at her daughter's explanation of her job. I could see the embarrassment there. And suddenly, so much made sense. Her parents didn't come not because they didn't want to, but because they worked themselves to the bone. We got to spend so much time with their daughter because we had the privilege to do so. My heart broke for them.

"That's wonderful," I said in earnest.

"Jem, I did actually bring you a present," Camden said and then looked to her parents. "If you don't mind."

Her parents quickly shook their heads. He took out a box and passed it to her. Jem squealed and ripped open the paper. She popped open the box. Her eyes widened.

"Oh my goodness," she whispered.

Then she withdrew the charm bracelet from the box. It was a duplicate of the one my father had given me all

K.A. LINDE

those years ago. And it had one lone charm on it—a crown.

"I... love it!" she gasped. "Help me put it on, Mom?"

"Sure." Liza secured it to her little wrist.

"There are extra links in the box," I told them. "So, when she gets bigger, she can still wear it if she wants."

"I am never taking it off," Jem said.

"What do you say, Jem?" her dad.

"Thank you!"

It felt right, giving her the bracelet. It wasn't fancy or expensive. But it started the tradition over with someone else who needed it.

"That is a very thoughtful gift," Liza said.

I glanced at Camden. And he nodded at me once. As if he knew exactly what I was thinking.

"Do you mind if we speak to you outside for a moment?"

Liza's eyes widened in concern. "Of course."

We left Jem to admire the bracelet and then exited her hospital room. Liza fidgeted, and Paul put a comforting arm around her shoulders. She smiled up at him. A unit. Two people who had had to deal with too much.

"I realize that we just met, and this might seem strange," I said. "But we love Jem. Both of us do. It might not seem like it, but she's really helped us."

"That's wonderful. We don't know how we got so lucky," Liza said.

"She's always been a ball of sunshine," Paul added.

"Her being here is likely a financial burden," I said as gently as I could. "And we're in a position to help."

"Oh no," Liza said at once. "We couldn't."

"I understand," Camden said. "But we insist."

Paul glanced at Liza. "It would help, honey."

"We can't accept money from strangers."

"It's for Jem," I insisted. "She's so much happier, having you around. We want what's best for her."

Liza covered her mouth and then began to sob. Paul swept her up into his arms. He held her as she shook and trembled with the weight of our offer. Paul just nodded his head.

"Thank you so much. We couldn't be more grateful." Tears even began to form in his eyes.

Liza stepped away from her husband and took my hands in hers. "You're a blessing."

I cleared my throat as a knot lodged in it. "Jem is the real blessing."

"She is, isn't she?" Liza whispered.

"Are you done out there?" Jem complained from the room.

We all burst into laughter at that. Well, she was still just a kid.

We traded information with Jem's parents so that we could help them in any way we could. After all this time of being the villain, it felt nice to be the princess that Jem had always seen me as.

We left the hospital hand in hand.

"You didn't even second-guess the offer," I told Camden.

He arched an eyebrow. "Why would I? I had the thought at the same time you did."

"We could probably help a lot more people."

He nodded. "We could."

"Probably the whole hospital wing."

He smiled and kissed me as the limo pulled up. "Perhaps the company could sponsor the entire ward."

My eyes lit up. "We should maybe ask the CEO."

"He says yes."

I laughed. "Deborah is going to freak out when I tell her about this new donation."

"Good. Shall we celebrate?"

"I believe we shall," I told him and hopped into the limo.

We picked up the rest of our friends—Lark and Sam, Court and English, Gavin, and Whitley. I noticed the two of them sat as far apart as possible. Whitley had reportedly had a huge breakup with Robert after the gala. I obviously hadn't been there to witness it. But it seemed Robert had initiated it this time. Whitley had just finished it. In her own... explosive way.

Despite Gavin and Whitley acting strange, the drive was fun. It took longer than expected to get to Hank's, but we had enough booze for a small country in the back of the limo.

When we finally arrived, we stumbled out in front of the establishment. All of us wore jeans and T-shirts. Sam was the only one who made it look normal. Southern boy that he was.

Court nudged Camden. "I'm still pissed that you hid this place from me for so long."

"Okay, little league coach," Camden shot back.

"Hey, that was different!"

"How?"

Court shrugged. "It was about me."

Camden arched an eyebrow. "Come meet my mom, jackass."

Court laughed, and the pair trudged through the swinging double doors. The interior was smoky and packed full of people. Wall-to-wall pool tables and clientele drinking cheap beer. It was the last kind of place that I would have wandered into, but I'd already been here once, and I understood why Camden liked it. There was no judgment here. It was a new world.

I led the charge down the main aisle, winking at Ricky, who whistled at me as I passed. And there was Mama Monica at the bar.

"Katherine!" she said, slipping out from under the bar to pull me in for a hug. "How is my gorgeous daughter-in-law?"

"Good. Thinking tequila shots tonight?"

Monica chuckled. "Aren't we always?"

She rounded on Camden and pressed an embarrassing kiss to his cheek. He just smiled at her. That was his *mom*. It was crazy and amazing.

Monica was likely the coolest person I'd ever met. She was so down-to-earth. Her advice so real. I was kind of sad that I hadn't known her all my life.

Monica hopped back under the bar and started lining up tequila shots for the entire party. Lark leaned in close to Sam and giggled. Once the shots were done, Lark held up her hands.

"Wait!" she cried.

We all looked at her expectantly. Waiting for a toast.

"Sam and I have something to tell you." Then she shoved her left hand into our faces. Where a giant diamond ring sat on it.

I squealed at the top of my lungs. "Oh my god!"

"Congratulations!" English cried.

"Ahhh!" was all Whitley could get out.

The guys patted Sam on the back. Acting like they'd known the whole time. Jerks! They probably had.

Monica started pouring new shots for Lark and Sam. "Double up for the engagement! Congrats, you two!"

We all held up our tequila shots and cheered for Lark and Sam. It couldn't have happened to better people.

"You know," Lark said after slamming back her second shot, "I'm going to need bridesmaids."

"Well, you were such a good one to me," I said with a laugh. "I could oblige."

"Me!" Whitley cried. "Please pick me! Oh my god, I've always wanted to be a bridesmaid. I'll plan the bachelorette party!"

Lark shook her head in bewilderment. "You're ridiculous. Yes, I want all three of you, of course!"

English grinned. "I'm so happy for you."

Then we all scooted forward and crashed into a four-person hug. It was bliss.

This was how it was all supposed to go. My friends all together, happy and healthy and drinking. My husband at my side, the new CEO of his company, with a relationship with his mother.

And as Monica filled up new drinks for us all, I held it out to Camden. A toast to us. For the beauty of finally getting to this moment.

"I love you," I told him, brushing a cherry-red kiss to his lips.

"And I love you," he whispered, bringing me closer. "Always."

EPILOGUE

"There is a literal parade of people in the waiting area to see you," Camden said with a shake of his head.

I laughed tenderly. "Not me. Her."

His eyes softened at the edges as he stared down at our daughter. All six pounds and four ounces of her. The tiny thing. And she was beautiful after eighteen painful hours of labor and an emergency C-section.

We'd decided on a name as soon as we found out that we were having a girl, but we hadn't told anyone. Not until today when all of my friends and family would show up to meet our baby girl—Helena Marie Percy.

We spent the next hour visiting with all those who wanted to see her. She was such a champ, too. Never complaining and loving every new person who held her. I grabbed a quick shower and dinner while everyone met our new addition.

By the time visiting hours were almost up, I thought I'd pass out from exhaustion and everything.

But then we were told that we had another visitor.

"Who is it?" I asked Camden.

But he smiled mischievously.

In strode Jem.

"Oh my god, Jem!" I cried.

She looked so grown up since the last time I'd seen her. Her hair was blonde and curly, creating an almost halo around her head. Her skin was back to its normal hue, and she no longer looked sick. Because she wasn't. She'd beaten her leukemia and passed her first-year checkup—cancer-free.

"Hi, Katherine," she said with a wide smile.

"It's so good to see you. Did your parents drop you off?"

"They're downstairs, checking out the gift shop," she told me. "Figured I was okay, navigating a hospital since I grew up in one."

That was a sad truth. But I was so glad that she was here. Paul had taken a job with Camden's company, and their income had stabilized so much that Liza could stay at home to help Jem catch up on her schoolwork until she could go to regular school again. She'd already been accepted into a private school in the city, and we'd offered to cover tuition. She had a bright future ahead of her.

Camden settled Jem into a chair by the window and then handed Helena over to her. She held her with such delicacy that my heart swelled in size. It was like having our two kids together. Even though Jem wasn't ours by law, she would always feel like she was.

A knock at the door pulled me away from them, and then in strode my mother. She'd been here all night with us. I'd thought it would be horrible, but it'd actually been such a relief.

"I brought another surprise," she said.

Then she swung the door open, and in walked my brother, David.

Tears sprang to my eyes. "David, you came!"

"Of course I did! I had to come. Plus, Sutton came with her brother Jensen and his wife, Emery. I thought it might be overwhelming the first day for all of them to show up, too."

"I missed you," I told him.

David dropped down and wrapped me in a gentle hug. "We'll have to find more times to fly out here. I want my kids to get to know their cousin."

I nodded. We'd never had that before. Our parents had kept us far from our relatives. Insulated us so that we could only be Upper East Side at heart. "I'd like that."

"In fact, Sutton requested that you come down for Christmas. She's been volunteering with the ballet, and I know that she would love to have your family out. Especially after I told her that you did ballet growing up."

"Actually, Christmas sounds great."

It wasn't like we were going to have a traditional Percy Christmas this year. It might be nice to go to Texas and start a new tradition.

"We'd love to," Camden said.

My husband shook hands with my brother, and I couldn't stop the tears forming in my eyes. At that moment, I felt like I finally had all my family together. By the time Jem and David had to leave with my mother, I was already making arrangements for them to come back. I hadn't known how much I needed them all here together especially for Helena's sake. I didn't want her to grow up the way that I had. I wanted her to know her cousins and to feel like she could do anything she wanted. As much as we all hoped she'd one day take over Percy Towers, I knew what that pressure did to a kid. It would be better to let her grow into her own potential. Live her own life.

I kissed her little head one more time after I finished breast-feeding and then handed her back to her father.

Camden easily took her in his arms and rocked her back to sleep. His eyes were only for me.

"Well," I said sleepily, "it seems the terms of our arrangement are complete now."

"Indeed it does."

"It looks like we might have to make a new one?"

"Oh?"

"How do you feel about a vow renewal?" I asked.

He raised his eyebrows. "We haven't even been married three years."

"I want to mean it when I say that I'll love you forever."

He sank onto the edge of the bed, holding our newborn baby between us. "A ceremony is just a ceremony. And I believe you now, here." He took my hand in his and looked deep in my eyes. "I vow to love you all of my days. To love and cherish you. For as long as we both shall live."

I swallowed hard and nodded, repeating the words back to him.

It wasn't before witnesses. It wasn't part of an enormous ceremony. It wasn't anything like the first time we had gotten married.

It was better.

Because it was the truth.

THE END

ACKNOWLEDGMENTS

Katherine & Camden came into my life three years ago as the villains I've always wanted to write. They were entitled, arrogant, and wholly uncaring. As I kept writing them through the Wrights then Cruel and finally to the Seasons, I started to think there was so much more buried underneath the masks that they showed the world. That they'd been hurt and they had enough money to make a racket about it. We saw them through the eyes of Katherine's brother, as the messed up little sister. We saw them through the eyes of Natalie, as the ultimate villain. Then we saw them through their friends eyes, as the people they were idolized to be. Writing who they actually *are* and peeling back the layers of to bring you who they are today in The Breaking Season was a treat. Thank you for coming on this journey with me.

And thank you to every person along the way who made this possible. But especially Nana Malone for help with Jem, look no one died! Sierra Simone, for loving my broken heroes and wanting to see them come to life. Diana Peter-freund for being the first person to say a reunion romance in the midst of an arranged marriage sounded like your jam. And my cadre of early readers who I wouldn't be able to get through this without—Becky, Rebecca, Anjee, Devin, and Katie. Not to mention Staci, for this brilliant cover, Jovana, for the amazing edits, and Dani, for championing this book! Last but not least, my husband Joel, who finds my twisted brain sexy.

ABOUT THE AUTHOR

K.A. Linde is the *USA Today* bestselling author of the more than thirty novels. She has a Masters degree in political science from the University of Georgia, was the head campaign worker for the 2012 presidential campaign at the University of North Carolina at Chapel Hill, and served as the head coach of the Duke University dance team.

She loves reading fantasy novels, binge-watching Supernatural, traveling to far off destinations, baking insane desserts, and dancing in her spare time.

She currently lives in Lubbock, Texas, with her husband and two super-adorable puppies.

You can reach her online at her website:
www.kalinde.com

Or Facebook, Instagram, and Twitter: @authorkalinde

For exclusive content, free books,
and giveaways every month.
www.kalinde.com/subscribe

CPSIA information can be obtained
at www.ICGtesting.com
Printed in the USA
FSHW021119270620
71530FS

9 781948 427418